ED MASESSA

WANDMAKER

SCHOLASTIC INC.

Library of Congress Cataloging-in-Publication Data

Names: Masessa, Ed, author.
Title: Wandmaker / Ed Masessa.
Description: First edition. | New York, NY: Scholastic Inc., 2016. | © 2016 |
    Summary: Henry Leach the Eighth is descended from a long line of wandmakers,
    but he still has not managed to make his very first wand do anything—and
    while he keeps trying he is also having to deal with a bully at school, and even
    worse, his eight-year-old little sister Brianna who has a positive genius for getting
    in his way.
Identifiers: LCCN 2015048828 | ISBN 9780545861748 (hardcover)
Subjects: LCSH: Magic—Juvenile fiction. | Magic wands—Juvenile fiction. |
    Brothers and sisters—Juvenile fiction. | Bullying—Juvenile fiction. |
    CYAC: Magic—Fiction. | Magic wands—Fiction. | Brothers and sisters—
    Fiction. | Bullying—Fiction. | Family life—Fiction.
Classification: LCC PZ7.M37345 Wan 2016 | DDC [Fic]—dc23 LC record
    available at http://lccn.loc.gov/2015048828

10 9 8 7 6 5 4 3 2 1   16 17 18 19 20

Printed in the U.S.A.   23

First edition, May 2016

Book design by Carol Ly

To Mom and Dad,
for setting the course and
making sure I never strayed
far from the path

PART ONE

Henry Leach the Eighth held the wand between the thumb and forefinger of his left hand with a delicate touch. *The Wandmaker's Guidebook* lay open beside him on his bed, propped against a pillow. The moon-and-stars pattern of his sheets framed the book, forming a natural extension of the page on which the constellations were illustrated.

He frowned as he focused, a pair of tiny thought lines bunched at the bridge of his nose. The book and bedsheet became one as his concentration intensified. It would work this time! He knew it would . . .

"Whatcha doin', Henry?" Brianna's shrill voice cut right through his concentration.

Henry yelped as he jumped off the bed, instinctively tightening his grip on the wand, afraid of dropping it.

"Get out, Brianna. This is my room." He squeezed the words out in a hush. At eight years old, Brianna was like a loose tooth that would never quite fall out—attached by an invisible thread, useless for doing anything, yet refusing to go away.

"Try and make me." She folded her arms across her chest. Henry looked down and imagined roots sprouting from her bare toes, embedding themselves in the carpet.

He relaxed his grip on the wand and gazed at it, wondering, *What if it really is capable of doing amazing things?* For all his practice, he'd seen no evidence that the wand was anything more than a fancy-looking stick, but maybe—just *maybe*—there was a little magic in it. All he needed was a little bit, and he could make her disappear.

"Let me see that," Brianna demanded as she reached for the wand.

Contamination!

His guidebook had explained the consequences of letting the wand out of his possession. Contaminated wands did bad things. And while he wasn't certain exactly what it took to contaminate a wand, he was pretty sure his sister could do it.

Henry quickly snatched the wand out of her reach and hid it behind his back.

"I'll tell Mom you're not sharing." A devilish smirk teased the corners of her mouth.

If there was anything more annoying than the way she snuck up on him, it was her tattletale voice, always threatening him with some parental punishment for crimes he didn't commit.

Henry wanted so much to believe there was magic in the world. What harm could it do to try?

The first full moon of spring hovered outside the window in a country-clear night sky. Henry focused on his wand and waved it over Brianna's head.

> *"Brianna is a pain in the rear.*
> *Make Brianna disappear!"*

He finished with a flourish and snapped his wrist, hoping to give the spell extra power.

Nothing.

Well . . . not nothing.

Brianna's smirk disappeared.

Her bottom lip puffed out.

Her blue eyes slowly sank into rising puddles of tears.

"Don't, Brianna," Henry pleaded. "Please?"

Too late. She inhaled deeply, and Henry knew he was in for a good one. He often thought of her as a volcano, gathering steam below the surface and . . .

"WAAA!"

There she blows.

"Henry!" his mother yelled from the bottom of the staircase.

"You brat!" he hissed, which served only to crank up her volume even higher.

Heavy footsteps tromped up the stairs toward Henry's room. They were not the footsteps of a small woman. Henry shoved the wand into his pocket.

"What's going on in here?" their father asked sternly from the doorway.

"Daddy!" Brianna squeezed out a few fresh tears before running to him. "Henry won't share." She flipped her long chestnut hair back and fluttered her eyes at him—the full look-at-poor-little-me treatment.

Henry cringed and braced for the worst.

Their father didn't say anything for a long moment, though. Instead, he sniffed the air from the doorway and gave Henry a curious look before finally turning his attention to Brianna. "Okay, Breezie. Why don't you go see Mommy for a minute?"

Brianna blinked. Henry could just about imagine her bewilderment—her time-tested tactic of getting him into trouble hadn't worked! Even stranger, no one had called her Breezie since she had come home from school in first grade and said it made her sound like a baby.

"Go on," their father urged. "Mommy has something for you." If he had mentioned what the "something" was, she might not have gone. But Brianna never could contain her curiosity. She left without another whimper, sticking out her tongue at Henry as she turned the corner.

Henry prepared to plead his defense. "Dad, she—"

"I know," his father said calmly. He grabbed a comic book from Henry's dresser and casually flipped through it as he looked around Henry's room. His nose twitched and continued to sniff the air. As he sat on the edge of the bed, he took off his glasses and rubbed his eyes, something Henry had noticed him doing a lot lately—as if he were constantly tired.

"Come here, Henry," he said, patting a place on the bed next to him.

There were times when Henry imagined he had a sixth sense like Spider-Man and could tell when something bad was about to happen. Not this time—his Spidey-Sense wasn't tingling.

But he wasn't quite ready to let his guard down. Brianna's tears had always brought him misery.

Seeing Henry's hesitation, his father smiled. "No lecture tonight. We just need to talk for a minute."

Henry hopped onto the bed. Side by side, Henry was struck, as he often was, by how much more he took after his mother. His light brown complexion and short-cropped black hair, courtesy of his mother's Navajo roots, were in sharp contrast to his father's fair Irish skin and reddish mop of curls.

"Dad, Brianna was—"

"How is your wand coming along?" his father interrupted.

Henry was surprised by the question. Since his father had gifted him the guidebook some weeks ago, he hadn't shown much interest in whether Henry was reading it or not, much less whether he was following its instructions for crafting and personalizing a wand. In fact, Henry had taken the task very seriously—but he knew adults had a tendency to dismiss such things as flights of boyish fancy.

He pulled the wand from his pocket, holding it lightly in his fingers—like the conductor of an orchestra with a baton—just as the book had instructed.

He'd taken steps over the last several weeks to infuse it with his personality. The bottom third of the wand was hollow, allowing him to insert several objects that reflected his interests:

A feather from a blue jay, his favorite bird.

A gray rock with a vein of pink quartz running through it—quite extraordinary.

A small vial of water from the fish tank in which he'd raised tadpoles into frogs. He reasoned that there must be something special about the water where such an amazing transformation had occurred, and he wanted to capture that quality in his wand.

He had also stained the wand, quite cleverly. From his room, he sometimes watched blue jays eating chokecherries in a tree tucked into the far corner of the backyard. He had gathered some berries that had fallen to the ground, mashed them into a paste, and rubbed the juice into his wand. He thought that this would form a further connection with the blue jays. And after all, purple was his favorite color. A good thing too, since it took weeks for the color to wash off his skin.

"It's looking fine, Henry." An odd gleam flashed in his father's eyes, for only a second. "In fact, it's looking better every day."

Henry twirled it delicately between two fingers, thinking about all the work he'd put into personalizing it. He was pleased with how it looked. He just wished that it would *do* something.

A quick spark prickled his fingers, like a shock from static electricity. He jumped, and for the second time that night almost dropped the wand. A curious smell drifted up—somewhat like the scent of charred wood.

"Careful, son," his father whispered in a strange voice. "You have something very special there."

Henry wanted to reply, but he was mesmerized by the tingling sensation in his hand.

Yes, thought Henry, *my wand is very special.*

His father's voice continued to drone, murmuring sounds like musical notes. Henry's vision became fuzzy around the edges, while the wand remained in perfect focus. From the blurred edges, his father's hand emerged, slowly reaching toward the wand.

Henry frowned. Something was not right.

The musical vibration of his father's voice changed to a lower, ominous pitch.

This time his Spidey-Sense did tingle. *Contamination!*

Something in his subconscious mind reacted, and a feeling like pins and needles raced down his arm and into the wand. A single spark jumped from its tip, and Henry was suddenly aware of his surroundings again. In one fluid motion he whipped the wand out of his father's reach and stared at him in surprise.

For a brief instant, Henry caught a glimpse of a swirling cloud—a miniature galaxy of spinning stars and vapor—that had replaced the whites of his father's eyes.

A gasp, or possibly a hiss, escaped his father's lips, and he rose quickly from the bed. Three long strides and he was at the window, his outline framed in moonlight.

Henry was frightened. But the fear was laced with curiosity.

"What was that?" he asked his father. "Was that . . . magic?"

From the day he'd been given the guidebook, Henry had dreamed of making a wand that would give him exceptional power. Things like transforming Billy Bodanski into a toad for bullying him on the school bus. Like turning Mary Cooper's tongue into a frying pan when she stuck it out at him for getting a higher score in math. Like changing toilet paper into enough money to buy his mother a new car, or at least a better one. And if there was still enough magic left, he'd poof a few dozen comic books for himself.

But things like that didn't happen for people like Henry. They happened in movies.

Theatrical special effects. Computer wizardry.

Yet maybe not.

Henry's father stared at him from across the room, holding his glasses in his hand. His eyes were soft and caring— and normal. Henry could easily have imagined the whole thing. If there was one thing he had an abundance of, it was imagination.

He looked down at his wand again.

"Henry." His father nudged him with an elbow.

Henry shifted his eyes from the wand to his father, who was sitting beside him on the bed. How had he gotten there from across the room so quickly?

And as he gazed into the swirling mass of stars that had reemerged within his father's eyes, an answer formed within Henry's eleven-year-old mind.

It never happened . . .

Musical intonations of his father's voice played softly in Henry's ear.

It never happened . . .

His father was smiling and nodding his head as if to confirm Henry's thought.

It never happened . . .

The music stopped.

Henry blinked as if he had just awoken from a midday nap.

He looked around the empty room, his eyes coming to rest on the wand, which was tucked neatly into *The Wandmaker's Guidebook.*

Someday he would get it to work.

Dear Coralis, My wand won't work.
I have done everything you told me. Please send
one that works. My sister is a pane.

Henry Leach VIII

Almost as an afterthought, Henry decided to check his spelling by using the dictionary, and he was glad he did. Very carefully, he copied the note onto a fresh piece of paper, changing *pane* to *pain*. He had nearly made a fatal blunder—calling Brianna a piece of glass. With a mistake like that, Coralis might throw the letter away without answering it.

Henry stuffed the letter into a plain white envelope, addressed it simply to *Coralis, Grand Wand Master*, and sealed it shut. He felt very important sitting at his father's desk in his home office, writing a note to the Grand Wand

Master himself! And he didn't think his father would mind that he used a sheet of his finest stationery for such an important occasion.

He stared at the envelope. Coralis had to be out there . . . somewhere. But all Henry had to go on was the guidebook that the Wand Master had written—and he hadn't chosen to share many personal details. In addition to instructions on the care and keeping of wands, Coralis's guidebook included fantastic information about the power of nature and exciting stories of the Wandbearers who had harnessed it. Yet there was virtually nothing about Coralis himself.

And despite Henry's best efforts, he'd found no information anywhere else. First he'd tried the library, but there were no records there for any other books written by Coralis—and in fact, the guidebook itself was missing from the library's database, as if it didn't exist. Next he'd used his computer time in science class to search for Coralis using every keyword he could think of. It had gotten him nowhere and cost him dearly—a D on a pop quiz the following day. Since science was his strongest subject, his teacher had been "concerned and disappointed." But Henry had kept his silence on his secret project and accepted the extra homework to make up for his poor grade.

It was almost as if Coralis didn't want to be found. And how could he mail a letter to someone who couldn't be found?

A slight breeze blew in through the open window, ruffling a few stray pieces of paper. Henry tucked a corner of the letter beneath a leather-bound book that lay on his father's desk.

The book itself caught his eye then. The walls of his father's office were lined with shelves full of books— impressive volumes of brown leather and gold lettering. But something about this one stood out. It appeared ancient, its cover and spine adorned with a mysterious symbol. There was no title or author name—at least, not in any language he'd ever seen before.

He briefly considered copying the fancy symbol onto his letter in an attempt to impress Coralis. He tried to focus on it, but every time he thought he had it, it would blur and squiggle in his vision—sunlight and shadow playing tricks on his eyes. Probably a bad idea anyway, he thought. For all he knew it might be a symbol for something like ballet, or cake mix, or even coffee, which his father had never liked in the past, but more recently couldn't get enough of.

Scanning his father's office, he found three other books that appeared of a set with the one on the desk. They were tucked out of the way on the tallest shelf. After a moment's consideration, Henry pulled his chair over and stood on it, retrieving them and stacking all four together upon the desk.

He ran his hand over the textured surface of the nearest book. Despite the warmth of the office, it felt cool. He glanced toward the open doorway, almost expecting to see his father standing there. He couldn't shake the feeling that he was seeing something he shouldn't see.

But that was silly. After all, they were only books. And wasn't he encouraged to read?

All the same, his hand shook slightly with anticipation as he lifted the cover. The spine crackled loudly. Even Henry, with as active an imagination as any eleven-year-old boy ever had, could not have anticipated what he would find when he opened the cover. Scrolled onto the endpaper in elaborate calligraphy were six unexpected words:

Yes, Henry, these are for you.

It wasn't the usual inscription of *To Henry, love, Mom* that many of his other books had. The way it was written, it was as if someone had anticipated this very moment, granting him permission to take them.

And he had never seen the handwriting before in his life.

It took several trips. The books were oversize and rather heavy. But he managed to carry them up to his room without any interference. He closed the door behind him and wedged a chair beneath the doorknob to lock out unwanted visitors named Brianna.

At the foot of the bed sat a green metal chest. It had belonged to his great-great-grandfather, who had been a brave firefighter many years ago. The name *Henry Leach IV* was stenciled on the footlocker in large block letters. He'd been thrilled when his father had given him the chest and told him the story of how Henry Leach the Fourth risked his life during the great San Francisco earthquake of 1906. Sharing his name with a true American hero made him proud.

Henry spun the combination lock to its secret code and slowly opened the lid. The chest contained many of his favorite and prized possessions. Some, like his rare mineral collection and *Millennium Falcon* yo-yo, he just didn't want Brianna to touch. But other items were ones he wanted *no one* to touch—like the wand secured within the guidebook.

Henry kept his guidebook neatly wrapped in the remains of a blanket he had carried everywhere with him until he turned four. The blanket's edges were frayed and torn. Stains from long-forgotten meals had turned the light beige to a mottled gray, not unlike the color of his cat. But it was still as precious to him as any treasure he owned. One of the first things he had added to his wand was a piece of thread from the blanket.

As he moved the bundled guidebook to make room for his new tomes, he had a sudden thought. He'd recently learned about a page in the beginning of every book that contains all kinds of information about the book's publication. Mrs. Verrity, the local librarian, called it a copyright page. Maybe Coralis's address was on that page in the guidebook!

Henry searched the book in vain. There was no copyright page, no information about who printed the book, nothing about the author. He wondered where his father had even purchased it. It was altogether unlike anything he'd ever found at the library: old and cracked, with handwritten advice scrawled in the margins.

"Henry!" Brianna called up to him from the backyard.

He looked out the window, ready to yell at her to leave him alone. Unfortunately, he could tell by looking what had happened.

Brianna held a sneaker by the shoelace at arm's length, pinching her nose with her other hand. "I stepped in poop, Henry," she whined. "Come clean it off."

It was a request he could not refuse. He had begged for a pet cat and had finally gotten his wish. (Actually, he had begged for an owl, but an emphatic *no* from both parents slammed that door closed rather quickly.) They had picked out a three-year-old cat from the animal shelter. The man from the shelter had not lied when he said the cat was housebroken. What he didn't say was that it hated to use a litter box, preferring instead to use the great outdoors. The whole backyard was its litter box, and it was Henry's responsibility to keep the yard clean.

"I'll be right down. Just don't try to wipe it off!" All she ever succeeded in doing was grinding it into all the tiny crevices that formed a flower shape on the sole of her shoe, making it that much more difficult to clean.

He quickly rewrapped the blanket around the guidebook and tucked it back into the chest, then closed and locked it before running outside to help his sister.

After the cleanup, as Henry hurried past his father's office on the way to wash his hands, he saw a sudden movement from the corner of his eye. He immediately reversed course and caught a brief glimpse of tail feathers leaving through the open window. He dashed into the room, arriving at the window just in time to see a large bird zoom around the corner of the house and out of sight. It had been much bigger than a blue jay, with gray, orange, and white markings.

He turned back to the desk to reach for the letter . . .

The letter! It was gone!

He rubbed his hand along the stubble of his crew cut, a subconscious habit that flared up whenever he became confused or flustered.

He was sure he had weighed it down. Quickly, he searched the room—over, under, and around the few pieces of furniture—believing a stiff breeze must have dislodged it.

Nothing. The letter had vanished.

Again Henry rubbed his head. Could the bird have taken it?

No, that was his imagination getting the better of him again. It had to be here somewhere . . .

"Henry!" He jumped as Brianna managed to sneak up on him. "I did it again." She held a soiled sneaker up, pinching her nose from the stench.

"Come on, Brianna! I just cleaned the whole yard!"

"You missed one," she said with her devilish grin. "And I found it."

Some time later, at a remote castle in the forests of Romania, a woman was shouting at a bear.

"Sophia!" Gretchen yelled sharply.

The large brown bear pulled her nose out of the compost heap too quickly, spraying bits of rotted vegetables into a nearby flower patch. Caught in the act, she pleaded with a series of grunts to be allowed to finish her midday snack.

"Bah!" Gretchen scolded. "You get too fat. Soon you will need a bigger cave to sleep."

Sophia snorted a reply that was just as insulting (if only Gretchen spoke bear!) before slinking away. She struggled fitfully to squeeze through the hole in the wall.

"Ha! You see? It is not the hole getting smaller. It is your bottom getting wider!" Gretchen laughed.

Sophia popped out the far side, then stood tall on her hind legs and roared—at either the hole or the woman on the other side of it—before ambling off into the surrounding forest.

"Ach, what am I to do with that animal?" Gretchen softly muttered a few curses in her native German before tending to the mess Sophia had left behind.

Gretchen's garden occupied a relatively small area of the expansive courtyard. Castle Coralis had been built thousands of years ago during an age of enlightenment. Though it was originally conceived as a center for learning, its outer structures had undergone significant change over the millennia, as men waged battle with increasingly sophisticated weaponry.

These days the fortress looked very much like a medieval castle without the moat. It was simple in design— basically a large rectangular courtyard enclosed by thick, twenty-foot-high stone walls. There were no turrets or spires. No ornate, grand battlements. The intent was to make it blend into the forest, and it succeeded. Unless you knew it was there, you wouldn't know it was there.

But like all good castles, this one had more than its share of secrets.

Atop the eastern wall, high above the courtyard, Coralis observed the woman and bear and allowed a rare brief smile to crease his timeworn face. "Worse than two old crones," he muttered to himself.

Gretchen squinted toward the sunrise, where the outline of Coralis made a striking image, nested in rays of sunshine. "*Guten Morgen,* Coralis. Will you be joining me for breakfast?" Her voice rose slightly, betraying a sense of hope. It had been too long since he had joined her for any meal, choosing instead to become more and more reclusive.

With a dismissive wave and a frown she couldn't see against the sunlight, the old man turned and passed from sight.

"*Ja*, same old story." Gretchen sighed. "What's a girl to do for company around here? Perhaps I should invite Sophia back for seconds." She shook her head sadly before heading toward the garden to begin the day's work.

As she sang and hummed songs from her childhood, her back bent low over the late-spring crops, Coralis returned to peer over the edge. From his hidden observation post, he watched his ever-faithful servant. Servant? Well . . . not really. She was the closest thing he'd had to a friend for over a century—since he had chosen the reclusive life of a hermit.

Her long, graying hair was pulled back and gathered at her neck. She'd accented her white blouse with a pink-and-aqua scarf. She reached into one of the many pockets of her loose-fitting tan cargo pants and pulled out a folded tissue containing a small stash of seeds.

He admired how skillfully she worked the soil, tending herbs and vegetables with a delicate touch. Not for the first time, he wondered how someone could work for hours in a garden and finish as fresh and clean as the minute she started.

Coralis breathed in the fragrant morning air, long and deep, then exhaled slowly, emptying his lungs. He closed his eyes and envisioned the castle as it was so long ago: vibrant with life and activity, a center for learning and philosophical debates. Wand Masters in animated discussions about the best ways of upholding their vows of protecting the Earth. It was when those healthy discussions turned poisonous that life within their ecosystem began to crumble. To this day, he could not identify with any certainty what caused the great rift within their ranks, but as they slowly drifted apart, only Coralis was left to maintain the sanctity of the castle. And it did not take long for his self-imposed solitude to turn him into a curmudgeon.

Gretchen had put up with him so far, but he feared even she had limits.

The shrieking cry of an aplomado falcon overhead abruptly interrupted his reverie. Despite his advanced age, Coralis's keen eyes were as sharp as the bird's. Immediately, he focused on the white envelope streaked with brown smudges that the bird grasped firmly in its talons.

The falcon's shadow passed directly over Gretchen. Try as she might to ignore it, her eyes, too, were drawn to it. A slight shiver raised bumps on her arms despite the heat. She rubbed them away, leaving careless smudges of dirt on her spotless blouse. Suddenly the day did not seem so promising.

This was no ordinary bird.

This was not to be an ordinary day.

The bird had a name: Randall. And when Randall stopped in for a visit, nothing good could come of it.

Randall circled teasingly, trying to provoke an annoyed outburst from the old man below. But Coralis was in no mood to play into Randall's cajoling.

Sensing the old man's foul mood, Randall released a small bundle hidden behind the envelope. The fresh carcass of a mangled rodent dropped with a splat at Coralis's feet with pinpoint accuracy.

"Get down here, you foul feathered fiend!"

Randall shrieked in triumph and dove quickly before Coralis's irritation could turn to anger. With amazing speed, he deposited the envelope and retrieved his meal in one fluid motion, gliding out of reach before Coralis's futile lunge could catch him.

"Keep it up, Randall, and I'll turn those feathers into scales!"

Coralis examined the envelope without touching it. Bloodstains had caused the brown smudges, some of which were not entirely dry. He glared at the rapidly shrinking dot of the falcon as he sped away. A pigeon would make a better mail carrier, but pigeons are unstable and messy—totally paranoid, dim-witted, and completely lacking in social skills and bathroom etiquette. As for owls—he grimaced at the thought. Never again would he use the conniving, untrustworthy beasts. People often mistook the impassive look on their faces as a look of wisdom. The truth was quite the opposite. No good ever came from entrusting an owl with secrets.

Finally, and with great reluctance, he picked up the envelope. A child's scrawl haphazardly addressed the letter to:

Coralis, Grand Wand Master

His frown deepened. Ridges of concern creased his forehead like waves on a stormy sea. He felt an energy pulse from within the envelope—familiar, yet not.

There was no return address, not even a stamp. And Randall had disappeared, not that he would have offered any intelligent answers. Perhaps someday, when he got tired of eating raw rodent gizzards, he would come back to the castle for good. But until that day, Coralis was content to let him suffer. If there was one thing that was not in short supply, it was time.

He pierced the envelope with a sharp fingernail and cautiously opened it, removing the single sheet of paper within. Then he stared for some time at the penciled note, seeing it but not actually believing it.

Dear Coralis, My wand won't work . . .

"Why, that impudent little . . ." His face reddened and his hands shook as anger boiled to the surface.

His wand won't work! "Of course it won't work, you impatient toad!" he shouted to the skies.

"What's that?" Gretchen had been watching from the garden, shielding her eyes from the blinding sun. In all her time at the castle, she had witnessed only one other letter being delivered. Several years ago, the largest raven she had ever seen brought news of the death of another Wand Master. It was an unfortunate accident. As the Grand Wand Master, Coralis was responsible for monitoring the ranks of the Wandmakers'

Guild and for making sure it flourished. As their numbers continued to dwindle, he'd had no choice but to write *The Wandmaker's Guidebook* in hopes of finding worthy recruits.

"Bahtzen bizzle!" He swore and shook the letter, ranting in angry circles before disappearing from sight. He was still yelling as he emerged from the castle, walking swiftly toward her. "Look at this!"

"Please try to calm yourself." She spoke in a reassuring voice, flexing her vocal cords so that a soft hum fluttered in the background. The technique was known among inner Wandmaker circles simply as "Voice," and Gretchen was one of the best with it. When applied correctly, Voice could stop a charging water buffalo in its tracks—as well as soothe a raging Wand Master.

The effect on Coralis was immediate. He stopped flapping his arms and waving the letter. He even blushed slightly as he composed himself and took a deep breath.

"Why don't I make you up some hawthorn-berry tea, and you can tell me what is so important," she suggested.

Coralis no longer fought the effects of Voice, as he had at one time. Gretchen suspected it was because he understood the damage that high blood pressure could cause. "Yes, that sounds wonderful," he said. "My aging heart could use a little help. Let us go to my Kunstkammer."

Gretchen tried unsuccessfully to mask her surprise. Coralis's Kunstkammer was his private workroom, where he spent the majority of his days. Even after all these years, she had never been allowed inside.

After a brief detour to the kitchen, she entered the Kunstkammer: a spacious, dimly lit room that was cluttered from floor to ceiling. Curiosity cabinets were filled to capacity with specimen jars, vials of colorful liquids, and taxidermy of some of the strangest creatures she had ever seen. A peculiar large rodent with a particularly nasty set of fangs stared at her with glassy eyes. It might have been long dead, but it still looked hungry.

Coralis leaned forward in his buffalo-leather armchair. The chair groaned—well, actually, it *moaned*. He took a cup of tea from her serving tray and visibly relaxed as he took a sip. "Mmm . . . just a touch of yarrow and mint. Excellent!"

Gretchen located a stool that looked harmless enough and dragged it from his workbench back to where Coralis sat, deep in thought. "You seem troubled," she said, dusting off the seat and sneezing in the process. "You really should allow me to give this room a thorough cleaning." As she sat, the wood seemed to soften and expand, making it very comfortable.

"Nonsense. A little dust never hurt anyone." He placed the teacup on a side table and saw the young boy's crumpled letter, and he scowled.

"I don't understand why the scribbles of a young boy would aggravate you so. You must have realized this kind of thing would happen when you printed the guidebook—after all, the instructions are not very clear."

"They're not meant to be clear!" he snapped, and smacked his hand against the leather, causing the chair to buck, four cloven hooves lifting off the ground. Gretchen jumped in surprise, but Coralis was unfazed. "It's why it's called a *guidebook* and not a manual!"

Despite his gruff tone, his eyes sparkled like stars in the night sky. "It's all that bahtzen-bizzle wizard claptrap! Don't writers understand how much harm is caused by spreading misinformation? And yet when I try to explain it to them, they twist it around, dress it up, and add concoctions of their own imaginings. All they have done is make a murky mess. Filled young minds with visions of fancy spells and trickery. But there are no shortcuts when it comes to true wand-bearing, and no sleight of hand when it comes to the natural world."

Coralis pushed himself up from the comfort of his chair, which promptly snorted in relief. "Oh, hush up, you old cow, or I won't rub you down later."

The chair sighed an apology. After all, there was nothing that the old buffalo chair looked forward to more than her weekly massage.

Coralis turned around just in time. "Willoughby! Get down!"

Gretchen spun around and ducked as a sneaky vine with teeth took a swipe at her, grazing her left ear. Another of his former apprentice's experiments gone awry. Not wanting to appear flustered, she leaped up and stepped over to the buffalo chair, which promptly fluffed at her, sending up a rather noxious plume.

"Still want to clean up in here?" Coralis smirked.

"It would appear the room can fend for itself." She looked around cautiously before choosing to lean against the weathered wooden workbench. A jar of very large orange-red Kinabalu leeches from Borneo squirmed at her approach, but the lid appeared to be tightly secured. The occupants of the jar reminded her why she was there. "What of this young Leach boy? The name is familiar, I think."

Coralis frowned as he paced back and forth, stopping to stare at the ceiling—or something beyond. "Yes. Henry Leach." He slowly ambled to the far wall, where a bundle of wooden poles with curious markings stuck out from an old clay urn. They rattled upon his approach. "Now then, settle down." His voice was tender, as if he were addressing a pet dog.

He selected a bluish-black pole with narrow white cross-bands that immediately went limp and wrapped itself around Coralis's right arm. It was a snake, Gretchen saw now. Stroking its head and whispering in soft tones, Coralis returned to his chair.

"Gretchen, I'd like you to meet Sallie." The serpent flicked its tongue in her direction.

"Nice to meet you, too," she said, squirming slightly under Sallie's reptilian gaze. Gretchen had a very easy way with animals, but was always leery of reptiles. It was her experience that they had a tendency toward unpredictability. "Is Sallie a . . . former apprentice?"

"No, she was the last person who attempted to clean this room." Coralis allowed a rare chuckle at Gretchen's stricken reaction. "Not really. In truth, Sallie has always been just as she is—a beautiful yet very deadly krait. I found her in my sleeping bag while camping in northern India—just before she found me. Isn't that right, my dear?"

The snake looked up at Coralis and appeared to smile. He continued to stroke the narrow head, much as one would a cat or a dog. For its part, the snake truly seemed to enjoy it, but rarely took its eyes off Gretchen.

"What is it about reptiles that is so unnerving?" she asked rhetorically. "And what of the Leach boy?" If she didn't know better, she'd say he was avoiding the subject.

"Humpf," Coralis growled. His frown returned. "Do you recall ever reading about a rather vicious earthquake that took place in San Francisco at the beginning of the twentieth century?"

"*Ja*. As I recall, it destroyed the entire city," she answered, wondering what the connection might be.

Coralis lapsed into silence while gloom gathered around him like a thundercloud. When he finally spoke, his dire tone sent a shiver down Gretchen's spine.

"There have been many times throughout history when bad things happened despite good intentions. Such was the case with the earthquake. While I was otherwise occupied, a conclave of Wandbearers convened in San Francisco. They had noticed signs of activity of a very dark nature. Henry Leach the Fourth, the great-great-grandfather of our young letter writer, was the Monarch of that conclave, and unfortunately he was up against a very powerful foe. A Wand Master named Dai She."

"I am not familiar with this name," Gretchen remarked, slightly confused, as she knew the Guild's history well.

"We don't like to talk about him." Coralis moved slowly past shelves filled with bottled specimens, tapping idly at jars as if coaxing the dead back to life. "As you know, I am the last of the direct descendants of the Aratta Wand Masters. I have always upheld their vow to protect the world. But throughout time, as more were trained in the ways of the Guild, there have been . . . defectors. Those who chose to follow the misguided teachings of a nefarious Wand Master named Malachai. They call themselves the Scorax. Dai She is Malachai's only offspring, and by 1906, he had gained considerable power."

Coralis hissed in a way that only Sallie could understand. Her head perked up and she followed his command, slithering into his robe and retrieving a small twiglike wand. It was pure white and no longer than his pinkie finger. "To find Dai She, the Wandbearers had to focus their combined energy through highly specialized wands, such as this one. Look closely," he told Gretchen. "You can see it pulse."

She leaned forward and opened her eyes wide in astonishment. "Why, it has a heartbeat!"

"Yes. It is strong and healthy. It is known as an Argus Wand. In principle it acts like a divining rod—the type that is used to find a source of water. But an effective Argus Wand will find anything the bearer seeks.

"The conclave had met for a solid week. They summoned clean, organic energy and filled their wands to capacity. Then they began their search—to no avail. They should have realized what was happening. Dai She was wielding incredible power, protecting himself from being found by deflecting their energy. But the conclave assumed they only needed more power. They funneled more and more energy into their wands—more than they should have dared. The result was . . . tragic."

Coralis paused for a long moment before turning his eyes back on Gretchen. "Does my story frighten you?" His concern was genuine. Gretchen had been living as an invited guest in his castle for almost ten years, but they rarely discussed anything at length, let alone something as serious as this. He never told her so, but he found her presence a great comfort.

He found her . . . compatible.

She put up with him and all his volatile moods and all his eccentric habits. And the castle liked her as well, which was quite important in the scheme of things.

"*Ja*, it frightens me, but I am not afraid. You are here and the world is still in one piece, so perhaps there is a happy ending." She spotted Willoughby the vine circling around the backside of Coralis's chair, which promptly snorted and kicked at it, sending the vine scurrying for cover.

"Not so happy," Coralis said darkly. "Imagine if I took your hand to help you up from the floor and suddenly let go. The motion would not affect me, because I was ready for it. You, on the other hand, would fall down hard because you didn't expect it. That is precisely what happened with the energy from the Argus Wands. When the power struggle between Dai She and the conclave suddenly snapped, it created a whiplash of energy that ran straight to the San Andreas fault line, causing the tectonic plates to shift.

"This sort of thing had happened before, but not beneath a city so heavily populated. Between the collapse of buildings and the ensuing fires, the city was decimated. Thousands of people died."

Coralis stroked Sallie's reptilian head as he spoke. If it were possible for a snake to purr, she would have done it.

Suddenly, the snake snapped her head around. A small black rat, barely noticeable, poked its nose out from behind a tall vat of brown liquid. Tiny ears perked up and whiskers twitched in alarm as the air became charged with signals of predator versus prey.

Too late. The krait uncoiled and raced across the flag-stone floor. In the urn, the rest of the pole snakes rattled and clanged against one another.

"Oh, all right." Coralis tapped a pale wand the size of a pencil against the urn. "Go!"

The room immediately erupted in a flurry of snakes and rats of all sizes. "Guess I was overdue for a little housecleaning after all," he said dryly.

"I think you are right. And it's good that I am not doing the cleaning," Gretchen said with a nervous tremor, stepping up on a workbench.

Activity in the room settled down quickly, the snakes proving to be remarkably efficient. When Gretchen finally turned her attention back to Coralis, he was deep in thought. He rubbed his hands as if fraught with worry. "What will you do now?" she asked him.

"It doesn't take a genius to see what's happening, but it does take a fool to ignore it." He picked up the jar with the giant leeches inside. "I have had my head buried in the sand. This letter . . ." He gently laid it on the workbench. "This is no coincidence. I knew it the second I touched the envelope. That falcon is five steps ahead of me, and it's time I caught up."

He put the jar down. "You've heard stories about the powers possessed by the seventh son of a seventh son?"

Gretchen nodded warily.

"Well," he said with a short laugh, "in this case, I can do you one better." Then his tone turned serious. "Young Henry is not your average boy. The Leach bloodline is strong, and he is the son of the seventh generation of Wandmakers on his father's side . . . and his mother's side, too. In our world, it is the equivalent of being a musical prodigy. He will have been born with exceptional skills. Whether or not he has the strength of character to use them wisely . . ."

He slapped both palms flat against the workbench and turned to Gretchen, his face filled with grim determination.

"Please fetch that confounded falcon. It's time for Master Leach to discover what he can do, and I have just the items to give him a proper nudge. Our feathered friend has a delivery to make."

Gretchen saw the spark in his eyes that she hadn't seen in too many years. "It's about time."

Henry hopped from the bottom step of the school bus to the curb. He casually took a few steps to the left. Then, as the bus began to roll by, he quickly reversed direction. Two ripe tomatoes and the remnants of a PBJ sandwich flew past his ear.

The back half of the bus cackled with laughter, led by none other than Billy Bodanski. "Leach the freak!" they chanted in unison.

"Hey, Leach, try a peach!" Billy yelled, tossing the fruit at Henry. Fortunately, it hadn't ripened yet and was hard enough to bounce off Henry's backpack, landing in the privet hedge that surrounded his front yard. He stared after the bus as it rounded the corner. From two blocks away, Billy's voice was still audible.

Henry dropped his backpack to the ground with a solid thunk. A tin containing some of his favorite rocks rattled inside as he dragged it up the sidewalk and tossed it carelessly onto the porch. He plopped down on the middle porch step and sank his face into his hands. "My life stinks," he mumbled.

He wiped his eyes with the sleeve of his jacket, glancing around quickly to see if Brianna was nearby. She had been getting much better at sneaking up on him lately. She wasn't due home for another hour, but there were days when his mother picked her up early from the after-school program. He couldn't understand why anyone would want to see Brianna for a minute more than was absolutely necessary.

He certainly didn't.

Henry stretched to reach his backpack and pulled a calendar from an outer pocket. He took a purple pencil and drew a firm *X* through the date, checking off the remaining days of school. "Only one more month," he whispered.

But a month of taunting and teasing was like a lifetime. Why couldn't Billy get eaten by a shark? Or if that was too much to hope for, at least catch a disease that would keep him out of school for a while?

Henry threw the calendar across the yard and into the hedge, where it dislodged the peach . . . which promptly conked a large gray bird on its head.

"What the . . . ?"

Henry raced over to the fallen bird and stared in wonder. He nudged it with his foot. Nothing happened. The bird was out cold.

"I hope it's not dead," he mumbled, and quickly turned around, sure that Brianna would be there watching. But he was alone. He bent closer to the bird and saw faint signs of life. Stupid Billy and his stupid peach!

Although it could have been worse. If Henry's name had been Andrew, Billy might have thrown a honeydew. That would have certainly killed the poor bird.

"Think, Henry!" He couldn't just leave it here. He ran his hand rapidly through his short hair. Then he noticed the long talons. "Bird of prey," he whispered. "Gray, orange, and white markings . . ." Henry's head snapped up, his eyes going wide. Could this be the same bird that had been in his father's office a few long and miserable weeks ago?

He quickly made his decision, bolting around the house to the garage at the back edge of their property line. He grabbed a pair of his father's thick leatherwork gloves and flipped over an old plastic crate, dumping his mother's gardening tools onto the floor. The crate had holes, but none big enough for the bird to escape. Then back to the bird he flew.

It was still out cold. Wearing the gloves for protection in case the bird should awaken, he gently lifted it off the ground. It felt odd to hold—alive yet limp, and lighter than he thought it should be.

The beak was razor sharp, pointed, hooked—perfect for tearing apart mice and rats. It was definitely some kind of falcon, but he would need his Audubon spotter's guide to identify it properly.

He lowered the bird into the crate with care and was about to take it away when he noticed a small parcel lying on the ground, wrapped in plain brown paper and tied neatly with a single piece of string. The bird had collapsed on top of it.

He turned the parcel over and there was his name: HENRY LEACH VIII, WANDMAKER.

"Oh!" Henry gasped and almost dropped it.

From the corner of his eye he saw the bird begin to stir. "Yikes!" He snatched up the crate and ran back to the garage, where he quickly located a piece of plywood that he placed over the crate. He then strained to lift a sturdy metal toolbox, which he plunked on top of the plywood. The bird was, after all, a large, powerful predator.

Breathing heavily, he slammed the door shut, flipped the light switch, and stared at the captive, unconscious bird in silence. Gradually his breath returned to normal. Ten . . . fifteen minutes, perhaps longer, he stared. Finally, his throat parched, he decided to get a glass of water.

"I'll be right back," he said to the bird, just in case it could hear him. He didn't want it to freak out and hurt itself. It would probably wake up with a lump on its head as it was.

He zipped across the yard and through the rear door, the wood-framed screen slamming shut behind him.

"Henry? Is that you?" his mother called from the basement, which she used as an art studio.

"Yes, Mom." He hoped his voice sounded calm. "Just getting a glass of water."

"Oh my, look at the time," he heard her say. "Henry, be a good boy and pour me a glass of iced tea."

Iced tea! Iced tea! There was a potentially dangerous bird in the garage that could awaken any second, and she wanted him to bring her iced tea? "Okay, Mom!" In his hurry, he spilled more on the counter than he got in the glass.

"I'll leave it out here, Mom," he said to her through the closed door. She started to reply, but he yelled, "Gotta run!"

The screen door slammed again as he raced across the yard and into the garage. He was so preoccupied with getting back to the bird that he sat down and stared at the crate for a full five seconds before he realized the bird wasn't in it!

The hastily built cage was completely intact—crate, plywood, toolbox—and sitting atop the toolbox, giving Henry the evil eye, was a large, angry falcon.

Henry swallowed with an audible gulp. He tried to remember what not to do when confronted by a predator. He had seen plenty of animal shows and even recorded a few to watch over again.

Don't look them in the eye—they could perceive this as a challenge and attack. Henry averted his eyes.

Play dead. Too late for that. But perhaps he could try holding his breath. He squeezed his eyes shut, took a deep breath, and held it as long as he could. He heard his heartbeat thrumming in his ears. When he could no longer stand the lack of air, he exhaled with a loud whoosh.

Too late, he realized his mistake. With a single flap of its wings, the falcon perched atop Henry's head, its sharp claws poking through his short hair and into his scalp. Henry winced but didn't panic. A small whimper escaped his lips, and the falcon hopped off, back atop the toolbox.

The toolbox that was on top of the plywood. Not knocked over and spilled on the floor—but right where he'd left it.

"How did . . . ?" he began, when the bird winked one eye at him.

"No way!" he whispered. The plywood was bulky, and the toolbox was filled with hammers, wrenches, screwdrivers, and even an electric drill. This was no small toolbox. Yet somehow, the bird had knocked them off, gotten out . . . and replaced them? He looked again at the sides of the crate. The only other explanation was that it had managed to squeeze through one of the holes . . .

The bird slowly shook its head from side to side. Was it reading his mind?

Henry nervously rubbed his hand through his hair.

The bird gave every indication that it could understand him. "That's impossible," he said aloud. Again the bird shook its head no. "You understand me?" Henry asked, not quite believing he was carrying on a conversation with a bird.

In reply, it waggled the feathers above its eyes, much as a person would wiggle their eyebrows. "Birds don't have eyebrows," he said.

The bird shrugged its feathered shoulders, rolled its eyes, and hopped down off the toolbox to the floor, where it picked up the wrapped parcel.

"For me?" Henry reached for the package, fully expecting the bird to fly off with it at the last second. But as he grabbed it, the bird pulled on the string with its beak. An assortment of crystals tumbled onto the ground, along with a polished black wand with three white pinstripes running the length of the wood. It was about the length of his hand and slightly thicker than his thumb.

"Wow!" he exclaimed as he carefully held it up, twirling it in the sunlight. The pinstripes were actually clear veins that ran all the way through the wood.

Mixed in with the raw crystals was an odd white cube made out of paper. Henry pinched it between his fingers. It popped open and spread out before him, and Henry saw it was a note.

Dear Henry,

Keep practicing. Patience and persistence will bring you success.

Remember, if it was easy, everybody would be doing it.

—Coralis

"Coralis wrote back to me." It was all becoming too hard to believe. "Then you must be the bird that stole my letter." He looked up to see that the falcon had moved over to the door and was motioning with its head for Henry to open it.

"Suppose I don't want to let you go? I have a lot of questions . . ."

The bird's mild manner swiftly disappeared. Its eyes turned mean and predatory. Its feathers fluffed out until it looked to be almost twice its original size. In a show of defiance, it fully extended its wings and let loose a terrifying shriek!

Henry almost poked himself in the eye with his new wand as he reached up to cover his ears, the noise deafening in the close confines of the garage. "All right! All right! Let me by!"

As if nothing had happened, the bird withdrew to its normal size and hopped out of Henry's way. In the open doorway it turned, winked once more, and rose majestically into the afternoon sky.

"Pretty bird!" Brianna called after it from where she stood on the back porch.

Henry smiled. "Pretty smart bird."

Henry made his escape after dinner.

He set the volume of his radio just high enough to be heard through the closed bedroom door, so it would appear he was still inside. Then, practicing the stealthy moves of a cat, he snuck out the back door and into the garage.

After locking the doors, he shimmied up a metal pole and hoisted his body over a ledge and onto a second-floor loft. It wasn't an easy move for someone whose athletic ability didn't extend much beyond walking, but it was worth it for the privacy. Other than an old car tire, an empty armoire, and plenty of cobwebs, the loft was empty.

When he'd first found this space, he'd instantly known what the children who'd found Narnia had felt like. He had discovered a place that was his and only his. And someday he would turn it into his own private workshop.

A small, dirt-encrusted window usually let in ample light. But the darkness of an oncoming storm left him nearly sightless. He felt around for the droplight, which was little more than a long black electrical cord with a light bulb at one end.

He turned it on and waited impatiently for his eyes to adjust; then he took a greasy old towel from the floor and draped it over the window—in case anyone from the house might look out.

Satisfied that he would not be disturbed, he began his preparations. From the bottom drawer of the armoire he removed the guidebook, along with the precious cargo that the falcon had delivered, a small feather the falcon had shed in the crate, his guide to rocks and minerals, the robe from his wizard costume, and last but not least, one of the old books he had found in his father's office. Getting it all up here hadn't been so hard once he'd tied a long rope to the plastic crate to haul things up.

A long, low rumble signaled the beginning of the storm. He dabbed at the sweat on his face—the garage was sweltering—and rolled his shoulders uncomfortably as a few drops rolled down the center of his back. It felt like bugs crawling on his skin.

He wasn't sure exactly what to do, but he hoped that once he got started, something like a Wandmaker's instinct might guide him. He placed the books side by side and was immediately rewarded for doing so when he saw that the symbols on the cover of each were remarkably similar. Up until that moment, he'd assumed the images on the cover of the guidebook were decorative pictures that looked cool but didn't mean anything.

BOOM! Thunder rattled the windowpane. The first drops of rain spattered against the roof in wind-driven gusts.

Even the towel over the window could not block the brightness of the next shaft of lightning. Thunder immediately followed, with a crack so loud it made his ears ring. Suddenly Henry felt very alone . . . and very foolish. This couldn't be the safest place to weather a storm.

He gathered enough courage to peek out the window and was greeted by a lightning strike that split the top of the tall oak tree in the neighbor's yard. He screamed and stumbled away from the window, falling entirely too close to the edge. In a panic, he swiped his arms across the floor, sending his neatly organized valuables to every corner of the loft.

Another blast hit too close. Then another! Henry curled into a ball and huddled on the floor. He felt a prickly sensation on his neck and knew exactly what it meant: He was in trouble.

Henry screamed. He was at the mercy of giant bolts of electricity. And he was certain that he was about to die.

Then, as suddenly as it started, it stopped. The sharp, crackling bolts receded into the distance, rolling onward to another town, another victim. When Henry was absolutely certain he was safe, he opened his eyes and was greeted with darkness. He felt his way toward the droplight.

"Ouch!" He nicked his finger on a thin piece of broken glass. One of the bolts had zapped the power box and exploded the light bulb. The thunder had been so loud that he didn't even hear it happen.

"Henry!"

Oh no! His mom must have checked his room, and now she was looking for him—probably with Brianna in tow. He couldn't let them find him in the loft. It was his private place, and he was determined to keep it that way.

As quickly as he'd ever moved in his life, Henry pulled the greasy towel from the window. The cloud cover had thinned, brightening the sky to a dull gray—just enough to see by. He began gathering up everything within sight and dropping his possessions into the armoire. He would come back when it was safe to take inventory.

In the far corner, he found the old book. He must have really been scared to knock it so far away. The book was open, and one of the rocks from Coralis's package was lying on top. He'd had some trouble identifying this particular rock, but eventually found it in one of his reference books. It was called ulexite.

At first it had looked like a plain piece of quartz in the shape of a rectangular block. When he'd accidentally dropped it onto a comic book he was reading, the words on the page were somehow projected onto the upper surface of the rock. It was like being able to read the book in 3-D! At the time, he thought it was pretty cool, but otherwise useless.

What he saw now, however, gave him a chill. All the books he had taken from his father's office were written in a language Henry had never seen and couldn't read. But as Henry moved the rock across the page, the words on the rock's upper surface appeared in English. The rock was some sort of translation device!

"Henry!" His mother's voice was closer. He had to hurry.

He swept up the remaining items, whipped off his robe, shoved everything into the armoire, and slid down the pole just as she appeared at the side door. "Oh, hi, Mom," he babbled nervously.

"Henry, why didn't you answer me?" She hugged him tightly. "Weren't you scared? Look at you, you're shaking."

Henry realized it was true—he was shaking. But not for the reasons his mother assumed.

If the ulexite let him read those ancient books, what secrets might he uncover next?

Who needs sports! Henry thought angrily as he stomped up the steps of the rear porch, making each plank pay the price for the humiliation he had just been through.

Stomp! Stomp! Stomp!

While he hated his baseball cleats, he liked the way the tough plastic soles made rock-solid contact. It felt doubly good to slam the screen door shut behind him.

It was even more satisfying to slam his bedroom door. He kicked off the first shoe, which hit the footlocker near his bed. The second shoe was fastened tighter, but rather than take the time to untie it, he yanked and strained at it until it finally popped off, flew across the room, and splashed into the tadpole tank on the nightstand.

All he wanted was to get back to his cache in the garage loft. Instead, he'd wasted the entire morning on baseball, and he knew better than to think he'd sneak past Brianna in the middle of the day.

"Henry?" his mother called up. "Henry, would you like a glass of fresh mint tea?"

Tea? Why would he want tea? Would it change him into a newt so he'd never have to play baseball again? Why did his parents insist on torturing him by having him play baseball? His ability to drop a fly ball was legendary, and he didn't even *have* a batting average—he struck out *every single time* he came to the plate!

The doorknob turned. He had hesitated too long.

A small hand extended through a crack, holding a glass of iced tea like a peace offering. It was followed by the doe-eyed face of Brianna. "Henry?" She said it so, so softly—softer even than a whisper.

"Go away, Brianna!" She had gone to the game and witnessed his public embarrassment.

"I like your uniform, Henry." There was a humming sound behind the words. He rolled onto his bed and faced the wall, willing himself to remain angry.

"Mommy says have some tea." Her voice fluttered like the musical warbling of a songbird.

He rolled partially back, enough to squint at her through the corner of his eye. "What are you doing?" he asked. "Why are you talking like that?"

"Like what?" Except for her hand and part of her face, she remained out of sight. "Mommy says to tell you, 'Don't shoot the messenger.'" Her voice remained soft yet amazingly clear, and so calm. An image of his worn and tattered security blanket from his toddler years materialized in his mind. He visualized it wrapped securely around the glass of tea.

He struggled to remain angry. "Tell her I don't want any." But it came out in a whisper. He slid off the bed, but instead of turning her away, he took the tea from her tiny, steady hand and was mildly surprised that the glass was cold and hard—not warm and soft like the blanket he had imagined.

"Thank you." His anger was gone, dissolved like sugar in his tea.

"You're welcome." She slipped away, silently closing the door behind her.

Henry examined the glass, his face a mix of confused curiosity.

His mind buzzed. *What just happened?*

The next week slugged along like a plow through mud. Every time Henry tried to retrieve his books and wands from the garage, either his mother or Brianna was there to run interference.

Henry, can you please do this? Henry, please play with your sister? Henry, we're going to the mall now.

The suspense was driving him crazy! He flipped through the remaining three books in the footlocker, which made him even more crazy, knowing he would actually be able to read them if he could get his hands on the ulexite. He kicked himself, not for the first time, for not thinking to take the stone with him.

He paced around the room for hours. He would stare at the tadpole tank, imagining his submerged baseball cleat had become an artificial coral reef (even if it was a freshwater tank). He tried to hide from Brianna with no success. It was as if he had a big bag of birdseed strapped to his back that dropped a trail of sunflower seeds—and Brianna was the lucky bird.

Finally, he caught a break on Saturday. Brianna had caught a cold and was taking a midmorning nap, while his mother used the time to paint in her basement studio. The moment had arrived.

Padding out the door in stocking feet, he sprinted to the garage, set a personal speed record for climbing the pole, and used the crate to lower his entire cache from the loft to the ground. He found it more difficult to sneak back to his room, his load of books weighing him down, but he made it. He flopped breathlessly onto his bed, smiled, and gave himself a high five.

Mission accomplished! Now he could get to work.

"Henry," Brianna whimpered from the hallway. "My head hurts."

"Go get Mom. She's in the basement."

"She won't answer me," she whined.

"Go knock harder. She probably has her earphones on." *She's probably just ignoring you, hoping you'll leave her in peace,* he thought. *I wish I had that choice.*

He heard her sit outside his door. When the sniffling started, he gave in. He knew from experience that when Mom got into painting mode, the rest of the world faded away. The books would have to wait—again.

He helped her up. Her hands were warm and clammy. Henry could see she really wasn't feeling well and led her to the kitchen. He offered her several choices of canned soup, which she turned down with dramatic looks that ranged from disgust to horror. But he eventually found something they could both sink their teeth into.

They were into their second round of peanut-butter-and-banana sandwiches when Mom emerged from the basement. *Finally,* thought Henry.

"Oh! Is it lunchtime already?" She hummed to the tune on her iPod, made herself a turkey sandwich, gave Brianna two aspirins, gave Henry a pat on the head, and disappeared back into the basement. When he heard the click of the lock from her studio door, he knew he was doomed. And as he buried his head in his hands, he saw Brianna smile.

The combination of nap, medicine, and food had revived her. Henry was stuck at least until dinner.

They played hand after hand of Go Fish. Every now and then he'd purposely slip and say "Go away," but she didn't rise to the bait. They sat together and watched an old black-and-white version of *Frankenstein.* Fortunately, Brianna fell asleep on the sofa before the scary parts came on. It would be his fault if she woke up in the middle of the night from a nightmare about dead monsters coming to life. Henry was fascinated by the movie—especially the scenes in the "la-*bor*-a-tory" with all the mad scientist equipment.

Not for the first time, he found himself wondering how much of what was in a movie was actually real. *Is it really possible to bring something to life with lightning?* After he'd witnessed the destructive power of lightning in the garage loft a few nights earlier, he found it hard to believe. But what if it *was* possible . . .

"Henry. Henry, get up." He opened his eyes, startled to see Brianna shaking him. "You fell asleep," she said, pushing him off the remote and switching to cartoons.

"Henry, when is Daddy coming home?" she asked. Her eyes were glued to the caped dog and his sidekick hamster on the television.

"What?" Still groggy, he looked at the screen to see if she was repeating lines from the show.

"When is Daddy coming home?" This time she faced him.

He had been wondering the same thing for days. It wasn't unlike his father to go away on business, but he had been gone for several weeks. The last time Henry had spoken to him was in his room the night Henry tried to make Brianna disappear. He couldn't recall their conversation, but for some reason, he was disturbed by the thought of it. He was sure it had to do with his wand.

"Henry!" Brianna snapped.

"I don't know, okay? Probably soon." She crossed her arms and scowled, unsatisfied. "Why don't you go get your crayons and we'll make a picture for him."

"Can we use your colored pencils?" She smiled mischievously. His colored pencils were forbidden to anyone under the age of nine (next year he'd change it to ten). But for reasons he couldn't explain, he found himself giving in to her more and more frequently these days.

"Okay, but you need to follow some rules . . ."

"No breaking!" she shouted.

"That's a good rule. What else?"

"Only use one at a time!"

"And . . . ?"

"Put them right back in the box—right in the same spot!" She squealed happily and ran up the stairs. Halfway up she stopped and turned to him. "Can I use your pencil sharpener?"

"No." Some things, like his Iron Man pencil sharpener, were strictly off-limits.

Brianna bounded up the stairs, not willing to push her luck any further. Henry smiled. She wasn't such a bad sister. He just wished she wasn't around so much.

His mother didn't emerge until almost six. "Oh, is it dinner-time already?" she said absently. "Guess we'll order pizza." This time she stayed out of the studio long enough to tuck Brianna in for the night.

She got as far as the doorway to the basement when Henry finally worked up the nerve to ask Brianna's question. "Mom?" Perhaps it was only his imagination, but her shoulders and back seemed to stiffen. "I was . . . that is, Brianna was asking about Dad."

"What about him, honey?" She smiled, but it looked strained.

"Well." Henry rubbed his head, realizing he probably should have thought it through before asking. "He's been gone a long time. Is he okay?"

"What an odd question!"

Henry blinked in surprise. The way she'd answered was . . . weird. Like fake happiness with a dash of nervousness.

"Oh, Henry. Everything's fine." She playfully rubbed his hair. "I really appreciate how you watched Brianna today. Why don't you go enjoy some free time and tuck yourself in when you're ready." A quick kiss to the top of his head and she was gone, but not before one last nervous glance over her shoulder.

It took a minute before Henry realized his luck had changed. He could finally get down to business!

Just as he'd suspected, the four symbols on the cover of the guidebook matched a symbol on each of the other four books. The ulexite didn't work on the symbols, but he was able to find one of the symbols repeated on the inside, next to a foreign word that the ulexite could translate.

"Yes!" He clamped his hands over his mouth as soon as the word escaped. His eyes blazed with triumph. The symbol meant fire! Knowing where to look now, he quickly solved the key to the remaining three.

Earth.

Air.

Water.

Now if he only knew what they were for.

The hours stretched well past his usual bedtime, but Henry wasn't the least bit tired. When he heard his mother humming her way up the stairs to go to bed, he quickly turned off the light and scuttled beneath the covers. A short time later, he was back at it.

So many of the words in the ulexite were unfamiliar to him, it was as if the stone were translating the words from one foreign language to another. The more he tried to read, the more confused he became. In a spiral-bound X-Men notebook he copied the words as they appeared on the ulexite. In many instances, the words were jumbled out of order and a sentence would read the way Yoda in *Star Wars* speaks— backward and twisted.

He left plenty of room in the margins to write short definitions of words he didn't know. There were so many, though, that he started writing the definitions in parentheses following the word. He was becoming frustrated. He had thought reading the books would be easy once he had the stone. But at this rate it would take years to read them all!

Henry lay down on the bed, exhausted. That was when he heard it. A single squeak.

He knew that squeak. It was the rear screen door. And it was just loud enough in the midnight silence of the sleeping household to get his attention.

Someone was coming into the house. He could hear footsteps. He turned off his flashlight and crept toward the door, giving himself two inches of an opening to look and listen.

The footsteps moved past the staircase. They walked to his father's office and stopped. There was a nearly silent click as the office door closed.

Henry rubbed his head, thinking desperately about what to do. He could use his baseball bat as a weapon, but he realized how hopeless that would be—he'd never hit anything with that bat. His eyes fell upon the black wand Coralis had sent to him, lying in a perfect patch of moonlight on the bed. It was a sign—he hoped. He would take the wand as protection and sneak up on the intruder while remaining undetected—he hoped.

If it was anyone other than his father, he would wake his mother and call the police.

By the time he got downstairs, fear had sucked all the moisture from his mouth and beads of sweat glistened at his hairline. He paused to gather his wits and plan his next move.

Am I nuts? he thought. *I don't have a next move!*

One of the beads started its descent, rolling past his right ear.

Blam!

Heavy objects were being slammed inside the office. He flattened against a wall. Another bead of sweat rolled past his left ear.

Blam!

Why would a thief be making so much noise?

Henry edged closer. The light spilling through a crack under the doorway hit his bare toes, and the noise abruptly stopped. He quickly stepped out of the light and held his breath. His pulse pounded a steady beat in his eardrums. He heard a tap-tap-tap at the office window. Whoever was in there opened the window, then sat heavily in his father's chair. The pounding in his ears grew louder.

The thief began to talk. Henry pressed his ear to the door. He was so relieved to recognize the voice that his aching lungs whooshed with relief.

The door swung open with lightning speed. A large shadow loomed in the doorway—it was his father. "Henry." His eyes bored into his son for a full ten seconds before he went back to his desk, leaving the door open.

Henry peered cautiously into the office. His father was alone with his back to the open window. Henry glanced quickly to the top shelf, and when he looked back, his father's narrowed eyes had zeroed in on him. "Good evening, son."

Henry wasn't sure what he'd expected, but his father's voice sounded calm. Normal. They could have been having a conversation at the dinner table.

"Hi, Dad."

"A little past your bedtime, isn't it?"

"Way past, sir."

His father smiled. "So it is."

Henry relaxed a little, enabling him to take in details: the crumpled suit, necktie off-center, smudged white shirt, dirty hands and nails. That was unusual. Henry was accustomed to seeing his father leave for work looking like a department store mannequin, and come home looking just as tidy.

"Who were you taking to?"

"I was reading out loud. It helps me concentrate."

"Oh." Henry didn't see any open books. "Are you reading for work?"

"In a manner of speaking."

Henry took another step toward the desk. For a second, the wand from Coralis seemed to tremble in his pajama pocket. His eyes widened, startled, before he decided it was probably just his imagination.

His father didn't notice. He appeared distant and preoccupied as he rifled through the desk's open drawers.

"You haven't been in here while I've been away?" he asked distractedly. "Have you?"

Henry's mouth went dry. "N-no," he said. He wasn't sure why he lied, but he had the sudden sense that his father wouldn't be pleased with the truth. He groped for something else to say—a safe topic that had nothing to do with wands or strange books.

"I've been playing baseball."

What? Where did that come from? Of all the things he did *not* want to discuss, this was possibly the worst.

"Your mother told me all about it. I heard it went well."

"Ha!" He didn't mean to laugh out loud, but it made his father smile, and there was warmth in it. "She must have been watching a different game."

"Guess it runs in the family. I wasn't much cut out for sports at your age either. I think I was referred to as a late bloomer. I had a great rock collection, though."

Henry perked up. His own rock collection was very much a work in progress.

"Want to see one of my most prized specimens?"

"Yeah, I do!" He crossed the room, approaching the desk. What had he been thinking? Was he really afraid of his own father? On the outside, he smiled. On the inside, he laughed himself silly for being cursed with an out-of-control imagination.

"Ow!" From out of nowhere a pain erupted in Henry's leg. The wand in his pocket was zapping his thigh with jolts of current.

He lurched forward, reaching out to his father for help.

The smiling, concerned parent of moments earlier flickered like a bad piece of film, replaced briefly by a scowling face he hardly recognized. He recoiled from Henry's outstretched arm with a hiss.

The pain had become a hot iron branding his side. Henry watched his father back away slowly from the desk. He no longer looked angry. Instead, he had the detached look of a scientist observing an experiment gone awry.

Henry could not take the pain any longer. With all the effort he could muster, he heaved away from the desk and landed flat on his behind, gasping for breath. He grabbed frantically at his shirt, hoping there wasn't a bloody, gaping wound.

There was nothing. Not a mark. Not a welt. Not even a slight discoloration.

The Coralis wand! He needed to put some distance between himself and the wand. He got as far as taking it out of his pocket.

"Where did you get that?" his father hissed, and lunged toward him like a cobra.

"Henry!" His mother's voice hit the room with a life-force of its own.

Young and old Henry snapped their heads toward her. "Mom!" young Henry cried with relief.

"Lois."

Henry's eyes widened. He had never heard his father address his mother with such contempt.

"Henry, get up to your room," she ordered. "Now."

He didn't have to be told twice. He scampered around the corner and flew up the stairs. Behind him, a door slammed and angry voices rose. Henry flung himself on the bed, covering his head with his pillow.

Eventually, the voices receded. Hours later Henry finally fell asleep, but his dreams were not pleasant.

On the way down the stairs the following morning, Henry began to wonder what the world's record for longest yawn might be. He seriously thought he'd topped it—he even had to rub his jaw to pop it back into place.

In the kitchen, his mother was busily cleaning the stove top. The slick black surface usually took no more effort than a quick wipe with a damp sponge, but today she attacked it like she was determined to rub a hole through it. He wondered what she might have cooked that left such a mess behind.

A box of cereal on the table had enough left for one last bowl, as did the carton of milk. She continued to scrub. He crunched on cereal with his mouth open—a serious no-no—loud enough to get her attention. But it didn't work. She scrubbed even harder.

Something was wrong. "Mom?"

"Oh!" She dropped the sponge and nearly knocked over a can of scouring powder. "Henry. Good morning, honey. Did you sleep well?" She wiped a fine mist of sweat from her forehead and tucked a loose strand of hair behind an ear.

Henry rested the spoon in the bowl. *She can't be serious!* "Mom, where's Dad?"

Her arms tensed and her voice strained to control emotion. "Why, he's away on business, silly. You know that."

"No, he's not! I saw him last night in his office. You were there!" Henry was surprised at the anger he projected.

Before she could answer, Brianna bounded into the room. "Hi, Henry! Hi, Mommy!" She ran into their mother with a tackling hug.

"Brianna, where's Dad?" Henry demanded.

"How should I know?" With a carefree bounce she started out of the kitchen.

"Wait a minute!" he barked sharply, and blocked her path. "Mom, what's going on?"

"Let me go, Henry." Brianna pouted.

"Henry, what's gotten into you? Leave your sister alone." His mother stepped toward him, almost threatening, but Henry refused to move.

"No. I saw Dad last night, and so did you. We were in his office! You yelled . . ."

His mother's finger snapped up, stopping Henry midrant. She squatted next to Brianna. "Honey, why don't you run outside and play. Mommy will be right there."

"Okay." Brianna looked like a frightened kitten as she bolted out the back door.

Henry turned on his mother, his frustration building. "I know you saw him because I was there with you!"

"Watch your tone with me, young man," she scolded. "And don't go frightening your sister."

"But—"

"No buts," she interrupted. "Your father stopped home to get something he forgot. Now I suggest *you* forget you ever saw him. We don't want to upset your sister."

"Mom, something's not right," Henry pleaded.

His mother's features softened. "You shouldn't worry. For all intents and purposes, your father was not here last night."

There was something about the way she said it. As if there was a hidden or double meaning.

And while he didn't really understand, he knew she was telling him the honest truth.

Henry stood outside his father's office, a nervous hand hovering over the doorknob. He cracked the door open. Despite what his mother had said, he would not have been surprised to see his father sitting behind the desk. He inched it open wider, Spidey-Sense on full alert.

Not only was the office empty, but it looked as if it hadn't been occupied in weeks. The window was closed, the desk was clear of papers, the chairs were in their usual spots. And yet . . .

He reached down to pick up a feather from the floor.

Henry had a new hideaway—a secluded, makeshift cave behind the garage that he made from a well-used picnic table, a stained painter's drop cloth, and a variety of scrap wood and logs that were drying out to be used in the fireplace. The cave was easier to get to than the loft, and he'd designed it to look like a scrap heap of random materials so as not to draw attention to it. The average eight-year-old girl would never suspect it was anything more than a pile of discarded remnants from household projects.

He brought the feather from the office, along with his very best Audubon spotter's guide. The detail in the book did not identify individual feathers, but he thought he might possibly get close by matching the colors of birds with those of the feather. Black and gray, maybe a little yellow?

He slammed the book shut in a huff. It seemed that almost every bird had black and gray feathers. And besides, what good would it do to identify a feather? How would that help solve the mystery of his father's sudden appearance, and even more sudden disappearance?

He was reminded of the feather from the falcon. He scurried into the garage and up the pole to the loft, where he took the feather from the armoire. Back in his cave, he studied the feather carefully. Having seen the bird up close, he had more to go on, and he found what he was looking for in the section about falcons. Mostly because of the unique tail feathers and coloring, he identified it as an aplomado falcon. The pictures that featured its beautiful light-orange belly and head were stunning, but he appreciated them even more for having seen one in the flesh (or was that feather?).

Could the two feathers be from the same bird?

Neither of them was very long—so not from the wing or tail. While the colors were similar, the markings were definitely different. But how different? Placing a small rock over each of them to keep them from blowing away, he zipped up the pole again, retrieving a magnifying glass. It was a gift from his father—large, heavy, and powerful—that had been given to him on his seventh birthday.

He tied back a section of the drop cloth, creating a tent flap to allow in more light. The feather from the office definitely contained a slight shade of yellow. Other than that, there was nothing different about it magnified than he had observed before.

The falcon feather, however, was so unusual he got chills. Each tiny filament bristled with life. They moved in a harmonious wave, as if this single feather were capable of flight all on its own! The movement was not visible to the naked eye, but when the feather was magnified, the effect was remarkable.

In his excitement, he bumped the other feather, nudging it closer to the falcon's. The reaction was that of a stray cat meeting a mean dog. Tiny pinpricks of light danced along the outer edges of the falcon feather as it recoiled in an effort to push away from the other feather. Henry tried a small test. The closer he brought them together, the more severe the reaction—like two positive magnetic fields repelling each other with invisible force.

"It has to be magic!" Henry whispered in awe.

"What's magic?" Henry flinched as Brianna managed to sneak up on him yet again.

"Brianna," he warned. "Stay out of here. I want to be alone, okay?"

She ducked beneath the flap and stepped inside. "What's magic?" she repeated.

He was about to yell at her to get lost when he noticed something peculiar about her. She had not made a move toward him. Instead, she stood to the side—stiff and straight, and . . . confused? This wasn't the typical meddling, interfering, annoying little-sister behavior. "What's wrong?" he asked.

She thought about that briefly and shrugged.

He decided he would need to pay closer attention to his sister. In the meantime, he offered to show her the feathers, but *without* the magnifying glass. Just because he was being nice didn't mean he trusted her.

It turned out she didn't need it.

"That one's from the pretty bird," she stated, pointing to the falcon's feather.

How could she know that? "What about this one?" he blurted out before he could stop himself.

"That one is bad." Her face puckered as if she got a whiff of curdled milk.

Henry nodded. He had a hunch she was right. "Brianna, if I show you my bird book, can you tell me which bird the bad one came from?"

It was like he pushed a magic button. Her face lit up with a smile and her eyes sparkled with the surprise of a long-awaited birthday present. The transformation caught Henry off guard. "Um . . . wait a minute . . ."

But it was too late. She scooted next to him and flipped through pages, pausing occasionally with comments like "Oh! Look at how blue this one is!" and "Henry, look! It's a pirate bird!" and "Can I buy one of these at the pet store?" This clearly wasn't going the way he'd expected. He must have been crazy to think she could help.

"OH!" She stopped abruptly, her trembling finger pointing to a page. "This one scares me."

She was pointing to a vulture.

Henry took the book from her and laid the bad feather on the page. The colors matched well and the shape was right. "That's the one, Henry. That's the bad bird." Her sparkle had gone, replaced by concern. "You should throw it away, Henry," she told him in a way that wasn't so much a suggestion as it was a command.

"I'm not throwing it away." It was a clue to the mystery surrounding his father's odd behavior.

"You have to." She stood, her hands clenched at her sides. "You have to throw it away, Henry." Her voice rose and her back stiffened. "Throw it away or I'm telling Mom!"

"Calm down," Henry pleaded as he recalled his mother's words: *Don't upset your sister.* "Here, look. I'm putting it away." He tucked the feather into the book at the vulture page. "I'll throw it away later, okay?"

Brianna's eyes opened wide. Her body trembled. "You're lying!" she shouted. "You don't understand!"

Henry reached for her to calm her down, but she quickly sidestepped his grasp, then angrily flung the tent flap closed as she ran away yelling, "Mommy!"

He flopped back down, panicky and confused. What was it about that feather that had set her off like a firecracker? He reflexively reached for his wand with one hand while pounding his forehead with the other. The wand grew noticeably warmer as Henry's grip tightened around it and he became more agitated. Brianna's voice carried as far as the entrance flap, the cloth barrier acting as a muffler, changing her words into garbled noise. What was she telling Mom?

The air inside the cave became a slurry, thickened with heat. He tensed up and gripped the wand even tighter. Had he not been so concerned about getting caught, he would have noticed the clear veins of the wand beginning to glow.

Voices approached the cave entrance. A small wisp of smoke curled off the tip of his wand, adding a tinge of sulfur like a snuffed-out match. When Brianna's small hand appeared and grabbed the entrance flap, he snapped. His impulse to lash out radiated through his body, ran down his arm, and flared into the wand.

A blast of heat, a spark of light, and a surge of power hit simultaneously. With a reflex born of panic, he rammed the wand into the soft sandy soil just as Brianna opened the flap. With an audible POP, a pair of moles sprang from the ground, flew a foot in the air, and landed in an unconscious heap of fur.

Even if he hadn't been stunned with awe, he wouldn't have been able to move quick enough to hide the moles.

Brianna yanked back the flap, flooding the cave with sunlight. It was like opening an oven door. Heat vapor formed a gust of wind that blew out of the opening. Brianna and their mother recoiled, shielding their faces with their arms for protection, and the cave was again plunged into darkness.

"Henry!" His mother's scream was a lethal combination of fear for her son's safety and anger that he was apparently playing with fire.

Startled back into action, Henry quickly reached for the moles, still unsure of what had happened. But just as he was about to touch them, they twitched back to life.

Again the flap opened, blinding Henry and the light-averse rodents, who staggered backward until they accidentally fell into their own hole.

If Henry thought the sunlight was bright, it paled in comparison to the anger that flashed from his mother's eyes. "Henry Leach the Eighth, *what* are you doing in here?"

He rubbed his head, searching for something intelligent to say. He looked at Brianna, who was staring slack-jawed at the hole. "I . . . um . . . was . . ."

But Brianna recovered faster.

"Tell Henry he has to share his bird book with me," she whined.

What? Wait . . . she wasn't ratting him out about the feather. Whether she meant to or not, she had given him an escape route. He reluctantly handed her the book.

"All you had to do was ask," he said sweetly. He turned to his mother for approval. Her face was scrunched into the strangest expression. She sniffed the air as if trying to identify an odor. She stopped abruptly. Her eyes glazed over and her face froze with an icy glare. She studied Henry as if seeing him for the first time.

"Everything is moving too fast. Please be careful, Henry," she said softly. "And always keep your sister by your side." And she walked away.

He continued to watch as she walked toward the house, as confused as he'd ever been in his life. Her shoulders were slumped forward and she slowly wrapped her arms across her chest as if warding off a sudden chill despite the summer heat. The screen door squeaked, and she was gone.

"Henry." He jumped. The happy Brianna from seconds ago was now possessed by her evil twin. "I'm flushing it down the toilet." She stomped out of the cave, composed herself, switched back to the happy twin, and skipped merrily away.

"This family just got a whole lot weirder," Henry said to himself. He reached tentatively for the wand and yanked it out of the ground.

A slight shiver ran down his back when he put the wand into his pocket. He shook it off with a shrug. Then he unpinned the flap, closed off the cave, and followed the path to the house.

In the darkness, the hole in the ground silently sealed shut.

CHAPTER
EIGHT

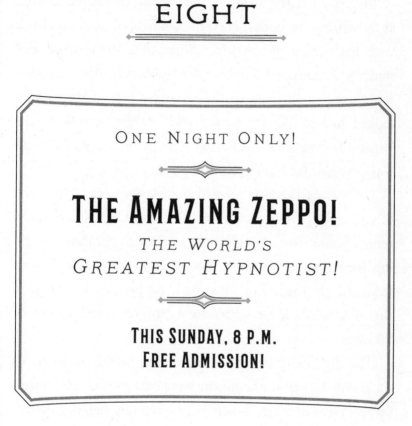

ONE NIGHT ONLY!

THE AMAZING ZEPPO!
THE WORLD'S
GREATEST HYPNOTIST!

THIS SUNDAY, 8 P.M.
FREE ADMISSION!

The sign stared back at Henry through the library window. He had arrived on his bicycle just as Mrs. Verrity was taping it to the front door. "Just a minute, Henry," she said, her voice muffled by the glass. "Is it straight?"

"Perfect, Mrs. Verrity." In a small town like Henry's, it wasn't unusual for local merchants to know the names of their best customers. And since school let out for the summer, Henry had become a library regular.

Over the last several weeks, Henry had continued to work at translating the books. He'd filled notebook after notebook with his neatest handwriting. Some of it made sense, but much of it sounded like complete gibberish. Also included within the main body of the text were lists of things that looked like recipes for what could qualify as some of the nastiest-tasting food on Earth—unless, of course, the food wasn't meant for human consumption.

He was particularly grossed out by one recipe that contained a scab from a cat's ear. Occasionally his cat would return home after a rough night in the neighborhood sporting fresh, oozing wounds. The thought of picking a scab from the cat made him shudder. And besides, he was sure that if he tried, he would receive a cat-scratch scab or two of his own.

The dictionary had become his best friend. So many of the words he saw in the ulexite were new to him. He looked up every one of them. When there was more than one definition, he wrote the one or two that best fit the sentence he was translating. As a result, his study habits as well as his vocabulary had improved remarkably.

One night at dinner, he slipped and used the word "transmogrification" when Brianna was talking about tadpoles turning into frogs. "Why, Henry, where did you pick up a word like that?" his mother asked.

"Um . . . I must have read it in a book," he answered, which wasn't a lie. But he made a mental note to be more careful.

The more he translated the old books, the greater his thirst for knowledge became. Whenever he arrived at a peculiar word or the mention of an exotic location, he felt compelled to do some research.

In this way he learned about the lost civilizations of Persia and about the wonders of the ancient world and the people who built them. And every path of research led him to forks that he would follow, until days had gone by and he realized he'd filled pages of a notebook with interesting facts and observations. Inevitably, some of these facts turned up later in his translations, giving him a sense of pride and accomplishment.

If only they would teach some of this in school. How much more interesting it would be.

But in the course of his research he also came across names and places that were remarkably difficult to learn more about. That's where Mrs. Verrity came in. "No one can know everything, Henry. The secret of possessing knowledge lies in knowing where to look for it." She had explained this to him on a rainy Saturday afternoon. He had been slumped over a table, frustrated by his Internet research, which was too often unreliable.

Mrs. Verrity worked alone, yet took the time to show Henry how to do research properly. And he soon found out that she was 100 percent right. He could find almost anything if he knew where to look for it—which included getting books on loan from other libraries around the state.

She had sent a postcard to Henry's home, preferring the postal system to deliver a message over the phone system—or, heaven forbid, the Internet! He was informed in her peculiar, backward-slanted scrawl that the book on alchemy he'd requested had been delivered—which was why he was arriving as the library opened the following day.

Henry scanned the rest of the front door, noticing for the first time all of the other events that were posted. Some had been there for weeks—possibly months. And yet it took the one about the hypnotist to get his attention.

What was it he'd read one day? You never know what you need until you find it. At the time it didn't make much sense. But suddenly it clicked. The unseen forces of the universe had conspired to bring him to precisely this place at precisely this time.

He was meant to go to the hypnotist's show.

———◇———

But by Sunday evening he was having second thoughts. It was possible the entire thing would be a waste of time. He had seen hypnotists on television. It always looked fake—like a staged performance. Getting someone to cluck like a chicken hardly seemed amazing. Any bully could accomplish a simple feat like that by waving a fist in your face instead of a shiny coin.

But what if this was the real thing? It could be the break he was waiting for in his never-ending battle with Billy Bodanski. What if Henry was able to turn the tables and have Billy do what he wanted for a change? It was an opportunity too good to pass up.

As they piled into the car, Henry's excitement grew, thinking about all the possibilities of hypnotism. They arrived at the library, and the car had barely come to a stop when Henry opened the door, ready to bound up the stairs and secure a front row seat.

"Henry," his mother said.

Oh no! He knew that tone. He knew what was coming.

"Take your sister." It wasn't a question.

"But—"

"No buts. You will take your sister. End of story."

Usually this sort of standoff ended with "and we'll go for ice cream later" or some similar bribe. Not this time. His mother's intensity was almost scary.

"Fine!" He felt his cheeks redden as his excitement changed to anger.

But Brianna wasn't moving. "Do I have to go, Mommy?"

Suddenly there was hope! Surely his mother would not force her little darling to do something she didn't want to.

"Yes." A single word uttered with power. He had never seen her so adamant about anything.

Henry's neck hair bristled. If his mom was scary before, she was downright frightening now. The car door slowly opened. Brianna stepped out and had barely closed the door before the car rocketed away, tires squealing as it turned the corner and disappeared.

"Wow" was all he could think to say. Mom had been acting even weirder than usual since the incident with the moles, but this was beyond weird.

He finally faced his sister, only to find her glaring at him. Clearly she was angry.

"Hey, it's not my fault." But as they continued their staring contest, it dawned on him that this might be the first time Brianna was forced to do anything she didn't want to. A now-you-know-what-it-feels-like smile crept onto his face.

"This isn't funny, Henry." Her gaze drifted upward. An extra-large full moon loomed on the eastern horizon.

Henry knew it was an optical illusion that made it appear bigger and closer than usual, and on a normal night he would find it an awesome sight. But tonight he found it . . . intimidating. He reached into his pocket for the safe and secure feeling of the Coralis wand and received the now-familiar tingle in his fingertips.

"I have a bad feeling about this," Brianna whispered to the moon.

Henry felt it too but wouldn't dare admit it to her. "Come on, then. Let's get this over with." He reached for her hand but she jerked it away and walked ahead of him.

Fine, be that way.

A sign on the wall read MAXIMUM OCCUPANCY 60 PEOPLE. Henry took a quick head count. Eleven people. No, make that ten people and one bully. And before he could catch her, Brianna went right to the front row and sat next to him.

The evening had just gone from bad to worse. And Billy's expression went from surprise to scorn. "Leach." It was only one word, but it dripped with poison. His soulless eyes drifted to Brianna. "And little Leach." A dim light clicked on in his brain. "Leach and slug—ha! Ha!"

"My name is Brianna." Her voice hummed. Henry felt the air bristle with tension. Billy's laughter faded. He struggled for something to say. His mouth opened and closed several times like a goldfish until he gave up and turned away.

Despite his earlier disappointment, Henry now found Brianna's presence somewhat comforting. *It pays to have an ally when facing the enemy.*

"Good evening, everyone!" Mrs. Verrity gathered the small crowd's attention. "I'd like to thank you all for coming on this very special night. We are honored to have a special guest with us this evening, who has taken a short break from her worldwide tour to give us a special performance."

Henry hoped the night would be *special*, but hearing Mrs. Verrity use the word so often gave him some doubt.

Wait! Did she just say *her* worldwide tour? For some reason he'd assumed the hypnotist would be a man. From the corner of his eye he saw Brianna smile—and Billy squirm, which made Henry smile too. Special or not, the evening had just become much more interesting.

"So . . . without further ado . . . I give you . . . the Amazing . . . Zeppo!"

A woman stepped from behind a screen in the corner of the room and strode purposefully to the center. She appeared to be younger than his mom and wore a simple white blouse with black pants. But while her appearance was ordinary—almost dull—her eyes shone with focused intensity. For several seconds she appraised her audience in silence, lingering slightly longer than necessary on Henry.

"Good evening." Her accent was thick and filled Henry's head with images of old vampires in dark crypts. She shifted her eyes without moving her head until they connected again with Henry's.

"I said, good evening."

Caught up in the moment, Henry replied, "Good evening." He didn't mean to imitate her accent—it just came out that way.

Billy snickered, and her eyes pounced on him with such force that he popped out of his chair and stood at rigid attention. "No, ma'am," he sputtered, though no question had been asked.

Brianna edged forward in her seat, clearly impressed.

"Yes, young lady." Zeppo addressed Brianna. "There is much power in the eyes as well as the voice."

Can she read our minds? Henry immediately tried to think of nothing—to make his mind a blank slate. But the thought of making his mind blank was still a thought! She would know what he was trying to do. There was no escape!

"There is no need for concern," she said to Henry. "Most people think hypnotism is nothing more than a cheap parlor trick." She looked at Billy, still standing. "Do you believe this?"

"No, ma'am." Henry had never seen Billy afraid of anything, but he was clearly afraid now.

The others in the room were all adults, but thus far, the Amazing Zeppo had addressed only the three children. Henry wondered whether she had some special power that worked better on kids.

"You may sit now." Billy did so without a sideways glance. Henry watched as a bead of sweat rolled down Billy's face. There would be no bullying tonight.

"Whether you know it or not, you are being hypnotized every day of your lives. You may wake up in the middle of the night, turn on your *television*, and before you know it you are inexplicably placing an order for *jewelry*."

Henry marveled at her speech patterns—the way she rolled her *r*'s and elongated words like "tell-u-vi-shun" and "jew-la-ree."

"Or perhaps you have the *urge* to buy a new *backpack* when there is nothing wrong with your old one." The words "uurj" and "bic-pic" stuck in Henry's head.

"There are many ways to convince us to do things we would not normally do. The brain is a very complex organ. And whether you know it or not, you are always open to suggestions, which makes it very easy to . . . mess with your *head*!"

She slammed abruptly on the word "head" and wheeled it right at Billy. He popped up again like his chair was electrified. The Amazing Zeppo widened her eyes—so did Billy. Then she narrowed them—so did Billy. It was like she was playing a telepathic game of Simon Says with him. With a simple hand gesture she sat him down.

"Can I go next?" Brianna asked boldly.

The Amazing Zeppo snapped her head toward Brianna. The air crackled with tension. Everyone except his little sister knew better than to interrupt.

"And where would you like to go, young lady? Perhaps to visit the restroom?"

A few adults chuckled softly, and Henry saw his sister stiffen. And before he could grab her hand to tell her to behave, she spoke back—using her newly discovered voice. "I think it's my turn next," she said with the background hum. But perhaps because she had been insulted, she gave it an extra punch.

"Yes," an adult said from the back of the room. "Let the girl go next."

And then another and another. "Yes, let the girl go next," they chimed in as Brianna's suggestion overwhelmed them.

As much as Henry wanted to turn around to see the look on their faces, his eyes were glued to the Amazing Zeppo. She was not amused—and she was not affected.

"You are an impertinent child!" She zapped Brianna with a buzzing hum of her own. And while it was directed at his sister, he also felt the sting of her power.

Brianna pushed her back against the chair, squirming into the same rigid posture as Billy and going just as quiet.

"Perhaps you have an interruption for me as well?" Zeppo asked Henry in a gentler way.

He tried several times to say no, but the word stuck in his throat. He panicked, wondering if she had hypnotized him into never speaking again, and vigorously shook his head no.

"Good. Then let us begin."

The Amazing Zeppo lived up to her hype. One after another, the adults submitted themselves to her power. One recited Shakespeare the way Yoda would say it. One thought the floor was molten lava and ran around looking for a fire hose. And one stomped on mints from his pocket, thinking they were giant cockroaches. She received a standing ovation at the end of the evening, accepting the praise with a humble, modest bow.

Before she left, she turned to Henry, Brianna, and Billy. With a simple hand motion she had them sit and wait while the adults filed out. Henry could hear them questioning one another—"What did I do?"—unable to recall their own silliness. When everyone, including Mrs. Verrity, had left the room, she shifted a chair to sit facing them.

She addressed Billy first. "The next time you think about doing something to harm Henry, you will cluck like a chicken and scratch your behind." She snapped her fingers close to his face and he immediately relaxed, though he also seemed dazed and confused. "Why are you still here? Go!" Billy hurried from the room.

"The simple minds are easiest to work with." She smiled for the first time. It transformed her face, and she no longer looked so terrifying. Henry smiled back.

"And now this one." She addressed Brianna. Henry noticed that while Brianna was quiet and attentive, her head shook with the slightest of quivers. "She is strong-willed, this one. You see how she fights me."

The Amazing Zeppo snapped her fingers. The effect was completely the opposite of what it had been on Billy. Brianna lunged forward as if she had been trying to get up all along. She caught herself and gulped down a big breath, ready to unleash her pent-up anger at having been restrained for so long—but was stopped by the raised palm of the Amazing Zeppo.

"Think about what you are about to say," she said sternly. "You are young and strong, but you are no match for me." Brianna clenched her fists but held her tongue.

"That is better." She smoothed the wrinkles of her skirt. "I am here because of you, you know, Henry." She tucked a loose strand of hair behind her ear.

Something about the way she did it made her seem younger, even as the seriousness of her voice sounded almost ancient.

"I am a Keeper," she said—then she laughed. "Though my boyfriend might not agree." She saw the puzzled looks on their faces. "Never mind. Bad joke." She waved a hand and started over. "You might think of me as a librarian. In our world—the world of Wandmakers—I am entrusted with keeping the ancient scrolls and documents safe. I also investigate . . . unusual requests made at more conventional libraries. You have quite the thirst for knowledge, young man."

Henry simply nodded, still unable to comprehend this new turn of events.

"How are your translations coming along, Henry?"

"I, um . . ."

"It's all right." She smiled again. "I'm sure you are doing okeydokey."

He laughed at her choice of words and the way she said them—like this was probably the first time in her life.

She nodded. "May I see the wand?"

He hesitated, but gave in to his instincts to trust her. His instincts were right—she made no move to touch it. "Yes," she said admiringly. "He must think highly of you to entrust you with such a powerful element. And rightfully so. You are the eighth. A special number, like the black ball in the center of a game of pool. The one it takes to win."

"What is happening?" He hadn't meant to ask anything, but now that he had, he realized it was exactly the right question. All the events of the past weeks were like pieces of an abstract puzzle. If she could give him an idea of how to start piecing them together, maybe he could understand the overall picture.

"The bad moon is on the rise, Henry."

"Bad moon," whispered Brianna.

"Do you mean a full moon?" He knew all the moon's phases, and "bad" wasn't one of them.

"The bad moon does occur when the moon is full, but only once every several hundred years. The moon holds great power, you see, and if the right person—make that the *wrong* person—was able to harness it, he or she would gain control over enormous destructive power. Does the term 'Scorax' mean anything to you?"

Henry squinted in thought. There was one brief mention in one of the books, but he hadn't been able to find it in any dictionary. "I've seen the word but don't know what it means."

Her voice lowered to a whisper. "It is the essence of evil. Whereas the Wandmakers' Guild is charged with protecting the world, the Scorax is here to destroy it. And while our order has diminished, their membership has grown exponentially. The lure of power is much stronger among those with evil in their hearts."

Henry swallowed hard. "What does this have to do with me?"

She smiled a sad smile. "You are special, Henry. But being special may not be enough. So listen to me carefully." Henry leaned forward again. "One of my most important jobs as a Keeper is to find things others miss—or have not yet discovered. I have found you, Henry. You are a child of two heritages. Some would claim you must choose between them. But only by bringing them together can you know yourself. And only by knowing yourself can you hope to overcome evil." Her eyes bored into Henry. "I am the first to find you. I will not be the last."

Suddenly he was frightened. "Come on, Brianna. Let's go." In his haste, he yanked her arm hard enough to elicit an "ouch."

"Henry!"

He stopped midway to the door.

"Follow your mother's instructions. And do not blame your father." She walked across the room to the screen in the corner and stepped behind it.

Brianna tugged her arm free from Henry's grip and ran to see what Henry already knew.

"She's gone!"

"We should wait for Mom," Brianna whined.

"We're not waiting." Henry forged ahead, not waiting for—but expecting—his sister to keep up.

"What if she comes and we're not there? She's going to be maaaaad."

Henry didn't answer. He didn't know why, but he knew that he had to get home in a hurry.

They were about to turn a corner that was partially obscured by a tall hedge when they heard a sudden movement—someone was lying in ambush.

"Billy!" Henry cringed. But as they rounded the corner, they could see Billy was tangled in the hedge, viciously scratching his rump. He clucked like a chicken.

Brianna giggled until she got the hiccups. Henry laughed too, and couldn't resist the urge to cluck back.

A few minutes later they arrived to an empty house. The back door was open and the car was gone. Brianna ran from room to room, calling for their mother. Henry could have told his sister to save her breath. Something had passed between them when the Amazing Zeppo looked deep inside him—like images of things to come. The empty house was one of them.

"Where is she, Henry?" Brianna was too confused to be scared, but that wouldn't last long.

"I don't know," he said, which was the truth. He watched as instant tears pooled in Brianna's eyes. "Come on. I'll make us some peanut-butter-and-marshmallow sandwiches."

It was a forbidden combination of eating so close to bedtime and eating something on their mother's banned list, and the sparkle of devilish mischief dried up the tears. She was already in motion before issuing the challenge, "Race you!"

Henry smiled at how easily he was able to divert her attention. Once they had eaten, he invited her to his room. The Amazing Zeppo had pretty much spilled the beans. If Brianna didn't know for certain, she at least suspected that Henry had been keeping some big secrets from her. And after seeing the hypnotist, Henry had to wonder if Brianna's strange voice wasn't its own kind of magic.

He removed the books from his footlocker and showed her how the stone could translate from the ancient language into English.

"It's magic," she whispered. "Like in the movies. Like a princess movie!" She squealed and ran off.

"Where are you going?"

"To get changed!" she yelled from down the hall.

He had definitely succeeded in getting her mind off their mother's absence, but it still nagged at him. *What am I missing?*

The full moon outside was bigger than ever, threatening to swallow the night sky. *The bad moon is on the rise.* The Amazing Zeppo's words. Words that meant nothing to him. He flipped open his notebook of translations to a page that referenced lunar activity. Then he opened the ancient book to the corresponding page. There was a crudely drawn picture of a large circle with interesting symbols inside it, and a line of text just below it. The ulexite hadn't translated any of that text, so Henry hadn't bothered to copy the image into his notebook.

An idea took form and gained momentum inside his head. He rummaged through his closet until he found an old piece of sidewalk chalk. It briefly occurred to him that his idea might not be a good one after all. But curiosity got the better of him.

Working swiftly, he re-created the drawing on the hardwood floor. When he was done, Coralis's wand tingled in his hand. He held it up to the moonlight. The clear veins began to glow. Quickly he flipped off the light switch and returned to the moonlit window. The wand brightened in his hand. When he dipped the point downward, the glow intensified into a single beam.

Henry had once had a flashlight with circular covers that would project images like the Batman symbol onto a wall. The effect now was very similar, as the beam of light illuminated the circle—but nothing outside of the circle. The beam stayed within its perimeter. Henry gasped as he thought his drawing of a winged symbol actually moved.

There! It *had* moved! And another had too! They were re-forming themselves to look exactly like the pictures in the book. He reached and was able to slide the book over without removing the light from the circle. With a good deal of effort, he managed to pick up the book and balance it so he could read it. *What am I doing?* A silent alarm went off in his head, but the moment was absolutely magical and he didn't want it to end.

Henry imagined what might happen if he were in a movie, and he began to read the mystery text aloud, sounding out the unfamiliar words. He was halfway through before he realized he didn't need the book. The words were in his head! If he closed his eyes, it was as if he could read them on his eyelids.

As he neared the end of the passage, the words on the page began to illuminate, whiteness now shining where black ink once appeared. And as he chanted the final word, he imagined himself a wizard and waved the wand with a flourish . . . just as Brianna reentered the room, dressed in her blue fairy-princess costume.

She stopped in the center of the circle with a smile on her face as bright as the light around her. She was on stage and reveling in the moment—a star performer!

A brilliant flash of whiteness exploded from the wand. The circle of light solidified into a cylinder that extended to the ceiling, trapping Brianna in the center of it. She screamed silently—as if the light had imprisoned the sound.

Henry panicked and began waving the wand in any and all directions, trying to undo whatever he had unleashed. "Brianna! Get out of there!" He tried to reach for her, but the light formed an impenetrable wall that singed his hand.

Her mouth formed the word "Henry" as she screamed his name over and over. Henry threw the wand on the bed and, in desperation, began rummaging through the footlocker.

What did I do?

He tossed out books, toys, and photos until there was nothing left but a lining of thin green fabric. In a rage born of desperation, he tore at the fabric, ripping it clear from the glue that bound it. A bright gold stone that had been stuck to the fabric flew across the room and began to glow.

A thin tendril of light—so thin and wispy it looked like bright smoke—snaked away from the cylinder of light and toward the stone. The tendril touched the stone tentatively— then pulled back like a mouse that realized it had entered a trap.

But it had already been ensnared by the stone. Not a stone, Henry realized—*a nugget of gold*. And the nugget was winning the battle.

As the thin strand of light flowed into the nugget, the cylinder began to spin, like a giant ball of yarn unraveling with ever-increasing speed. Henry shielded his eyes as it spun faster and faster. Brianna was nothing but a blur that got smaller and smaller as the cylinder shrank away.

And then . . . it was gone.

And so was Brianna.

But what remained was a small blue hedgehog, wearing a tiara.

PART TWO

Dai She ran his stubby fingers over the map on the table as if it were a sacred relic. Unable to deny his pleasure, he laughed, and his high-pitched giggle wrenched through the small confines of his workroom, almost shrill enough to blister the paint off the walls. On an impulse, he touched the map lightly with his wand. It rippled in response. That simple touch, he knew, had sent a shock wave through the tectonic plates under the Indian Ocean. A tsunami would hit the coast of Sri Lanka within a few hours.

Oh, the fun he was having!

The Corsini Mappaemundi had changed hands several times over the course of its long existence. Created by the great Wand Master Epifanio Corsini almost four thousand years ago, the map had first been stolen from the High Council of Aratta's safe repository by Dai She's father, the infamous Wand Master Malachai. It had eventually been recaptured by a group of sanctimonious monks in the Himalayas—only to be re-stolen by Dai She. His father would have been proud if he were still alive. Especially if he could have witnessed the devious method Dai She had devised to steal it . . .

Everyone was afraid of something, and Dai She was a master at twisting that fear into its most horrifying forms. He had decided to go biblical on the monks, tormenting them with the ten plagues of Egypt from the Old Testament.

Turning their water supply into blood was child's play. Their screams had made him giggle with glee and fueled his wickedness. He was just getting started.

Unleashing a horde of frogs wasn't deadly enough for his taste. So he made sure the frogs were not only poisonous, but also an invasive species that would wreak havoc on the local environment for years to come.

It was fun to watch the monks gag on a plague of gnats, which he had waited to release until they had all gathered at an outing far from any protection.

Next, he added his own sick twist by using large, biting horseflies as plague number four. They were relentless and merciless. Seeing the itching welts they left behind gave Dai She so much joy that he did a little dance.

The next plague called for killing their livestock, but that was too easy. Instead, he hypnotized one of the monks into believing all of their cattle and goats were demons, then sat back and watched as he took their lives. Dai She's pet, a king vulture named Viktor, ate well that night.

Plague number six—boils—was the most fun of all. Dai She took immense pleasure in causing others physical pain. A few boils—red, pimplelike abscesses of the skin—could be manageable, but Dai She left no room for comfort. He made them erupt on the bottoms of the monks' feet and completely covered their torsos . . . especially their backsides. There was no relief. The monks could not comfortably stand, sit, kneel, or lie down.

The plague of hail covered the ground three feet thick and partially collapsed their roof.

The few crops that survived the storm were wiped out when he released millions of hungry locusts for plague number eight.

If he were following the plagues by the book, number nine should have been three days of darkness. But Dai She was so sad that there was only one plague to go that he hid the sun from them for a month. And in the meantime, he took the opportunity for a nice vacation at a villa in Italy, resting up for the grand finale.

According to the Old Testament, the tenth plague had been the deaths of the firstborn. Dai She was stumped. What if all the monks were themselves firstborn? He didn't particularly want them to die, just to suffer as long as humanly possible.

He was still pondering his dilemma when he returned to the monastery and heard the wailing. As it turned out, he'd needed only nine plagues. The monks had gone stark raving mad.

Dai She simply waltzed in and took the map while whistling a happy tune.

C old, damp, and miserable—three words that could have described either the weather or the person in it.

Gretchen had tried to offer Coralis advice on what to expect with modern-day travel. "I read newspapers!" she had scolded. He should have paid closer attention. The last time he had reluctantly flown in an airplane, it had had propellers, and he had entered it via a portable staircase on the runway tarmac.

Today, just the process of going through security was a nightmare. A uniformed woman with a badge had even made him remove his coat. Of all the nerve! But he got the last laugh when their so-called X-ray machine failed to penetrate the invisibility shield that protected his wands.

Gretchen had also tried to talk him into first-class seats, but he'd insisted on what they called "coach." He'd pictured a horse-drawn carriage in the sky. But there was nothing coachlike about it. In a coach he would have had room to stretch his legs and would not have been crammed into a seat meant for a child, stuffed into a row with two more adults, one of whom snored loud enough to wake the dead.

He had come close to leaving the plane by fading himself through the walls of the fuselage, but traveling at five hundred miles an hour at thirty-seven thousand feet was too much of an obstacle to overcome—even for someone with his abilities. At one point he tried to escape from his misery by entering a "restroom," but quickly retreated to his seat when he realized it was the airline's version of a practical joke.

The simple act of leaving the airport required a torturous ride in a leaky taxicab. The downpour slowed traffic to a crawl, but eventually he arrived at the corner of Second Avenue and Third Street in Manhattan.

He was sorely tempted to kiss the ground after the nightmarish ride, if not for the distinct possibility of coming into contact with some form of deadly fungus or parasite lying in wait on the filthy sidewalk. He waited patiently for the cab to turn the corner before continuing on his journey.

The city had changed enormously since his last visit. Buildings were too tall. Road maintenance was entirely inadequate for the amount of traffic. Yet once he got his bearings, the street grid became familiar. One block away, near the corner of Second Avenue and Second Street, was the unmarked and seldom-used entrance to a members-only tavern. Coralis stepped through the entrance into a small foyer. On the opposite wall, a heavily paneled door made of chestnut and inlaid with sets of ancient runes carved from blue-green amazonite provided a formidable barrier to anyone who might stumble upon the entrance. In every major city in the world, enclaves like this were managed by

Wandbearers as a refuge. Places where they could sit among their own kind, share stories of their travels, and discuss recent discoveries in the science of Wandulurgy.

They were also safe havens for those who needed them.

Coralis reached for a chain he wore around his neck: an iron pyrite flower pendant that sparkled with energy. He had worn it for over three hundred years, since it was presented to him as a gift from a shaman in the Peruvian Andes.

Touching the pyrite to the runes in a diagonal cross sequence unlocked the door. He let himself in and reversed the pattern to reseal the door. He entered a long narrow room with tables lining one side and an ornately carved breakfront that served as a bar on the other.

A single patron sat in the farthest booth, quietly eating a bowl of stew, reading a book about a boy wizard. Gretchen had recently introduced him to some of the current literature— all balderdash! Coralis gnashed his teeth and vowed to have a long talk with the author. Her facts were all wrong.

Coralis removed his dripping trench coat and sodden hat, and a row of pegs shaped like dragon claws flexed to grip the coat and hat firmly in their talons. The proprietor, a woman in her mid-hundreds (but who looked much like she was in her mid-thirties) leaned casually across the bar, resting on her elbows and smiling.

"Molly." Coralis had not seen her in over fifty years, but she hadn't aged a day.

"Coralis." Her voice, with its lilting Irish accent, was just loud enough to reach the patron in the back, who promptly dropped his spoon, splashing thick drops of gravy onto his gray flannel shirt. He looked up sharply from his book like a boy caught with his hand in the cookie jar.

Coralis's reputation as a despiser of books about wizardry stretched to every corner of the Wandmaker universe. He was a stickler for facts—not fiction.

Coralis placed a fist on the bar top and extended two fingers. Molly set out a cocktail glass and selected a bottle containing a glowing blue liquid, filling the glass to the two-finger line. Three short taps on the glass with a pencil-sized wand of rutilated quartz, and Coralis brought time within the bar to a standstill.

"Ah, that's better." He stomped over to the patron, who had frozen holding a spoonful of stew just shy of his mouth. "What have we here? Do even the First-Order Wandbearers fancy themselves to be wizards these days? It's no wonder the world is in such a rotten state."

"I was going to warn him you were on your way here, but I figured, why spoil all the fun." Molly had a round face and a pleasant smile. She was a first-generation immigrant—one of the first Irish to settle in what was known as the Five Points neighborhood of Manhattan. Her father had been a Wandbearer Monarch who'd died in the great gang wars of the 1850s.

She had all the right qualities to make her an excellent Wand Master, but chose to live a quiet life in relative obscurity. Still, she was a street-tough New Yorker, not to be trifled with.

"Your message said it was an urgent matter," he said brusquely. "I hope it has nothing to do with wizardry."

"You'll not need to take that attitude," she scolded. "If I say it's urgent, then bet yer finest wand that it's darned important."

"Humpf." He turned the patron's spoon to a slight downward angle. "Let's get to it, then."

Using an amber amulet with markings similar to those on the padlocks at the castle, she unsealed a hidden door adjacent to the restrooms. "Need to use the facilities, sir?" she asked.

Coralis scowled. "I may be old enough to be your great-great-grandfather, but my kidneys work just fine."

"I meant nothing by it, sir. It's just that it must have been quite a trip for you."

"I have witnessed the horror of the modern-day restroom and have no intention of subjecting myself to such humiliation," he growled.

"Ah." She tried unsuccessfully to suppress a rueful smile. "I think you'll find my water closet a wee bit more accommodating than those on the plane."

She pointed to a door marked wc, and as the door closed behind him, he said to himself: "This is more like it."

Upon exiting, he nodded humbly. "Thank you," he said. "It's good to see the world has not lost all sense of civility and decency."

Molly stifled a laugh as she led him down the exposed staircase. It was thirty-seven steps down—no landings. "How was your trip?" she asked.

"My trip was the painful equivalent of having four teeth extracted," he grumbled. "Why people choose to travel like that is beyond comprehension. Crying babies, cramped seats. The only bright spot was that people had their heads buried in electronic gadgets—no mindless chitchat. But there are much better ways to travel. Surely this 'emergency situation' isn't as dire as all that."

"We'll see." At the bottom of the staircase was another door. "I have a feelin' yer gonna eat them words."

Coralis was about to contradict her—but when he saw the two figures on the other side of the door, he realized Molly had been right.

"Pass the saltshaker," he said.

Though not as extravagant as Coralis's Kunstkammer at the castle, Molly's was nonetheless impressive. If one knew where to look, some of the rarest curiosities in the natural world were available from New York City merchants. It was obvious Molly knew where to look. The twenty-by-twenty room was a Wandmaker's gold mine. Coralis had seen it all before, of course—except for the unusual bundle in the far corner.

Molly adjusted the blanket that was wrapped around the two sleeping figures. A rodent-sized ball of blue fur uncurled from her slumber and yawned. She blinked rapidly, taking in the sight of not one but two adults gawking down at them—then bit her still-sleeping companion on the arm.

"Ouch!" The boy rubbed his arm, then his eyes. "Oh!" He scrambled to sit up, suddenly aware that the Wand Master had arrived.

"We have company," said the hedgehog.

"It can speak!" Coralis said as he leaned in for a closer look.

"And bite," Molly warned a second before the rodent nipped at him. "She's not very happy, I'm afraid."

The boy sat huddled in silence, his back to the wall. "And what about him?" Coralis asked.

"His name is Henry and he can hear you," snapped the hedgehog. "Ask him yourself."

"Humpf! Do not test my patience, young lady," warned Coralis.

"Or what? You'll turn me into a toad? You think that could be any worse than a spikeball?"

"I didn't mean it," Henry said, barely audible. "It was an accident."

"An accident?" Coralis stroked his chin thoughtfully. "Must have been a very potent one to do this to a young girl."

"Someone was dumb enough to give Henry a *real* wand," she said.

Molly stifled a laugh. She seemed to enjoy the hedgehog's cantankerous attitude. "There is something else you should probably see, Coralis." She flipped the light switch, which should have shrouded the room in darkness. Instead, the young boy glowed like a twenty-watt bulb.

"What on Earth?" Coralis leaned closer, and the brightness intensified. He immediately backed off. "Young man, who are you?"

Henry opened his mouth as if to speak, but the words dried up in his throat. However, the hedgehog seemed to have no such trouble. And her words were as sharp as her teeth. "He's Henry Leach, and I'm his sister, Brianna, and by the way—"

"It can't be . . ." This time it was Coralis's turn to go speechless.

Brianna's tiny nose wiggled in irritation at being interrupted. "Well, now that you know who we are, maybe you can tell us who *you* are," she demanded.

"He's Coralis," whispered Henry. "The Grand Wand Master."

"Coralis . . . huh . . . Hey, wait a minute!" exclaimed Brianna. "You're the one who got us into this mess!"

"Young lady, I don't think—"

"You're telling me!" Her spiky fur bristled angrily. "The next time you go giving out magic potions, leave my ding-a-ling brother off your list. Some grand wizard you turned out to be."

"What?" Coralis exploded.

"Uh-oh." Henry yanked the blanket over his head.

"How dare you call me a wizard, you . . . you . . . bilious blue blemish!"

"Hey! Now you wait a minute!" She waddled up to him and slapped at his boot. "I don't know what 'bilious' means, but I know what a 'blemish' is and I-have-never-had-a-zit-in-my-life!" She poked his foot with her paw for emphasis at each word.

Molly snorted loudly as she tried to contain herself, but then burst out laughing. "Oh, this is precious." She leaned her back to the wall, laughing till she was short of breath. "The great Coralis—scolded by a hedgehog."

With no warning, Coralis bent down and scooped up Brianna. She squirmed in his grip and was about to clamp down on a finger when she saw the deadly scowl on his face and thought better of it. "That's the first wise decision you've made since I met you," he grumbled. "And you!" he addressed Molly. "Get rid of the buffoon upstairs so we can discuss this matter in comfort . . . please."

When Coralis removed the time-freeze, the patron's stew promptly spilled in his lap, courtesy of Coralis's earlier prank with the spoon. Molly was still mopping up the mess when Coralis emerged from the basement, followed by the trembling form of Henry holding his sister.

"Mmmm. That smells delish!" Brianna's whiskers twitched happily.

Coralis growled and led them to a booth.

"If it's any consolation," said Molly, "the boy appears to be a vegetarian."

"Humpf," he grumbled, but appeared pleased by the information, and Henry suspected that Coralis himself was a vegetarian. "Drink this." He handed a glass of yellow liquid to Henry. "It will help calm your nerves."

Henry quickly ran through a list of yellow fluids in his head, trying to determine whether he should obey. Was this a test of some kind that would establish him as an apprentice?

"Drink it!" Coralis bellowed.

Henry jumped, then quickly swallowed it in four gulps. The mixture was surprisingly tasty. He licked his lips. The accident had done for Henry's senses what it did for Brianna's mouth. All five were elevated. "Lavender, I believe, with a twist of peppermint leaf. Safflower would give it the color." He glanced nervously at Coralis, hoping he hadn't messed up.

A cagey smile crossed the Wand Master's lips. Henry relaxed.

"Let me see your wand." A light sparkled in Coralis's eyes.

Henry sensed another test. He reached into a hidden pocket on the inside of his jacket where he kept his wand. The second he touched it, he began to glow even brighter. Henry winced—not from any pain, but because he didn't know how Coralis would react to seeing how badly he had failed. He quickly put the wand back in his pocket. "I'm afraid I'm not getting along with it too well these days." He lowered his head.

"Yes," said Coralis thoughtfully. "We shall need to tend to that first, won't we. Why don't you tell me what happened." He looked at his watch. "I believe we have time. Start with the day Randall delivered the wand."

"Randall?" Henry asked.

"The falcon," Coralis clarified.

"Pretty smart bird," said Brianna, making Henry smile.

"Not as smart as he thinks," said Coralis.

Molly served a round of herbal tea, Brianna's in a bowl.

Henry started his tale several times, each time realizing he had left something important out and starting over. Eventually, he covered all the events from the time his father left to the time his mother left. Toward the end, his voice wavered as the reality of his situation hit home. He and Brianna had been abandoned.

"And how did you end up here?" asked Coralis. "It's not exactly a landmark establishment."

"Excuse me?" Molly scowled. "It's a fine refuge for the wayward traveler. But I can see I'm not appreciated. Remind me to change the locks on the door."

Brianna giggled. Molly winked at her.

"After the accident"—Henry looked warily at his sister—"we waited till morning for Mom to return. When she didn't show, I searched her studio. And that's when we found the note—plus five hundred dollars. It told us exactly what to do to get here. That was a few days ago. Molly has been really nice. She even took us to the Museum of Natural History!" Henry's spirits temporarily lifted as he recalled the great exhibits—especially the one called *Dragons: Separating Fact from Fiction.* By the end of the tour he was certain they must still exist in some remote corner of the world.

"What of the boy's mother?" Coralis asked Molly. "Did she send word to you that the children were en route? Or did she push them from the nest, hoping they could fly on their own?"

"Aye, she called."

"Mom's instructions were very clear," Henry bristled, determined to defend her. "She liked using buses and showed us how to use them when we were little kids . . . um . . . littler kids." He handed a crumpled piece of paper to Coralis. "Bus routes, times, getting on behind an adult so the driver wouldn't think we were traveling alone. Where to go and how to act in the city." He pointed to the last line. *Always act like you know what you're doing and no one will question you.*

"Who knew Henry was such a good actor?" Brianna gave him a good-natured nip.

"It's all right, Henry. Your mum did what she had to do." Molly then addressed Coralis. "Do you know her family?"

"I know of it," he said.

"Well, believe me, she would have done this only as a last resort. Her words were cryptic, and it was obvious something had frightened her." Molly stopped to choose her next words carefully. "There was another presence—her word, not mine. She feared for the children's safety, so she sent them here and hoped to lead it away from them."

Coralis cupped his chin in his hand, deep in thought. The silence droned on. No one wanted to be the first to break it. Even Brianna kept her sassy comments to herself. "This is serious, but I urge you two not to worry about your mother. She has a fine lineage and I'm sure was properly trained to deal with adversity. But as for you . . . I must say, young man, usually it takes years of apprenticeship to make a mistake of this magnitude. That you were able to accomplish it on your

first try says quite a deal about your abilities. Even though
you got it all wrong."

"It was an accident!" pleaded Henry. "Nothing should
have happened!"

"Then why am I stuck like this, Henry? Undo it, please!"
Brianna sobbed a marathon of squeaks and squeals.

Molly cradled her. "There, there, little lass. Coralis will
see to it now."

"I'll see to nothing if I can't get to the bottom of it!" he
boomed. "Henry, stay on course. What else did you bring
with you?"

"Nothing. The books are too big and heavy. I might have
carried one, but not all of them. And . . ." He wasn't sure
how to continue.

"Keep going, Henry," Molly urged.

"And I was afraid to touch the gold stone. The way it
glowed, I thought for sure it would burn me."

A sudden realization struck Coralis. The ashen look on
his face said it all. "Oh my." He slumped in his seat.

"Coralis." Molly rushed to his side. "What is it? What's
wrong?"

"Henry, did this nugget of gold pulse? Did it seem to
drink the light the way you might drink a glass of water?"

Henry recalled the event all too vividly. "Yes. That's
exactly how it looked."

Coralis's eyes, fraught with worry and concern, roamed
across the dark ceiling. When he finally spoke, it was with
the weight of time pressing down on him. "In 1906, a terrible

earthquake shook and nearly destroyed the city of San Francisco. The cause of that earthquake was not what you believe. Yes, tectonic plates shifted. But the *reason* they shifted was due to a great battle that was fought between a brave conclave of Wandbearers led by Henry and Brianna's great-great-grandfather and an evil Wand Master named Dai She."

"The evil snake." Molly shivered. "I know of the legend."

"A legend based in fact." Coralis nodded. "Dai She's incredible power should have sent the entire city plummeting into the water, but your great-great-grandfather got lucky. The city was home to a federal mint that housed some of the purest gold on Earth. When the conclave managed to repel Dai She's energy, the gold *attracted* that energy.

"A large mound of it sucked in every remaining wave of bad energy and trapped it. And as the gold tightened its grip, it shrank to the size of a nugget. For years I tried to talk Henry into giving it to me, but he refused. He felt responsible for the devastation and wanted to keep the gold to remind him of his failure. And now, after all these years, it has fallen into the hands of this young man."

"But . . . but . . ." Henry furiously rubbed his head. "I don't have it! I mean, I left it home! I didn't know what it was. I was scared . . ."

"Calm down, Henry." Coralis reached to pat his arm. "We need to go to your house anyway to retrieve the books. The nugget is not going anywhere."

"Sir." Molly's voice trembled slightly. She gently lowered Brainna to the table. "The first time . . . the gold trapped negative energy. Is it safe to assume that it would only attract more negative energy?"

"Yes, my dear Molly," he said. "And therein lies a rather big problem."

Henry could hardly stand it any longer. He had made so many mistakes. He suddenly wished he had never laid eyes on the *Guidebook*. "What did I do?" he moaned.

"Well, my dear boy, if I am correct, I believe you have succeeded in capturing moonbeams in your aura. And not the pleasant variety, either."

"That sounds bad." Henry slumped forward and buried his head into his arms.

"Relax, Henry." Coralis stood and smiled at him. "Our adventure is just beginning."

But he kept a final thought to himself: *The worst may be yet to come.*

THIRTEEN

The rain had slackened, but the wind still whipped in crazy circles. Henry thought it was remarkable how it seemed to come from every direction at once.

Brianna, however, did not appreciate the elements in quite the same way. "I told you to buy a poncho yesterday—but no, don't bother listening to me. I'm an animal now, Henry. I can sense things like rain coming . . ." She continued to chitter away, concealed within Henry's jacket. At first he worried that anyone who overheard would assume that Henry was talking to himself. From his research about the moon, he knew such people were called lunatics—crazies! Of course, that was before advancements in technology. Now passersby would more likely assume that he had a cell phone or an iPod making noise in his pocket. These days, it was impossible to tell the nuts from the normals.

Henry tightened his hold on his sister to give her as much shelter as possible. He tried to make it a habit to learn something new every day. On this day, he'd learned something about fabric—specifically the difference between water-resistant and waterproof. An involuntary shiver passed from his damp neck to his shoulders to his chest.

Brianna felt it. "Don't you go getting sick, Henry!" After a few precious seconds of silence she mumbled, "Oh man. I sound just like Mom. I'll shut up now."

Coralis walked ahead of them, moving with speed and urgency. Molly, who'd closed up shop for the day, caught up to Henry and huddled a motherly arm around his shoulder. "We're almost there. But pull your hood closer to your face. You're glowing like a firefly."

They approached a door marked 41½. It was in the center of a row of buildings that had obviously not seen repairs since the day they were built. Several vagrants gathered in a tight group around the rusted gate that barred the entrance. They turned to say something to Coralis but thought better of it and hastily retreated down the block.

A slight smile pinched at Henry's lips. He had only just met the Wand Master, but already he could imagine what Coralis might have said, or the look he might have given, to make them leave so quickly.

The gate opened easily despite the rust, and Coralis led them down a short flight of stairs to a formidable door covered in graffiti. A sudden gust of wind doused them with another bucket of rain. "Bahtzen bizzle! Confounded elements!"

Brianna giggled, which prompted a glower from Coralis before he set to work, deactivating a locking mechanism similar to that at the tavern. They all stepped into a pitch-black foyer. "Remove your jacket, young man. It seems your condition will be useful after all."

Henry did as he was told, but also thought to retrieve his wand, increasing his skin wattage.

"Ah! Now you're thinking!" Coralis said lightheartedly.

Henry grinned at the compliment.

They proceeded down a long hallway, where they came upon yet another door. "There are sure enough locked doors around here," Brianna said, voicing exactly what Henry was thinking. "Hope there's a treasure chest waiting for us."

"Yes, and it contains a muzzle for small animals," snapped Coralis.

Brianna fluffed her bristles, which poked through Henry's shirt.

"Ouch! Easy, Brianna."

"Sorry. He's such a grump."

Henry listened carefully to the verbal code that unlocked the door. It appeared to be the same for each door, and he thought that if he heard it again he might be able to commit it to memory. But there were no more doors, only stairs—again. Henry began to wonder if the entire world of Wandmakers was underground.

Brianna poked her nose out. "Where are we? It smells like . . . something rotten."

Henry had started to pick up the odor as well—mold, mildew, decay.

"Mind your manners, young lady," Coralis scolded. "Have some respect for the dead."

"We are in a cemetery," Molly explained before Coralis could say more.

"Wait a minute!" Henry stopped at the foot of the stairs. His voice echoed back from several directions. "You mean we're *underground* in a cemetery? Like where the bodies are buried?"

"It's not like that," she said. "This is the New York Marble Cemetery. All the people here are interred in underground vaults made of solid white Tuckahoe marble."

"Wow," Brianna said, "even the cemeteries in New York are strange."

"Well, there's a lot of history here. After the yellow fever epidemic in 1822, which took the life of my older sister, Mary Claire"—Molly paused briefly to utter a blessing—"the city banned traditional earth burials south of Canal Street. Later, they extended the ban, first to Fourteenth Street and then all the way to Eighty-Sixth Street. But they still allowed burials in private family vaults like these."

"Is your sister buried here?" asked Brianna.

"No. We were very poor and couldn't afford a private burial. And so many people were dying from the fever." Molly dabbed the corners of her eyes with a handkerchief. "Poor Mary Claire joined the thousands that were buried in a potter's field that is now called Washington Square Park."

An ethereal voice sounded from next to Henry. "Oh, how I love hearing a true historian," it said.

"Ahh!" Henry ducked and ran, tripped, and sprawled into a damp, slimy wall. "Who's there? Who was that?" He looked all around, but couldn't find the source of the voice.

"Don't worry," Molly whispered softly in Henry's ear. "Most of them are friendly."

"Most of who . . . ?"

"What are you babbling on about?" Coralis hissed.

"Oh, it's just an unexpected visit from John," Molly said lightly.

"Wh-h-ho's John?" Henry stuttered.

"He's a dentist and a mean one!" snapped Coralis. "And he loves to pull children's teeth. Now can we stop this incessant chatter and get moving? There are urgent matters to attend to!"

"Coralis, please! You're scaring them. Do you want them to be afraid of all spirits?" Molly pleaded.

"Nonsense," he said dismissively. "John Greenwood! Show yourself."

A fuzzy apparition materialized between Molly and Coralis, gradually taking the shape of a middle-aged man in a finely tailored suit. His eyes were downcast, as if he had just received a scolding from a teacher. "I didn't mean to frighten anyone. You know how I love guests, and it's been so long since any children visited."

A tiny squeal of alarm peeped out from Henry's pocket as Brianna shivered.

"Henry, Brianna, meet John Greenwood, dentist to George Washington," Molly announced.

"G-G-G-eorge Washington . . . as in the first president?" Henry asked.

"The one and only!" said John. "I was a bit of a master with ivory, if I do say so myself. And George was so generous with his praise after I made the most exquisite set of teeth for him." He pulled a letter from his jacket pocket. "January 6, 1799. And I quote, 'His prices are very moderate, as no person can excel him in facility and neatness of performance.' Naturally, I raised my rates after that." He winked at them.

Henry couldn't help but like the man. "So who else is buried here?"

"Oh, I have lots of friends. Let's see . . . There's Cornelius DuBois, and Benjamin Wright—but don't get him started about that canal of his or you'll never get to leave. 'Erie Canal' this and 'Erie Canal' that. If you ever get caught by him, just start talking about the Panama Canal. That will shut him up." He laughed.

"I heard that, Greenwood!" a disembodied voice boomed nearby.

"Oops! Time to go." He faded away as if he had never been there.

"Wow," Henry whispered. "That was really a ghost, wasn't it?"

"Don't call them ghosts," Molly confided. "They prefer to be thought of as people. Use their real names."

"Are you just going to stand there all day?" Coralis thundered from up the tunnel.

They resumed their walk, passing vaults on either side. "Do they haunt people?" Brianna whispered, popping her head out.

"No," Molly answered in a whisper of her own. "The walls of the vaults are inlaid with phantom quartz crystals, which calm the spirits of the dead. Only restless spirits haunt people."

At the end of the tunnel, they entered the open vault on the right. It was bigger than Henry had imagined, and it was also empty. Now what? He watched Coralis walk to the back of the vault and withdraw a small yellow wand from the folds of his coat, which he used to trace the rectangular outline of a door onto the wall. Then with a slight tap of the wand to the exact center, the solid rock swung outward. They stepped through, and the pitch-darkness on the other side seemed to absorb some of Henry's glow. He couldn't see far, but he could sense the spaciousness of the room they'd entered.

Click.

Henry closed his eyes against the sudden brightness. When he could see again, he saw Coralis standing near a wall switch, grinning somberly beneath a series of wall sconces. Henry couldn't disguise his disappointment. He had been hoping for something much more magical than electricity.

Coralis must have been able to read his expression. "I hope you haven't been completely corrupted by misguided notions of 'wizardry,' boy. Now come here. We have much to do and little time to do it."

Henry examined the cavernous room as he approached Coralis, soaking up every detail. Light glittered and danced as it reflected off the tiny quartz crystals embedded in the ceiling. *They look like stars,* thought Henry. As he focused on an area directly overhead, it hit him. "They *are* stars," he whispered in wonder.

"Stars?" Brianna poked her nose out to see what her brother was talking about.

"The quartz in the walls. It's been arranged to look like the constellations!" He spun in a circle. "There's the archer, Sagittarius, and the Gemini twins. Oh! And there's the southern hemisphere!" Henry pointed to another set of constellations across the room. "This is amazing!"

"Very perceptive," Coralis said, and Henry thought he caught a hint of genuine admiration in the Wand Master's voice, but it was gone just as quickly. "Now stop babbling like a disturbed child and get over here. Mr. Osborne!" Coralis boomed, and Henry turned to see the spirit of another well-dressed man on the far side of the room. The man cringed and began to dissolve into the wall.

"Not so fast!" Coralis hurried over and took a small parcel from the spirit. He opened it to reveal several sparkling gemstones, which he brought to a cabinet. Henry caught only a glimpse inside, but the cabinet appeared to contain a gemologist's dream selection of minerals from around the world—some of which he'd never seen before, even in books.

"Your days as a mercantile agent are long over, William," Coralis said, returning the gemstones to their proper place. "And the market for these is well beyond your reach."

"I am sorry, sir." Mr. Osborne's voice was full and deep. Henry could easily imagine him bellowing from a podium. "I was simply . . . cleaning them for you. Are you certain you don't need to have any of these fine samples appraised?"

"I am quite certain."

"Very well, then. Good day to you all."

"That's the problem with these old haunts," Coralis grumbled as the spirit faded from view. "Too many temptations for the poor bored souls left behind." He opened a small drawer in the cabinet and selected a clear quartz ring that fit him perfectly. He then led Henry to a large ebony desk, the top of which was inlaid with swirls of iridescent opal. "Give your sister to Molly."

Henry reluctantly handed Brianna over. He hadn't realized how much he depended on having her with him. He suddenly felt very alone as he faced the scowling Wand Master.

"Take off your coat and give me your hands." Henry did as directed, and Coralis roughly grabbed his wrists and placed his palms directly on the center of the desk. The opal coursed with energy, rippling through a dazzling display of color that ranged from orange to purple to brilliant blue.

"Good," said Coralis. "We still have time." He released Henry's hands and the opal's colors diminished, settling on a warm amber infused with blue highlights.

"Still have time for what?" Henry asked nervously.

"Don't worry, my boy." Coralis looked at Henry, kindness seeping into the creases of his frown and softening the edges. "What Bella told you about the bad moon . . ."

"Bella?"

Coralis chuckled. "I almost forgot. You know her as 'The Amazing Zeppo.' Did you have any idea what she meant by 'bad moon'?"

"No, sir."

"There will be time for explanations later. For now, let's deal with the immediate problem."

Coralis reached into a desk drawer and took out a large leather-bound book, covered in runes and fastened together with clawlike hinges that bit firmly into all four corners. He whispered a phrase in Latin. Several of the runes shifted and joined together, forming the shape of a keyhole. He placed his index finger over the shape and pressed firmly. The book gave a barely noticeable sigh. The hinges relaxed their grip and the rigid edges of parchment rippled, almost with relief, as he reverently opened the book.

He once again gripped Henry's hands, but gently this time. His eyes danced with anticipation. "Let us begin."

FOURTEEN

Dai She arrived in Mexico City on the Nightmare Flight. What was supposed to be a four-hour, non-stop flight had encountered bad weather and an endless series of mechanical problems.

Three forced landings and seventeen hours later, Dai She finally emerged into an overcrowded airport terminal to the stares of hundreds of people who had apparently never before encountered a quasi-albino—a short, round one at that.

Dai She had always been round. He'd always been very, very pale. But the feature that drew the most attention was the large orange birthmark that covered his entire nose. As a child, he'd suffered the incessant teasing of his peers. Their cries of "Frosty the Snowman" had haunted his nightmares for years.

Already in the foulest of moods, he glared at a young girl who stood staring at him, openmouthed in wide-eyed wonder. "It's not polite to stare, little girl!" he snapped at her.

The fact that she didn't understand English didn't keep her from running to her equally frightened mother, screaming all the way.

Dai She had grown to expect people to gawk at his condition over the years, which is why he seldom ventured out of his secluded estate. But the fuss from these people was beyond rude. Perhaps, he thought as he walked into a restroom, ivory-white skin and facial birthmarks were even rarer in Mexico.

And then he looked in the mirror.

He nearly screamed! His face was blotchy with swollen hives. The second he touched one, it began to itch. There was only one thing he knew of that could cause this reaction—rodents! Among all the other maladies he suffered through his childhood was a severe allergy to rodents—mice, rats, squirrels, hamsters, gerbils, even the dog-sized capybara.

As he hurried out of the restroom to find a pharmacy, he nearly collided with a man he recognized from the flight who was carrying a small crate. A tiny pink snout with white fur and pale whiskers wiggled through a breathing hole—mocking him, albino to albino.

"Ahh!" He screamed in horror and roughly shoved the unwary man out of his way. The crate clattered to the ground, and a hinge broke free upon impact.

One of the interesting facts about rats is that they can squeeze through openings no bigger than a half-dollar coin. The gap in the crate was slightly larger than that. Fleeing its smashed cage, the rat skittered behind the nearest large object—the leg of Dai She. The sound of a grown man screaming in fright was too much for the poor rat to take.

It, too, screamed.

The high-pitched squeal doubled in intensity as the dancing trunk of a leg stomped down heavily, catching the tip of the long pink tail.

Irrational terror gripped both large man and small beast as they simultaneously lunged for the safety of the restroom. Dai She ran blindly ahead until he was stopped by a wall, at which point he turned and fell, nearly breathless, into a stall, where he sat blubbering like a fool, holding the broken door closed with his feet.

The rat took a different path. It turned left and hugged the base of the wall, squeezing through the gaps between the stalls until it arrived at the last one, where it hid behind a toilet occupied by a large man. Its rapid rodent breath was masked by the sound of whimpering sobs.

"Gigi," called the man with the crate. "Oh, Gigi."

The rat, upon hearing its name, stepped cautiously from behind the toilet. It almost made it out of the stall unnoticed— but then Dai She saw it out of the corner of his eye.

"Aiii!"

Dai She jumped straight up, stomping wildly until one foot landed squarely in the unflushed-by-the-previous-occupant toilet bowl.

Gigi spotted her broken cage, along with the familiar face of her owner, and raced to safety, happily leaving the blotchy man with the smelly, wet feet behind.

An hour later, his face smeared with anti-itch cream and his shoes still damp, a somewhat composed Dai She warily left the confines of the restroom. And just when he thought his day couldn't get any worse, he arrived at the baggage claim only to find that his suitcase had been lost.

Viktor, meanwhile, was having troubles of his own. Airlines will allow many types of pets to travel with their owners, but for some reason Dai She did not understand, the no-fly list includes vultures. Unable to travel with his master, Viktor was left to his instincts to find his way to Dai She's destination. For several hours he hugged the coastline, soaring on wind currents that enabled him to cover maximum distance with minimal effort.

Vultures are best known as scavengers, but their diet extends beyond roadkill. As Viktor flew, he kept an eye out for potential meals along the cliffs. He could hardly believe his luck when he spotted an abandoned nest with two large bluish-white eggs.

Just as he approached the rocky ledge, however, the wind shifted. Instead of making a graceful (by vulture standards) landing, he slammed headlong into the cliff.

Viktor fell beside the nest in an unconscious heap.

Dai She had previously arranged to have a private jet take him a few hours north to Chihuahua City, where he had a car waiting for the next leg of his journey. But because of his excessive travel delays, the jet took off without him. What little Spanish he knew allowed him to successfully negotiate new transportation with the seedy owners of a small propeller-driven aircraft. (Calling it a plane, he decided, would be giving it too much credit.)

He finally settled into the open-cockpit backseat of what he surmised to be a crop duster, which held only enough fuel to take him to Los Mochis on the Mexican coast. The aircraft's name was stenciled on its side. An hour into the flight, Dai She puzzled out the rough translation: *Smoke and Choke*. And that it did.

Exhaustion had left him weak. He hadn't eaten in almost a day and wouldn't dare drink the water. On a trip through Mexico many years earlier he had learned a lifelong lesson when tiny parasites in the water gave him a severe case of diarrhea—or as it was best known, Montezuma's revenge.

Despite his physical and mental fatigue, he managed to find his way to the Los Mochis train station, where he caught his first break. The Copper Canyon train was just about to depart for Chihuahua City. His spirits soared when he saw that the train also stopped in Cuauhtémoc. The promise of rest, relaxation, and a good meal occupied his thoughts as the train rumbled out of the station.

Six separate canyons make up what is commonly known as the Copper Canyon. Formed by a half-dozen rivers, it is more than six times larger than the Grand Canyon and offers some of the most breathtaking scenery in the world. The railway had taken nearly a hundred years to build, and it featured three dozen canyon-spanning bridges and close to one hundred tunnels.

Dai She didn't care about any of this. Things of beauty were lost on him. Feats of engineering left him indifferent. He did, however, happen to glance out the window as the train passed over an exceptionally deep gorge. The power of nature was something he could appreciate, and water was one of its most impressive forces. Water had shaped the rock over the centuries, as if the rock were nothing.

Finding a way to harness nature's power to do his bidding had consumed him for his entire life.

Power was all that mattered. Power meant control.

Turning a blind eye to the stares of tourists who packed the train, he closed his eyes and slept.

When Viktor awoke, he wasn't alone. A very large, very angry giant condor was perched in the nest, glaring at him.

The condor is in fact a relative of the vulture—but this was not to be a happy family reunion. Viktor barely had time to clear the cobwebs from his tiny brain before he was unceremoniously grabbed by the neck, throttled soundly, and thrown from the ledge.

Fortunately, instinct took over. He spread his wings wide and let the currents lift him along until his head cleared. Many miles later, he realized the cliff face was on his left instead of his right.

He was going in the wrong direction.

A jarring stop woke Dai She from his slumber and the inspiring dreams of world domination. A raucous commotion filled the car as dozens of tourists gathered their luggage in their haste to disembark at the town of Creel. Gay laughter and excitement permeated the air, and Dai She was jolted back to reality.

Thoroughly disgusted at the frivolity and with many more hours of travel ahead of him, he elected to remain in a state of mock hibernation until the train got moving again and the annoying happiness settled back into a quiet calm. But within moments he sensed a presence in his personal space, and when he opened his eyes, he found himself looking into the face of a wide-eyed child, leaning over the seat in front of him. The young boy smiled, which did nothing to improve Dai She's disposition.

The boy's father was preoccupied with his phone, littering the train car with colorful language directed at a lack of cell service. "Sit down, Charlie. It's rude to stare at . . ." The father finally looked up from his phone into the blotchy face of the passenger behind him. He smiled nervously as he tugged on Charlie's shirt. "Just sit," he whispered.

"Can I have the window seat?" Charlie jumped like a boy with a spring-loaded butt.

"No." His father began snapping pictures with his phone, slyly adjusting the angle to get a photo of Dai She in the seat behind him.

"Come on, Dad," Charlie pleaded. "I want to look for chupacabras." He bounced several more times and flipped back around to face Dai She.

"There's no such thing," his father said firmly. "Now, stop your foolishness."

Dai She had no intention of engaging anyone in conversation, least of all a happy child. But something in the father's dismissive tone struck a nerve. Dai She knew what it was like to be belittled.

"You're very mistaken," he told them. "Chupacabras are most certainly real. I've encountered one."

The boy's eyes lit up. "Really?"

"Now hold yer horses, fella. Don't go fillin' the kid's head with nonsense." The man's pride had been pricked enough that he put the phone down.

Dai She stared at him for a brief moment. A sneer curled the corners of his mouth, his thin lips taking on the appearance of a hungry reptile's. "Intelligent life-forms such as the chupacabra rely on the ignorance of people like you. It will wait until it finds you alone, perhaps hiking along a secluded trail. And at the most unsuspecting moment it will show itself.

"Your measly brain will have only seconds to process the terror of bristling fur and blood-drenched teeth. The end will be painful. It prefers its meals alive. Your terror will add seasoning to your flesh. And you can die knowing you have made it happy."

"Cool!" the boy shouted.

"Charlie!" The father quickly gathered their belongings and hustled Charlie into the adjoining car, but not before the eager child gave Dai She a thumbs-up.

Dai She sat back, savoring the man's discomfort. Much like the chupacabra, he relied on the ignorance of humanity.

Suddenly it occurred to him that the facilities of the train station promised to be more hygienic than those on the train. He roused his bulk out of the seat and hastened out onto the platform. For the first time since this miserable trip had begun, he was truly happy.

But the happiness was short-lived.

He emerged from the restroom.

The train had departed.

Part of Dai She's problem was that being dastardly and diabolical doesn't make you many friends. You're required to keep your plans to yourself. Trust is not part of your vocabulary. Consequently, he had no one to turn to for help.

He had two choices: wait twenty-four hours for the next train, or find another means of transportation. Forced into a vigorous negotiation with a cabdriver, he eventually left Creel in the confines of a battered green-and-gold taxi.

The cab, as could be expected at this point, broke down on a remote dirt road. Dai She was a large man with active sweat glands. The lack of air conditioning had turned him into a sopping wet mess. Not even the breeze blowing through holes in the floorboard could help. However, there was one small consolation. As soon as he stepped out of the cab, road dust clung to every pore of his exposed skin. For the first time in his life, Dai She looked tan—enough so that he had no problem hitching a ride on a passing bus.

By the time Viktor realized he was flying in the wrong direction, he had more than doubled the time it should have taken to rendezvous with his master. He knew that Dai She would punish him in some way—probably by withholding a few meals.

Even so, turning around was out of the question. Viktor wouldn't risk another run-in with the condor.

So he headed inland, hoping to find another route to his master—and perhaps some fresh roadkill to tide him over.

Dai She giggled, high and shrill. A very sound sleeper, he was gradually awakened by a tickling sensation on his left foot. His giggle died. The goat that was licking his toes didn't stop until Dai She had given it a sound kick. He slumped back against a stack of crates that held a variety of fruits and vegetables in various stages of decay, wondering if this journey could get any worse.

Besides the decaying fruit and vegetables, the bus also contained goats, chickens, and a single dirty brown goose that gazed at him over a warty orange beak. If the goose had half the brain it was born with, it might have thought it was looking into a distorted carnival mirror. Instead, it waddled up next to the tan man in the mottled yellow suit with the blotchy orange nose and settled in for a cozy nap.

To the casual observer, they could have passed for siblings.

Viktor had flown for hours without finding a single morsel of roadkill. Exhausted, lost, and very hungry, the vulture decided to rest his weary wings. He settled on a rusted brown bus, which was kicking up a trail of dust mixed with gray smoke from a failing exhaust system. With a loud THUMP he landed on its roof and skidded to a grinding halt in the dead center.

Once the offensive smells of burning oil cleared his senses, he detected a scent that was much more appetizing. It was coming from inside the bus. The odors of rotting fruit and fresh fowl renewed his hunger. The only sound louder than the rickety bus was that of his growling stomach.

He was in the middle of planning a strategy for getting at his next meal when another odor came forth—one that was very familiar. Could it be?

Keeping his balance on the moving bus was not easy, but he carefully made his way to the edge, gripping the smooth surface as hard as he could and peering over the side.

Dai She squirmed uncomfortably on the floor. His make-shift seat had become unbearable, as had the stench. Surely walking was a better option.

Something moved near the top of the dirt-encrusted window. A shadow? Curious, he stood and wiped the glass with a filthy, damp rag. A face looked back at him—a face only a mother (or a master) could love. A face he had never been happier to see.

Viktor.

Dai She opened the window and Viktor poked his head in. But any elation at seeing his companion quickly dissipated when the bus driver slammed on the brakes, then turned in his seat to vehemently voice his objection. Dai She's translation skills weren't the sharpest, but he understood the essence of the driver's highly animated speech.

Either it goes or you go.

But there were limits to Dai She's patience, and they had just been reached. He had not become the vilest Wand Master of all time by accident.

The bus driver was in midrant when Dai She's pupils narrowed to thin vertical lines—the eyes of a snake. He concentrated on the driver's thoughts and sought out his personal fears.

Spiders. Too easy. He smiled.

The first indication the driver had that there was a problem was the distinctive sensation that something was climbing up his leg. Dai She expected some hysterical screaming, but the reaction was even better: The driver was paralyzed with fear, unable to move, unable to speak.

Then Dai She made the large, hairy black spider disappear in a single puff of smoke. "Start driving," he commanded.

Either the driver thought he had imagined the feeling of a spider on his leg, or his mental capacity was too limited to connect the dots. He began to rant about Viktor once again, raising a hand and pointing at the vulture.

This time, two spiders the size of dinner plates appeared out of thin air on the man's arm. A gargled scream caught in his throat as he began to shake in fright. So that there was no misunderstanding about what was happening, Dai She waved his hand over the spiders, and again they disappeared. "I said," he commanded menacingly, "drive the bus."

The driver slowly backed away from Dai She's snakelike glare. But instead of returning to his seat, he made a mad rush for the door. A half-dozen hairy arachnids blocked his way and he flopped backward into his seat, blessing himself with multiple signs of the cross for divine protection.

"Drive now, or I will tell them to attack. And when they are done, I will have a snake swallow you whole." A large boa constrictor slithered across the floorboard, tongue flicking, eyes full of hunger.

The driver started the bus and ground the gears in a panic.

"Thank you." Dai She smiled. The spiders and snake disappeared and his eyes returned to normal. It felt good to be evil, to intimidate the clueless and the helpless.

It had been a rough journey, and it wasn't over. But he was beginning to have some fun.

High overhead, a lone bird of prey soared in wide, lazy circles, a mere pinpoint of movement against a pale blue sky. Even if he had not possessed the keen eyesight of a falcon, Randall would have been able to follow the plume of dust that trailed behind the bus from miles away.

It had taken a bit of an adjustment to slow down into a gliding pattern. As a rule, falcons prefer speed. But stealth was much more essential to this mission.

He wondered if Coralis had any idea what was going on. As much as he wanted to return to his mentor and fill him in, he couldn't let Dai She out of his sight—not until he knew what the evil snake was up to. He watched as a pair of pale hands reached out of the bus to take the vulture inside.

Casting aside pangs of hunger and thirst, he continued his lonely vigil.

FIFTEEN

Henry had finally fallen asleep. Coralis watched him curled up in the corner of Molly's basement on a makeshift bed. The blanket moved slightly as Brianna shuffled into a more comfortable position.

The procedure had been painful for the boy. His aura was strong and protective—Coralis had rarely seen the potential for such power in one so young. But it also meant that a higher concentration of energy was needed to extract the moonbeam. Stubborn tendrils of light had held on to Henry like a desperate man clinging by his fingertips to the edge of a cliff. Despite Coralis's efforts to lessen the pain, Henry had cried out. He said it felt like pliers pinching and pulling at his skin. When the angry moonbeam had finally snapped free, Coralis had trapped it within a rutilated quartz ring he wore on his left hand—a gift from a Mayan high priest.

He held the ring up to examine it once more. Light pulsed briefly, almost in contempt over its imprisonment. A bad sign.

Normal moonbeams are docile, eager to be absorbed and easily acclimated to their new environment. The moonbeam

Henry had absorbed was something else entirely. And if it was any indication of what was in store for them, then Coralis had every right to be concerned.

Randall and Bella were right after all: A bad moon was on the rise.

And it had nearly claimed its first victim. Given enough time, the moonbeam might have completely overtaken Henry's aura. It would not have been the first time a promising young apprentice had been lost to the elements of evil.

The creases on Coralis's face softened as he scrutinized Henry from across the small table. It occurred to him that he had just thought of the boy as an apprentice.

Henry awoke to Brianna's gentle nudging.

"What is it?" he mumbled.

"I smell breakfast," she said excitedly.

A moment later the door opened and Molly entered the room carrying a tray of tea and fresh-baked cranberry scones.

"Breakfast is served," she announced, rousing Coralis from his slumber. The Wand Master grumbled unhappily.

"Thanks, Molly. I'm starved," said Henry. He crossed the room to help, taking the tray from her and arranging place settings at a folding table.

"Such a polite boy," she said admiringly. Then she winked at Coralis, who scowled. "Oh come on now, Coralis. Henry has shown remarkable character for a boy his age. Especially in these times, when good manners and common courtesy have been all but abandoned."

Coralis selected a scone, silently acknowledging her comment with a thoughtful tilt of his head, and Henry blushed. As the Wand Master popped a bite of his scone in his mouth, he seemed to sense two beady eyes boring into his back. "Is something bothering you, young lady?" he asked Brianna without turning to face her.

"Speaking of manners!" Brianna snapped. "Do you always talk to people with your back to them?"

Coralis did not try to hide his annoyance as he turned, glaring menacingly at the hedgehog. "Feeling rambunctious, are we?"

Her spikes bristled. "I'll show you ram . . . whatever!"

"Brianna!" Henry shouted. She had seen the extent of Coralis's power the same as he had. Did she honestly believe that getting under his skin was a wise move?

"First of all," Coralis growled, "rambunctious means wild and unruly—like you. And secondly, if you have a question, just come out with it. *With* some respect," he added.

Brianna's face turned purple as a flush of red anger blended with her blue coloring. Henry saw the tiny digits of her paws move as she counted to ten. He turned away as the beginnings of a smile tugged at his lips. It was good to see her trying to control her temper tantrums, and given Coralis's mood, it was a wise choice.

"Fine." Her voice shook slightly. Counting to ten hadn't worked. "You've taken care of him; now what about me? All he had was a lighting problem. Look at me! I'm an eight-year-old girl. I used to have beautiful auburn curls, not blue spikes!" A sob crept into her voice. "Why don't you use some of that hocus-pocus on me?"

"There, there." Molly reached out to pet her but drew her hand back quickly when Brianna bristled and snarled at her.

"No!" she yipped. "Do not pet me! I am not to be petted—ever again! It's my turn, Mr. Wizard—or whatever you are. Wave your magic wand in my direction. Or aren't you up to it?"

Henry had seen many of Brianna's outbursts in the past, but he'd never witnessed the kind of venom she spat at Coralis just now. He wondered if the moonbeam had affected more than just her physical appearance. "Brianna!" he hissed in warning.

But Coralis surprised them all. "The girl has a point," he said slowly. He stroked his chin in thought as he paced to the door and back. "Her situation is more . . . complex."

He reached down to pick her up. To Henry's surprise, she let him. "There are powerful forces at work here, the likes of which have not been seen for hundreds of years. In order to undo what has been done to you, I will need to understand all the forces that were involved. Otherwise, I could make things worse."

"How could it be worse?" She whimpered sadly.

"I once saw a young man changed from a box turtle into an ordinary rock. No longer able to speak, he will spend eternity alone, forever encased in stone. Think of this the next time you toss a stone into a lake."

"Was there nothing you could do to help him?" Henry gulped.

"Nothing. By the time I got involved, the forces that were responsible had been twisted beyond recognition." He turned back to Brianna. "Sometimes we should leave well enough alone."

"You mean I might stay like this forever?"

"I mean we gain nothing from rushing the matter." Unexpectedly, he smiled. "Besides, judging by your quills, I can see you are a remarkable little princess in any form."

Brianna ran a paw over her face, accepting the compliment, yet slightly embarrassed.

"Don't worry, young lady. We'll get you straightened out."

SIXTEEN

Henry had heard the word "ransacked" before, but it wasn't until he stepped through the front door of his home that he could appreciate what it meant. What started with a few pieces of overturned furniture in the living room rapidly escalated. Cabinet doors in the kitchen had been yanked off their hinges and their contents tossed violently onto the floor. Very few pieces of his mother's china had survived the onslaught. Herbs and spices, their bottles shattered, dusted the mess with a fragrance Henry would forever think of as the scent of anger.

"Wow! Somebody hated this kitchen worse than Mom did!" said Brianna.

It was true that their mother could never have been accused of loving to cook, but what they witnessed here went beyond a mere dislike.

Henry had a brief panic attack when he thought of what might have happened to his cat. But he knew from past experience that she couldn't be caught if she didn't want to be. And she was very efficient at raiding the neighbor's cat dish for food, as well as making meals of the prolific rodent population. The cat would be fine.

Surveying the wreckage of the kitchen, Henry was suddenly very relieved that Coralis had accompanied them from New York. The old Wand Master had grumbled most of the way, as they traveled by subway train and bus and chartered car. But he'd insisted that they needed to do this together.

Before they'd departed Molly's tavern, Coralis had chosen a coat very similar to his own from a closet full of strange apparel and given it to Henry. He explained that it was constructed from very special fibers and was the preferred garment of Wandmakers. And to someone who liked pockets as much as Henry, it was a dream come true.

Molly had bid them a tearful good-bye. Unaccustomed to physical displays of affection, especially from someone as pretty as Molly, Henry had blushed furiously when she'd squeezed him in a tight hug. Brianna had teased him about it for hours.

"Bahtzen bizzle!" Coralis's shout pulled them away from the horror of the kitchen to a worse horror—their father's study. The large immovable desk had been upended and now leaned at such an extreme angle, it looked like it should topple over. But the gaping gash it had wedged into the wall held it like a clenched fist. Every book had been ripped from the shelves, and in some cases torn in half.

"What about our rooms, Henry?" Perched in Henry's pocket, Brianna looked up to him with moist eyes.

"No need to bother," said Coralis grimly. "I've already looked. They are in no better shape than this." He smiled cagily. "And yet, amid the rubble, the intruder missed this." He tossed the gold nugget to Henry, who, for the first time in his life, caught something without dropping it.

Henry immediately flipped it back to Coralis. "Yikes!" He had seen what that gold was capable of doing and his mind reflexively screamed *Danger!*

"Relax." Coralis pressed the nugget into Henry's palm. "It's quite dormant for the time being. We may need it later, so it's best that you hold on to it for now. I also found this." He reached inside his coat, where he had tucked a book away.

"My guidebook." Henry frowned. Immediately after the accident, he'd put the book away, wishing he'd never set eyes upon it.

He thought back to the day he'd received the guidebook. He remembered the way his imagination had run rampant with the possibilities of wielding a magic wand. But the accident had changed all that. "What do you want me to do with it?" he asked.

"There is something inside that belongs to you." Coralis opened the compartment that held Henry's first wand. "Once a Wandmaker has infused a wand with his power, he must never allow it to leave his possession. This wand is now as much a part of you as your left foot."

Henry carefully extracted the simple, purple-stained wand and felt the familiar tingle in his fingertips. "Thanks, but—"

He was about to ask what good the wand would be to them now, but he was distracted by a leather-bound tome on the floor. "Coralis, what is this? It looks like it's been burned."

Coralis took the book from his hands and sniffed it. "Hmmm . . . not good." He mumbled something softly and ran his thumb over the brown edge. Tiny fingers of sparks spat and popped on the page. "Not burned. Scorched. And not from a match. You saw the sparks. They are a reaction due to residue from elemental energy." He saw the puzzled looks on their faces. "Someone was looking for something. And not just any someone. Only someone with the skills of a Wand Master could do this. Whoever it was used a Conscindo Wand. It is designed to destroy—the Latin definition literally means to tear apart. As you can see, it works."

"But who would do this?" Henry asked.

"And why couldn't they look without making such a mess?" added Brianna.

"To answer your question"—he addressed Brianna— "I believe the intensity of this mayhem was intentional. It is entirely possible that whoever did this found what they were looking for and created this mess to throw us off. But it is also possible that he could *not* find it and threw what you might call a temper tantrum."

"You said 'he.'" Henry moved to face Coralis. "Why did you say 'he'? You know who did this, don't you?"

"Allow me to answer a question with a question, Henry. The last time you saw your father, was there anything odd about his behavior?"

"Yes," Henry answered. "It was right here in this room, too."

"Describe in as much detail as possible everything you can remember about the night you spoke to him in this room."

Henry closed his eyes and forced himself to recall that frightening night. It should have been so easy. He thought he would never forget the look on his father's face, but his recollection failed him. It was all fuzzy around the edges— like looking at a 3-D photo without wearing the special glasses that would bring it into focus.

He frowned in concentration, then absentmindedly reached into a pocket. As his fingers contacted his wand, a surge of energy flooded his body and his eyes shone with clarity. Suddenly the room was just as it had been that night. The desk was upright in its proper place, the books were on their shelves, and most shocking of all, his father was sitting at his desk. Henry gasped, almost releasing the wand.

"Tell me what you see." Coralis's voice was inside his head, urging him on.

"He's here!" Henry was startled by his own voice.

"Henry, do not be afraid," Coralis whispered as he cupped his hand around Henry's. "I am with you now."

And indeed he was. Henry could clearly see Coralis standing behind his father, but even more remarkably, Henry saw another Henry standing beside the desk. The entire scene replayed itself just as it had happened that night, right up to the point when his mother charged into the room.

Coralis released Henry's hand and the room reverted to its state of disarray. "What just happened?" Henry's voice crackled and he coughed, his throat dry and mouth parched.

Coralis said nothing as he led Henry into the kitchen, where they managed to find an unbroken glass. It wasn't until his fourth glass of water that his thirst was quenched.

"Young man, are you quite sure you have had no formal training?" Coralis asked.

"No, sir." Henry righted a chair and sat heavily, his body drained of energy. "I've pretty much memorized the *Guidebook*, but . . . wait!"

He bolted from the chair and raced out the back door, Coralis a half step behind. Into the garage and up the pole to his loft in record time. "It's still here!" he shouted. He slid down the pole and jubilantly waved his notebook. "He didn't know about my private room!"

"Bahtzen bizzle!" Coralis exploded. "Slow down! What do you have there?"

"My notebooks!" Henry danced happily, unmindful of Coralis's growing irritation. "They're my notebooks—the ones I used when I translated the big books." The smile on his face stretched from ear to ear.

"Look!" He flipped through page after page of meticulous notes and definitions scribbled into the margins. "I didn't have any training, but I must have learned something on my own!" He handed the notebooks to Coralis, bursting with pride.

Coralis scanned the pages, murmuring to himself. When he stopped, he slowly closed the notebook, looking a degree paler.

"What's wrong?" asked Henry. "Did I do something wrong again?" His voice cracked, this time from worry. "I used the ulexite you sent me," he said defensively. "Why would you give it to me if I wasn't supposed to use it?"

"Are the books up there, too?" Coralis nodded toward the loft.

"They're in my room. Come on, I'll show you." He ran back to the house and held the door open for Coralis.

But Coralis did not follow. Instead, he stepped from the garage and looked skyward, deep in thought. Henry slowly returned to his side. "They're not there, are they?" he asked, but he knew. "That's what he was looking for, wasn't it?"

"Yes, Henry."

"They're important, aren't they?"

Coralis chuckled. "Yes, Henry. They are very important."

Silence again as Coralis continued to search the heavens. "What does it mean?" Henry asked softly.

"It means . . ." Coralis moved his thoughtful gaze to Henry. "We have work to do."

SEVENTEEN

R andall was faced with a most difficult task: to see without being seen. He could perch atop a tower and easily observe all that took place in the village below, but he did not want to draw attention to himself. He was fairly certain he had not been spotted by Dai She and desired to keep it that way. And he also had to be mindful of the sharp eyes of the vulture.

The bell tower in a church provided the refuge he needed while allowing him a clear view of Dai She's misshapen form. It was almost comical watching the openmouthed stares of children as he rumbled past them on the crowded streets below.

Cuauhtémoc was a thriving municipality. It was apparent there were many different cultures at work here. Colorfully clothed schoolchildren and dark-suited professionals—doctors and lawyers—meandered the streets in equal numbers.

When Dai She entered a clothing store, Randall took the opportunity to look for the vulture. It would be as out of place as he was and probably tucked into its own hiding spot. As he scanned the rooftops, his stomach reminded him just how long it had been since he'd eaten. He had seen marvelously delicious apple groves on the flight in and promised himself he would get back there as soon as possible. Long flights sapped a lot of his energy, and he had taken entirely too many of them in recent weeks.

But his own hunger gave him an idea. He expanded his olfactory sense, seeking the scent of carrion. Even in a town like this, there had to be a rotting animal corpse somewhere that would appeal to a hungry vulture.

His acute vision pierced the alleys, methodically searching. Several rats in garbage bins sent his hunger instincts to the edge of flight, but he managed to squash the urge. His persistence was rewarded on the south edge of town, far in the distance, where he found Viktor tearing into an armadillo carcass. He was jealous of his enemy's feast, but realized it was one less worry for him. The vulture would be occupied for some time.

A short while later Dai She emerged from the clothier, and a sharp squawk resembling laughter escaped Randall's beak. The tailor had probably done the best he could, but he obviously wasn't used to patrons of Dai She's unusual proportions.

The Wand Master now sported a pink shirt with ruffles down the front and a tan sport coat that had been "stretched" by adding a piece of green canvas that ran down the center of the back. The shiny black pants had been similarly stretched with vertical patches of paisley running from the waistline all the way down the legs. And topping it all off was a large gold sombrero.

He looked like a drum major from a hideous marching band. If his intent was to blend in with the locals, he would have been better off going to a costume shop.

But the comedy of the moment fell away as a large black sedan pulled up to the curb. A tall Caucasian man in a tailored suit stepped from the driver's side. He met Dai She and shook his meaty hand firmly. Neither man smiled. It was a meeting of business more than pleasure. And there was a powerful presence about the man.

Randall stretched his senses the way Coralis had taught him. This stranger was powerful, and he was hiding something— Randall could *feel* it.

The stranger had an air of familiarity. Randall had never laid eyes on him before, but he *had* seen those facial features. The shape of the mouth, the curious expression. So similar to . . . Henry? Could it be . . . ?

A sharp, sudden cry shattered his concentration. Close by. Too close!

Viktor raced into his field of vision. The two men jerked their heads toward the vulture's war cry as Randall tried a last-second lunge to evade his powerful opponent.

The last thing he remembered was a shout from Dai She as Viktor crashed into him.

The bell rang a single ominous note when Randall's head collided with it.

EIGHTEEN

"She is quite good." Coralis looked from canvas to canvas, examining the extensive collection of paintings that had occupied the majority of Henry's mother's time.

"Do you really think so?" Brianna probably had never given it much thought. The few times she and Henry had ventured into the basement studio, they weren't encouraged to stay. "Do be a dear and give your mommy a few minutes" was a typical dismissal of any intrusions.

"Yes, indeed. You can tell from the extraordinary detail that she truly immersed herself into the painting."

While Coralis and Brianna bantered aimlessly, Henry paced the floor like a monkey in a cage. This wasn't right—at all! They should be doing something. Coralis should be using his skills to locate the books so they could get them back. But even if Henry was the only one concerned with the urgency of their situation, something else wasn't right. Finally he blurted it out. "Why is this the only room in the house that wasn't trashed?"

Coralis did not answer immediately. Instead, he cocked his head like a dog that doesn't understand a "go fetch" command. "Didn't you feel it as you walked in?"

"It?" Henry glanced back at the doorway. Unsure of what "it" was, he scanned for evidence of something hanging from the ceiling or protruding from the floor.

"Hmmm." Coralis scowled. "There is still much you need to learn. Come over here," he said as he stepped closer to the door. "Now hold your wand out at arm's length and trace the outline of the door."

"Oh!" Henry jumped as the wand tugged at his hand as if it were magnetized. "What is it? What's making it do that?"

"That, dear boy, is a protection spell." Coralis smiled, enjoying the moment as teacher.

"Protection for what?" Brianna asked. "There's nothing here but paint."

"Not from what . . . from whom. Put your wand away, Henry." Coralis took a seat, rubbing his knees. "Do either of you happen to know your mother's maiden name?"

The question was answered by a blank look.

"Your mother's name before she married your father," he clarified.

"We never met anyone from Mom's side of the family," said Henry.

"And she never talked about them either," Brianna said. "Even though we'd always ask why we didn't have a grandma or grandpa like a lot of our friends."

"But there was that one time," Henry continued. "Remember when that old delivery van pulled up one day and how Mom flew into a panic?" he asked Brianna. "We asked what was wrong but she told us to stay put as she ran out the door. I could have sworn she said 'Mom' as the van pulled in, but the way she yelled at the old woman I thought I must have heard her wrong."

"But if that was her own mother, why would she yell at her?" Brianna angrily nudged Henry's foot. "She wouldn't do that! You must have messed that up, too." She nipped at his shoe.

"Hey, cut that out! I didn't mess anything up. I know what I heard. And I also know she told the woman to never come back."

Coralis growled softly, just enough to get their attention. "What kind of van was it? Can you recall the color? Any markings? What was she delivering?"

"White!" "Green!" They responded simultaneously.

"It was white with green letters," Henry stated emphatically.

"Oh yeah?" Brianna's fur bristled with agitation, not wanting to be outdone. "It had a pretty picture of something like fruit or vegetables."

"No, it wasn't," Henry argued. "It was wheat or something. Why else would it say Granoble's Granary?" His eyes bulged. "Wait! That's exactly what it said! I remember now because I had to look up the meaning of *granary* after she left."

Coralis's lips twitched in a half smile. "It's amazing what the mind can recall if you just stop thinking."

"And I'll tell you what else I remember." Henry was on a roll. "It had Arizona license plates."

"Do tell." Coralis leaned forward.

"And . . . and . . . well, I guess that's it." Henry's shoulders slumped. "That's not enough, is it? It doesn't tell us anything."

"On the contrary." Coralis walked to a series of paintings on the far wall. "Have you ever been to Arizona?"

"No." Brianna jumped in before Henry could answer.

"Did your mother ever talk about it? Perhaps she spent some time there. Did she like southwestern artifacts, perhaps an occasional cattle skull?"

"Ew, gross!" Brianna wrinkled her nose.

"No, she didn't," said Henry, but he leaned into a painting as he began to understand Coralis's line of questioning. "That's what all these paintings are. They're of Arizona, aren't they?" And for the first time, Henry witnessed the extent of his mother's talent. The flowers, the cacti, the reptiles, the rock formations: Every painting was of something best described as southwestern, and though he'd never been there, the images captured a sense of place brilliantly.

"Why would she paint these?" Henry asked, but it was of himself. He leaned in closer and squinted at a tiny black vertical line in the bottom right corner. A mistake? But the paintings were perfect—even Coralis thought so. Why wouldn't she cover over the mistake with a dab of brown paint to match the rest of it? Startled, he swung back around to face Coralis. "It's not a mistake!"

"Of course it's a mistake if you thought of it," Brianna said, bristling.

Henry didn't acknowledge her. He quickly went from painting to painting, locating other ones with marks on them. "Look!" He anxiously grabbed canvases from walls and easels and stacked them along a baseboard. "They're numbers!"

"They're not any numbers I ever saw," Brianna countered.

"They're Roman numerals!" Henry clarified. He quickly rearranged the paintings in order from I to IV. The effect was incredible. The four paintings formed a single tremendous landscape. "Ha! Look at that!" He turned to gloat at Brianna on the floor, but instead found her cupped gently in Coralis's palm, dumbfounded and speechless.

Henry looked back at the mural. "Whoa," he whispered.

"Indeed." Coralis stood next to him.

"Is that, like, one of those optical illusions?" Brianna asked.

"Something like that." Henry knew what he was looking at but couldn't make any sense of it. There were four paintings and three seams between them. Along the right edge of the first painting was what looked like a fluffy cloud or possibly a windblown dust devil. Along the left edge of the second painting was a continuation of that cloudiness. But what it actually formed when the paintings were pressed together was a mushroom cloud. The kind an atomic bomb would create.

Similarly, between paintings two and three was a large snake riding on the back of a long-horned goat. And between paintings three and four was a man's face, so lined with wrinkles it almost blended into the mountain range behind him. Henry rubbed his head. None of it made any sense. Was his mother just being creative, or was she trying to tell them something?

He was about to ask Coralis when he saw how intently the Wand Master stared at the face in the painting. "Joseph," he said softly.

"You know him?" Brianna asked.

"Yes." Coralis frowned. "It would appear pieces of the puzzle are coming together. And it is imperative that we finish the puzzle before anyone else does."

"So you never suspected a thing? She never told you anything about her lineage? Never discussed anything like natural elements? Never took you rock hunting or exploring for herbs? Nothing like that?"

Coralis had been peppering Henry with questions from the moment they left the studio. Now in the kitchen, he foraged for a bite to eat while Henry sat at the table with his head in his hands.

"No, nothing at all. Not even a hint." He thought hard. Until the day he was given the *Guidebook*, all he knew about another side of reality was what he read in books about magic and wizardry. He had never suspected he would possess any kind of special power within himself. But then events had spiraled quickly. And now, not only did he find out he had his own special powers, but his parents did as well.

Dad had given him some signs lately. But Mom? Really? Whatever her reasons, she had chosen to hide her true self from them. And she'd done a good job of it. Did Dad know? He had to . . . right? Maybe that was what had brought them together in the first place. And if he did know, maybe he was going after her right now . . . while they sat around doing nothing.

"We have to go. Now!" He bolted from the chair.

Brianna looked up from a bowl on the tabletop where she nibbled on dry cereal. "And how exactly are we going to get there? It's not like we can fly. Next time you poof me into something other than a girl, make it something that can fly . . . or become invisible. At least that would be useful. What can a hedgehog do?"

"I don't know. Maybe we can drive." But even as he said it, he doubted Coralis would be up to spending several days and thousands of miles behind the wheel of the car.

Coralis set a plate stacked with peanut-butter-and-jelly sandwiches on the table. "This is all I could find worth eating. If your mother had any culinary skills, she was as good at hiding them as she was at hiding her heritage."

"Watch it!" snapped Brianna. "That's my mother you're talking about."

Coralis started to retort but was interrupted by an outburst from Henry. "Oh!" he said. "I just remembered! Mrs. Verrity took a trip to Arizona last year. I'll bet she could help."

"And who, pray tell, is Mrs. Verrity?" Coralis asked.

Brianna rolled her eyes and nudged Henry's hand. "That would be his bookworm buddy. Library, here we come."

"Well, hello, Henry!" Mrs. Verrity gushed. "It's been so long since I've seen you. I thought you forgot about me." Her eyes glittered behind glasses with bright red frames. A beaded turquoise chain attached to the glasses draped loosely around her neck.

"Hello, Mrs. Verrity. This is my . . . um, uncle. Uncle C." Henry hadn't thought about introducing Coralis and fumbled for something to say at the last minute.

"My name is Coralis. Pleased to meet you, madam," he said, bowing slightly.

"Oh! Such a proper gentleman." She toyed with her chain coyly. "Coralis. What an unusual name. Where have I heard it before?" Her thoughts seemed to drift.

"Nowhere!" Henry almost shouted. Mrs. Verrity remembered everything, and he might have carelessly mentioned the name during one of his visits. He needed to distract her. "We're here to do some research."

She smiled broadly. "That's my Henry. Always the inquisitive one."

"Geek," Brianna chirped from Coralis's pocket.

Fortunately, Mrs. Verrity was already on her way to the lone computer at the information desk. "You must be very proud of your nephew. He's one of my best customers. So many interests. Which reminds me, Henry. I just ordered a new book about alchemy. I'll be sure to notify you when it arrives."

Henry stole a quick look at Coralis to see his reaction and was rewarded with a brief half smile. "Not many young minds seek a challenge," said Coralis.

"No." She sat and entered a password. "Too many distractions for today's youth. Makes me feel like an old relic."

"Ha!" Coralis's laugh was genuine. "I know the feeling all too well. But you, fair lady, are far from a relic."

"Oh my . . . thank you." She blushed.

Brianna stirred in his pocket. "Get on with it and stop flirting," she hissed.

Mrs. Verrity tilted her head. "Did you hear something? It sounded like a voice—a very small voice."

Henry thought fast. "Have you been reading *The Borrowers* again, Mrs. Verrity?" He gave her his best smile.

She smiled back. "It's either that, or the ghosts in this drafty old place."

"Actually, Mrs. Verrity . . . ," Coralis interjected.

"Please call me Cloris."

"Um . . . yes. Well . . . Cloris, Henry's question has to do with travel."

"His interests tend to be a little more unusual than that. Travel . . ." She turned to Henry. "Let me guess: You want to know about time travel! There's the Einstein variety, of course, or the *Wrinkle in Time* method . . ."

"No, ma'am. Not time travel. Regular travel." She looked slightly disappointed, but Henry pressed on. "Didn't you go to Arizona last year?"

"Oh, yes!" She clapped her hands giddily. "A simply wonderful adventure. I planned it all myself, you know. But Arizona is a very large state. Did you have a particular destination in mind?"

"Monument Valley," Henry said, which was the location Coralis had identified in his mother's mural.

"Oh, how splendid!" She clapped her hands again. "You can follow the exact route that I took several years ago. Follow in my footsteps, so to speak." She giggled.

"And how would that be accomplished?" Coralis asked. His voice was kind, but Henry sensed impatience just below the surface.

If she sensed it as well, she didn't let on. "See these lines?" She directed them to a large wall map of the United States and pointed to a series of crosshatched lines that meandered through the states. "These are railroad lines. That's why they look like train tracks. Lots of people prefer to travel by train. It provides a fascinating look at Americana. Passing through all those small towns and farms in America's heartland. Simply wonderful!"

"Is that how you went? Could you show us the route?" Henry asked.

"I'll do you one better than that." She leaned into Henry and whispered as if they were coconspirators in a crime. "I'll let you borrow my travel diary." She added a wink, sealing the deal. "I like to think I keep much better notes than any of those travel guides."

Henry thanked her profusely for the diary, promising to return it safe and sound, although he hadn't the foggiest idea when that would be. Following an awkward good-bye, during which Coralis forgot Mrs. Verrity's first name, they returned to the house. Not since the falcon, Randall, dropped into his life had Henry been so excited . . . and nervous. Were they really about to take a train all the way to Arizona?

He racked his brain. What did he know about Arizona? They had deserts and roadrunners and coyotes . . . but that was in cartoons. And hummingbirds! He knew that from his Audubon book. He'd never seen a real hummingbird.

He took his wand from his pocket on their way back home. Excitement ran from his arm into the wand, and the veins of clear crystal glowed in response.

Henry, Brianna, and Coralis left the house well before the sun had crested the horizon. And given the gloomy forecast, they knew they might not see the sun at all that day. They were heading for the train station several hours away in Pittsburgh. It wasn't the closest station to the house, but it was where Mrs. Verrity began her journey and was one less train connection on the first leg of their trip.

Of all the strange things Henry had witnessed recently, seeing the old Wand Master behind the steering wheel ranked perhaps higher than it should. There were some odd sounds from the engine and more than a few exclamations of "Bahtzen bizzle!" But eventually they were on their way.

Brianna slept on the backseat, curled comfortably in one of her favorite sweatshirts. Henry continued to read Mrs. Verrity's diary with the aid of a battery-operated book lamp. He didn't think Coralis needed to know it was an official Harry Potter book light.

"Henry," Coralis said softly. "Why don't you put that foolish light away."

Henry snapped it off too quickly. He fumbled to catch it as it slipped from his grasp. "Sorry, but how will I read in the dark?"

Coralis smiled but never took his eyes off the road. "I believe it's time I became a responsible adult again." The glow of light from the dashboard cast his face in shadow. Crow's-feet crinkled the corner of his eyes. It was the first time Henry saw him as more of a friend than a craggy old Wand Master. "It's time we accelerated your training."

Henry's heart skipped a joyful beat. "But . . but . . . do you really think I'm ready?"

Coralis chuckled. "No one is ever ready for the odd and unusual turns of life, but preparation for the unexpected is helpful. Now take out your wand."

Henry put the book light away and did as instructed. The wand felt more comfortable with each touch. It was now more a part of him than any of the treasures he had collected in his loft.

"You feel it, don't you? The wand is you and you are the wand. It is an extension of your inner self. By concentrating through it, you can enhance your natural strength and talent."

Strength? *He's never seen me swing a baseball bat,* thought Henry.

"Strength of the mind and spirit can overcome most physical challenges, but only if you have the confidence in yourself."

Henry thought back to the ball field. He knew he would strike out every time he came to the plate. What would have happened if he'd projected the confidence of hitting the ball as he glared at the opposing pitcher? Would it have helped? He almost smiled. It certainly wouldn't have hurt.

"Now concentrate on the wand and think of the power of the sun." Coralis's voice pulsed like a heartbeat in Henry's mind. He gripped the wand tightly and thought of the superheated gas that gave the sun its brilliance.

Without warning, blinding light erupted from the wand. Coralis stomped on the brake as the car swerved violently, tossing Brianna to the floor. In a panic, Henry yelled, "Dark!"

The wand immediately dimmed. Coralis regained control of the car and eased to the shoulder, waiting for his eyes to adjust from the momentary blindness.

Spots swam in front of Henry as if someone had taken a flash photo in a dark room. "What happened?" His voice cracked, betraying his fear of Coralis's wrath.

Coralis's shoulders began to shake as he suddenly erupted in laughter, shocking Henry. "My boy, you just taught me two valuable lessons. Never underestimate your student . . . and give better instructions." He continued to laugh until a few teardrops squeezed out and ran down his cheeks. "That was a good one," he finally managed to say. "We're going to make a heck of a team, Henry."

A muffled, irritated voice piped up from the rear. "You've never seen him swing a bat."

By the time they arrived in Pittsburgh, the sky was in full graydom. Coralis had spent the rest of the drive teaching Henry how to apply a measure of control over his powers. The only other hitch occurred when Coralis paid cash for the train tickets.

"Well, I'll be," said the cashier, holding up several odd-looking five-dollar bills. "I haven't seen a Lincoln porthole in years!"

"Is it still good?" asked Henry, hoping Coralis wasn't trying to use counterfeit money.

The old man behind the counter winked at Henry through his bifocals. "More than good, young man. This is what we used to call a silver certificate, which meant it was backed by silver instead of gold."

He saw the blank look on Henry's face. "Kids these days," he said, and winked at Coralis this time. "Gotta teach 'em everything." Enjoying the moment, he removed his glasses and began polishing the lenses in true professorial style. "Used to be that paper money was backed by gold—which meant that if you had a mind to, you could take your paper to the US Treasury and exchange it for gold. I don't know anyone who ever did that, but that was the theory. But at some point, the government saw they were running out of gold reserves and occasionally printed silver certificates—which were backed by silver. Are you still with me?"

Henry nodded, secretly enjoying the impromptu history lesson.

"Sometimes, when they printed silver certificates, they got fancy and put interesting designs on them. And sometimes they simply gave the design a bit of a twist . . . which is what you have here."

He took out a newer five-dollar bill and laid them side by side. "This particular bill was printed in 1923. See here how they placed the portrait of President Lincoln in a nice round circle? And how they outlined the border with the words 'The United States of America'? That's why they called these porthole notes—because it looks like the port-hole on a ship."

He looked up at Coralis. "Are you sure you want to give these up? They're probably worth more than five bucks."

Coralis gave no indication if he was mad at himself for choosing outdated currency. Henry imagined that much of the currency the man had collected over the years must be priceless, but the bill in question looked innocuous enough. He never would have guessed it was anything special.

"Will they get us to Chicago?" Coralis asked.

"Oh, indeed they will!"

Coralis winked conspiratorially back at him. "Then they're all yours."

The cashier printed the tickets and handed them to Coralis with a business card. "The name's Harry. Harry Wilson. Let me know if you ever have any more gems like this you want to get rid of."

"You'll be the first to know. Now come along, Henry. We have a train to catch."

As they turned to leave, the cashier said hopefully, "Don't you need a return ticket?"

"Afraid not, good sir. From Chicago, we're bound for the Southwest Chief to Arizona," said Coralis.

The smile on the cashier's face lit up almost as bright as Henry's wand. "Well, you're in luck! I can sell you those tickets from here, too. And I can give you some tips for the ride. I used to be a conductor on that line years ago. My son took my place."

"Well then, *you're* in luck," mimicked Coralis. "I just happen to have a few more of those certificates."

By the time they left, they had more useful information than anything written in Mrs. Verrity's diary. "It's amazing what you can learn just by being nice to someone," said Coralis.

"It didn't hurt that you just gave him something he can sell on eBay," piped in Brianna. Coralis's eyebrows arched quizzically.

Henry and Brianna shared a giggle. "We'll explain it to you later."

Randall awoke to pitch-blackness. Slowly his senses returned. His body was tightly bound and his beak clamped. A blindfold wrapped his head. Yet from the continuous jostling motion and muffled voices, he determined he was in the trunk of a car.

His talons were not bound, which gave him some hope. But as he moved one, he understood why. A small bell had been loosely tied to one of his legs, and it immediately jingled. The noise was very small but clearly enough to alert Viktor, sitting in the backseat, who screeched a warning like a junkyard dog.

The car came to a halt, tires grinding on loose gravel. The trunk opened and he was lifted out—carefully, to avoid contact with his razor-sharp talons. It was the first time he heard either of the voices clearly, but he could tell whose was whose. The higher-pitched, irritating voice could only belong to Dai She. The deep, smooth tone that reeked of venom belonged to the other man.

"So, Mr. Leach, our guest has regained consciousness."

The hands that held him tensed. "First, let me congratulate you on giving away my identity," Henry's father growled. "Second, I insist that you use my chosen name from this point forward."

"As you wish, Markhor." It was clear to Randall that Dai She did not like being corrected. He detected a subtle power struggle between the two, seething beneath the surface, which he could possibly exploit later. "But may I also remind you that you have not proven yourself worthy of the Wand Master rank."

Randall was quite familiar with the hierarchy of the Wandmakers' Guild. Once a Wandmaker succeeded in making his or her first wand, they became a Wandbearer. With extensive training and practice, a student would advance to First, Second, and Third-Order Wandbearer until reaching the status of Monarch.

From there, only the elite few achieved the rank of Wand Master. It was at that point that the individual could choose a new name befitting their rank.

Henry's father had apparently chosen Markhor—"the snake eater."

Markhor's hands tensed again in response to Dai She's insult, but the man offered no rebuttal. The power Randall could sense in those hands was indeed great . . . and muddled. As if two overlapping forces struggled to control the same body. He didn't know how to decipher this. Perhaps there was still more to learn from Coralis.

He quickly suppressed the thought. If Markhor was indeed this powerful, he might be able to see through the falcon to his true essence.

And that would ruin everything.

Perhaps Dai She was worried—as he should be. While he may have convinced himself of his superiority, there was a long history of students surpassing their teachers in the realm of Wandmakers.

Randall detected movement. "This is quite a collection you were carrying, young falcon." He could hear Dai She examining the pack of miniature wands and elements from his small, customized pouch. "Why would someone take the effort to train such a bird?"

Randall was lifted, turned, and examined. "Perhaps not trained as a bird." Markhor's voice had an ominous undertone.

Randall suppressed the urge to lash out with his talons, knowing it would give him away. Feigning ignorance was his best strategy for the moment. But Markhor was not easily duped. "Would a bound bird be so submissive?"

"Don't be a fool!" Dai She snapped. "It's nothing more than a passenger pigeon in disguise. What we need to find out is to whom he was delivering this precious cargo." Dai She's stubby fingers pinched his beak tightly. This time Randall did lash out. He quickly brought his talons up and raked at Dai She's hand, drawing blood and a pitiful scream. "You idiot! Bind those wretched talons," he shrieked.

Markhor cleared his throat. Was he laughing at Dai She? "As you wish." Randall was firmly pinned to the ground by a large foot while hands deftly tied his talons. He was placed back in the trunk. "We should get going soon. We want to get to the caves before sunset."

The lid slammed shut, sealing Randall with nothing but his thoughts, the foremost of which was: *This is not going to end well.*

Coralis allowed Henry and Brianna to sleep on the train ride from Pittsburgh to Chicago. When Henry awoke, he saw that it wasn't just for their benefit. Coralis's head was bent at an unnatural angle against the windowpane, almost guaranteeing a sore neck.

With Brianna wrapped safely under the seat in a blanket, Henry took advantage of the clacking of railroad ties to stand without disturbing anyone and head for the nearest bathroom. The train rocked violently, knocking him off balance as he closed the door behind him, and he decided it would be much safer (and less messy) to sit than stand. But as he pulled his pants up, his wand tumbled from his pocket and rolled beneath the sink.

Henry froze. He had read about the lack of sanitation in public bathrooms. What might the contamination do to his wand? Several wild scenarios ran through his mind, ranging from accidentally spreading disease to unsuspecting travelers, to giving janitors the ability to see through walls.

Using a clean wad of toilet paper, he gingerly picked it up. The water was probably filtered, but just to be safe, he wet a small area of his pants and rubbed the wand against it—his theory being that at least the pants were connected to him.

He examined it in the unnatural light of the fluorescent bulb for any signs of cracks or damage. Not only was it his prized possession, but he needed to show Coralis he could be responsible. He was relieved to see the wand was intact, and he felt certain he'd done the right thing.

The mirror hanging over the sink was covered with a film of hazy grime and soap stains. He took the wad of toilet paper, dampened it, and wiped a small section of the surface—then gasped in shock. Right in the center of his chin was a large red pimple! How long had it been there? Why hadn't anyone told him? And why hadn't he noticed it sooner?

So much for his powers of observation. He frowned at it, focusing his will to make it disappear. Unconsciously, he lifted his wand. The pimple ripened to a deeper shade of crimson and began to blister. He almost dropped the wand in a panic and tried desperately to reverse his train of thought. But it was too late! The pimple continued to fester.

Contamination! No! This couldn't be happening. He had messed up royally! He continued to stare helplessly, and at first didn't notice the subtle change in the grime on the rest of the mirror. Gradually the images in the haze moved into his field of vision—and Henry realized he was witnessing a scene taking place far, far away.

Two people were driving in a car, an ugly vulture perched on the console between the seats. Henry seemed to be watching from the car's rearview mirror. The two people faced each other, arguing. The passenger was a heavy man with skin too white and a face marred by a large birthmark. He appeared to be shouting, but Henry couldn't hear any sound.

He sensed . . . evil. It coalesced into an angry red aura that surrounded the mirror. Henry was frightened but could not take his eyes away.

Finally, the driver thought wiser of his actions and turned away from the passenger. His eyes casually glanced at the rearview mirror, then at the road, but quickly stared back into the mirror. It was as if the driver could sense him watching. Then the driver smiled at him—a horrible, cruel smile—and Henry cried aloud.

The sound broke the connection. Henry startled, splashing water all over the front of his pants, and fell heavily onto the toilet seat, gasping for breath. *It couldn't be!* Then a tiny scratching at the door made him jump, bringing him back to the moment.

"Henry," a small voice whispered. "Are you in there? I have to go!"

"Just a minute." Henry took several deep breaths to compose himself, then took one last look in the mirror to make sure the images were gone. The memory of what he had seen rushed back, but the mirror was clear. And even more remarkably, so was his face. The pimple had vanished.

He opened the door a crack and Brianna rushed in. "Turn around, Henry, and don't look," she said testily. Seconds later she tapped at his foot. "Okay, I'm done." He saw the small wet spot she'd left behind in the corner—right where his wand had fallen.

An involuntary shiver reminded him of the contamination. He knew he was going to have to tell Coralis and face the repercussions.

Brianna giggled. "Henry, you wet your pants."

The walk back to his seat felt like a death march. He thought of a prisoner taking his last steps toward his execution. Coralis was awake. Henry sat silently and stared at the water mark on his pants as Brianna curled back into her makeshift nest and instantly fell asleep.

"What did you see?" Coralis's voice was grave.

Hope and relief flooded Henry's emotions. "How did you know I saw something?"

"I didn't," he said, "until now." He shifted toward Henry, his face a mask of compassion and understanding.

"I dropped the wand. I dropped it, and I tried to clean it, but then I saw . . . it was my father." The words stuck in his throat and the tears finally came. "It was my father . . . and he was *terrifying*!"

Coralis reached over and pulled Henry close. Henry let himself go, the bottled emotions of fear and uncertainty pouring out.

"When you are ready, you must tell me everything. But quietly. There is no need to wake your sister—no need to frighten her." Coralis stared out the window into the gloomy, overcast skies, knowing how difficult the road ahead was going to be. And regretting the loss of innocence of a young boy who was in over his head.

In the annals of Wandmaker history, the creation of the Corsini Mappaemundi stands out as one of the greatest man-made achievements. Now several thousand years old, its parchment remains as fresh and pliable as the day it was born.

Born?

Yes, it is a living thing—an organism that changes over time, a reflection of the Earth's surface. But the genius of Epifanio Corsini also foresaw the need to transport the map in a convenient (and undetectable) way. Which leads us to its most remarkable feature.

In order to carry the map from one place to another, the owner could wear it.

If one places the parchment against the skin and seals the edges with the Corsini Wand, the map becomes a part of the carrier, where it then lies temporarily dormant until removed. If someone had the gross responsibility of removing Dai She's shirt, he or she would be greeted with what appeared to be a large tattoo.

But there is a catch—there is always a catch . . . a price to pay.

The map cannot lie dormant for long. Given the way the Earth's surface is constantly changing, the map is most healthy when it can change simultaneously. As a dormant object, the changes in the map are stored. If the changes, such as large tectonic plate shifts, occur while the map is being worn, it will begin to itch. But as anyone who has ever worn the map could tell you, don't try to scratch!

Even in a dormant state, it is protected by the spells woven into it. The slightest of scratches will leave behind lifelong welts—like cuts from a whip that have healed.

This was one important fact Dai She was not aware of. The last Wandmaker to wear the map died long ago, and that vital piece of information died with her.

And so it was that just after Henry had seen his father in the car mirror, a 9.0 earthquake struck the coast of Japan. And Dai She made the mistake of scratching.

"Aieee!" he suddenly screamed, squirming violently in his seat. "Stop the car! Stop the car, you idiot!"

Markhor slammed on the brakes, surprised by the outburst, hoping neither Dai She nor his moronic vulture had seen the image of Henry in the mirror. "What's wrong now, oh great Wand Master?" Markhor knew he needed to tone down the sarcasm. He could not afford to reveal too much. But playing the servant to Dai She was grating on his nerves.

"My back! It's burning!" Dai She threw open the door and tore off his jacket, flailing desperately at his back with arms too short to reach their destination. "Don't just stand there like an oaf. Do something!"

Unaware of what lay hidden beneath the shirt, Markhor ran his fingertips across Dai She's back. "Aieee!" Dai She screamed as if he had been branded with red-hot iron.

Markhor barely noticed. His hand had been thrown violently backward, repelled by an unseen force of incredible power.

"What did you do to me, you fool?" Dai She screamed.

"You need to remove your shirt." Markhor remained calm. His tone was commanding.

Dai She's reaction was swift. "No! Never!" Then an 8.0 aftershock hit. He screamed again. "All right! All right!" Pink buttons flew in every direction, lost to the Mexican desert.

Markhor smiled behind Dai She's back. "Is that what I think it is?"

"It doesn't matter what you think, fool, help me get it off!" He twitched and squirmed in fits of pain.

Markhor could not take his eyes off it. The legendary Corsini Mappaemundi covered the entire flabby white surface of Dai She's back. He was simultaneously fascinated and repulsed—and very curious. He knew precisely what the map was, and even felt a sudden burst of pride that Dai She had managed to liberate it. But he decided that playing dumb was in his best interest. "How do I remove it?"

"And you call yourself a Wand Master." He bent at the waist and rolled up his trousers, frantically removing something taped to his calf. "Use this!" He thrust the Corsini Wand at Markhor. "Touch this to the edges of the map. Gently!"

Markhor relished the familiar warmth of the wand, which pulsed as if begging to be used. The color of leathered skin, it was bent slightly at the tip—like an old man's finger. The second the wand touched the surface, a small edge peeled away from the skin.

"Faster, you idiot!"

But Markhor had had enough of Dai She's attitude. "No."

"What do you mean, no? I command you to remove it at once!"

"Say please." A smile creased his face as a plan took shape. Another aftershock. Another scream. The smile widened. Blazing fury erupted in Dai She's bloodred eyes, but he was helpless and he knew it.

"Please," he growled.

With all the tender loving care of a sculptor wielding a chisel, Markhor began removing the map, pausing only once as another aftershock rippled under the surface. He had not known the last Wandmaker to wear it and was thoroughly dumbfounded when he discovered why it caused so much pain.

While the map was two-dimensional to the eye, it was three-dimensional in effect. The upper surface showed changes to topography—forests thinning, cities expanding, rivers widening and contracting. The opposite side reacted to shifts in tectonic plates. As Markhor separated the map from

Dai She, the underside folded along a crease into a knifelike edge, catching a sizable slab of skin in a firm, pinching grasp.

Dai She screamed in agony until the crease released its hold, leaving behind a fresh, raw welt. With one corner to go, Markhor paused again.

"Why are you stopping? Remove this abomination at once!" he wailed.

"Not until you tell me the details of your plan." Markhor stepped away, dangling the Corsini Wand like a carrot.

"I will tell you *what* you need to know only *when* you need to know. And that is my decision to make. Not yours."

"Fine. Then I'll just leave the map right where it is." He edged the wand toward his pants pocket.

"You can't leave it like this! It will become damaged! Then everything will be ruined!"

"Then make me your partner. Give me the information, or I swear I will leave you here in the middle of the desert and your precious vulture can pick your bones clean." Markhor's tone had the hardness of steel with an edge of undeniable truth.

Dai She's eyes darted to the road they had traveled and the mountains yet to come. A temper tantrum of epic proportions welled inside. Viktor had seen that look before, and edged slowly out of sight behind the car, wishing he were inside the trunk with the falcon.

But Dai She knew that as long as Markhor had the Corsini Wand, he also had the upper hand. "All right." His teeth gnashed like the sound of grating sand. "I will tell you."

Markhor smiled again and withdrew a small blue wand from his pocket. "And you will tell me the truth."

Dai She recognized it as a Wahrheit Wand—named for the German word for truth. A rich, dark blue, it was constructed from the gemstone spinel. On its own, spinel contained no natural power, but when etched with the correct sequence of ancient Germanic symbols, it became an extremely powerful tool. In the right hands, the crystals would glow in the presence of a lie.

"Be mindful of the enemies you make," Dai She said, his voice soft but menacing.

Markhor's smile vanished. Dai She may have looked and acted the clown, but his power was undeniably great. "You are right," he said humbly. "I will not be your enemy. Nor will I be your friend. But you need an accomplice, and in that I am a willing partner. If you want to succeed, I will need to know what we are doing."

Dai She's face was a mask of stone, but he knew he had achieved a small victory. Markhor still knew enough to respect his power, and in the end, that might be the only thing that could keep Markhor in line. "Remove the map. Then keep the wand until you are satisfied I am telling the truth. But you must promise to return it to me—for one is useless without the other."

"You have my word."

And Dai She explained the plan.

And in the trunk, Randall heard every word.

And he knew he must escape.

As it turned out, they arrived in Chicago with time to spare before their connection to the Southwest Chief. Using Mrs. Verrity's journal, Coralis found his way to the site of the old train station, the historic Great Hall lined with gigantic marble pillars. "What say we venture into the city for a brisk walk before being cramped up on another train?"

Coralis's mood had improved since Henry told him the details of the incident with his father. However, Henry had the feeling it was for his benefit. All pleasantries aside, he still held on to a nagging guilt that he had messed up. And with that in mind, he was more than willing to go for a long walk that would shift the focus of conversation.

They meandered along the busy streets, staring upward at the marvelous architecture. They stopped to read plaques outside the Chicago Board of Trade and gawked open-mouthed at the amazing public library building. A large sculpted owl gazed down upon them as if they were its next meal, making Henry's stomach rumble.

"I heard Chicago deep-dish pizza is supposed to be really good," said Henry.

"Perhaps. It hadn't been invented yet when I was last here," said Coralis.

"You've been here before?" asked Henry.

"Several times, though the last time was a sad occasion. It was during the Great Fire."

"What's so great about a fire?" Brianna squeaked from within Henry's jacket.

"It became known as the Great Fire because before it was over it had burned down most of the city. At that time, most buildings were made of wood and the region was experiencing a terrible drought." His face darkened with a scowl. "Hundreds died, hundreds of thousands were left homeless, and thousands of buildings were destroyed. And for nothing. I warned them it was coming and to be prepared, but the politicians scoffed at me and banished me from City Hall."

"You knew the city was going to burn down?" Henry asked incredulously.

"No, of course not!" Coralis snapped, then calmed. "Sorry. It's still very upsetting and it happened over a hundred and forty years ago."

Henry shook his head. He knew Coralis was very old, but it still baffled him. "Then what did you warn them about?"

"The comet. By my calculations, Biela's Comet was due to pass close enough to Earth to shed some of its mass, and I wanted to collect some fragments that I suspected would make their way through the atmosphere and to this region. It would mean getting my hands on some valuable elements—but it was also a potential hazard to the people of the city."

"As things fall through the atmosphere they burn up, don't they?" Henry asked, recalling information from his science book.

"Yes, they do. But they weren't about to believe me—an old coot, an out-of-towner. Perhaps you could have talked more sense into them, Henry. In any case, some of the fragments did make it through. Very unfortunate. Hot, fiery coals from the heavens that ignited upon impact." Coralis paused, then laughed. "And they blamed it on some poor old woman's cow! Said it kicked over a lantern!

"Well, now you know the truth, Henry. Straight from an eyewitness. And I'll give you another tidbit to chew on. That comet caused three other fires that same night within several hundred miles of here, and one of them killed *thousands* of people! But because it wasn't *Chicago*, it didn't get the same amount of press."

"And did you get what you came for?" asked Brianna.

"Yes, I did, little one. And I've never seen anything like it before or since." He squinted in the hazy gloom. "I'm almost afraid of it, though I've yet to determine what kind of power it contains. It's a big universe, and there are many things we will never understand about it. In the meantime, it is under lock and key and hidden well within the confines of my castle."

"You live in a castle? With princesses?" Brianna asked hopefully.

"Ha! No princesses . . . though Gretchen is a magician in the kitchen."

The two children stared at him, mouths agape.

"What?" asked Coralis.

"You . . . you're married?" asked Brianna.

"What? Goodness no! Whatever gave you that idea?" A light touch of rosiness colored Coralis's cheeks.

"You're blushing!" shouted Brianna.

"You are, sir," Henry added with a short laugh.

"Bahtzen bizzle!" Coralis turned abruptly and walked at a brisk pace, shouting over his shoulder, "Keep up if you expect to eat anything."

"Henry, he was embarrassed," Brianna said gleefully.

"I know! So who do you think Gretchen is?" asked Henry.

"Coralis and Gretchen sittin' in a tree, k-i-s-s—"

"Shhh!" He clamped a hand over her mouth. Then he bent down to give her a light kiss on the nose. "But I think you're right." And they shared a private giggle as they scrambled to catch up.

"Whoa! What is that?" Henry ran ahead of Coralis, up several flights of stairs in a large open plaza. An enormous silver object—oblong, curved, and reflective—sat in the center of a paved area. "This is so cool!" He ran around it, then under and through the center, watching how his reflection distorted in the curves. "Look, Brianna!"

He took her out from his jacket and held her nose up to the surface. "Wow! What is this thing?"

"Did that mouse just talk?"

Henry gasped and quickly shoved Brianna back under cover. He'd been so caught up in his excitement that he'd forgotten about her predicament. Had he begun to accept it as normal? Regardless, the small boy standing next to him must have been there all along and Henry never took notice. "Um . . . no . . . of course not. Mice can't talk."

"I'm a hedgehog! And don't be so rough!"

"That one does," said the boy with a British accent. "Can I hold it? I've only seen talking mice in the movies, and Mum says they aren't real."

Henry thought wildly about how to escape from this. "It's a . . . it's a . . ." Then it hit him. "I'm practicing to be a ventriloquist!"

"What's that? I can hardly say the word. Ven-tri . . ."

"Ventriloquist. I can project my voice without moving my lips so that it sounds like my stuffed toy is talking."

Brianna squirmed angrily. "Stuffed toy? I'm your sister, Henry!"

"Wow! That was really good. Your mouth never moved. I'm Michael. Who are you?"

"Henry. And my stuffed . . . um, sister is Brianna."

"Can I try her?" He smiled broadly and held out his hand.

"Henry, perhaps you can introduce me to your young friend." Coralis's reflection loomed up behind him, looking none too happy.

"My name is Michael. Are you a wizard?" He extended a polite hand in greeting, which Coralis shook.

"Why would you ask such a question, Michael?"

"Oh, I dunno. Guess you just kinda look like one. Maybe it has something to do with the talking mouse."

Henry continued to watch the scene play out in the reflection rather than face the Wand Master.

"A talking mouse, Henry?"

Henry attempted to speak several times, but was truly at a loss for words.

"Why don't you let me hold on to your toy for you until we leave."

"Yes, that's a good idea," he said, suddenly relieved to unload Brianna.

"Michael!" a woman yelled from across the plaza. "Time to go!"

"But there's a talking mouse here, Mum!"

"Michael, we've been through this. Mice simply cannot speak. Now come along."

"See?" He faced Henry with sad eyes. "She just never believes me." Shoulders sagging, he walked toward his mother.

"That was careless, Henry," Coralis said. "You can't let your guard down. Do you understand what that means?"

"Yes, sir. I'm sorry. But I've never seen anything like this and I wanted Brianna to see it, too."

"It *is* pretty cool," she whispered in his defense.

"Yes, apparently people call it the Bean. But a sign over there refers to it as the Cloud Gate. A much more appropriate name. It looks very much like a blob of mercury, don't you think?"

"Yeah!" said Henry, glad to have changed subjects so easily. "Just like the mercury in the glass tube of Dad's barometer." He immediately, involuntarily shuddered at the mention of his father, and quickly checked the mirrorlike surface of metal for any sign of him.

"It's all right, Henry," Coralis said, as if reading his thoughts. "He's gone for now."

But as they turned to walk away in search of hot dogs and pizza, nearby, a distorted image of a fatherly face gradually dissipated where no reflection should have been.

And it appeared to be smiling.

At 3:00 p.m. sharp, the Southwest Chief left the Chicago station on its long, winding path to the West Coast. Mrs. Verrity's diary continued to be incredibly accurate, and Henry wondered how she could watch the sights and record them at the same time.

With bellies still full and a few hours until dinner, they retired to the first-class sleeping car that Coralis had reserved. Henry hadn't really known what to expect from their room, and he was amazed at how tiny it was. He'd assumed "first class" meant something a little more fancy than two seats and a bunk bed crammed into a room the size of a walk-in closet. But at least they had their own bathroom.

Coralis checked the schedule and saw there were to be half a dozen stops before they would arrive in Kansas City later that night, which would be their next opportunity to disembark and stretch their legs. He wanted to make the best use of their time before then. Henry's apprenticeship had officially begun.

Coralis removed a weatherworn leather satchel from one of the many inner pockets of his trench coat and withdrew from it several packets of herbs, which he mixed together in a small ceramic bowl. "This is to relax your mind." He tapped the bowl lightly with a clear crystal wand and an intoxicating aroma filled the compartment.

Henry's eyes drooped and his head nodded forward until Coralis gave him a light pat on the cheek. "Sorry, Henry. I forgot to adjust the mixture to compensate for your size and age." He smiled. "I believe these lessons will be as good for me as they are for you."

He removed a small pinch of herbs from the bowl and popped it into his mouth, swallowing with a wince. "Yuck! Always bitter when dry. Especially the chamomile."

Within moments, Henry's eyes were focused and his body relaxed.

"When your mind is clear, it can more easily absorb information. And not only absorb it but store it."

"What's the difference?" asked Brianna. The effects of the herbs were even greater on her small size, and from her drowsy state, she appeared to be sleep-talking.

Yet Coralis addressed the question as if she were fully awake. "The human mind is among the most complex structures on the planet—better than any supercomputer. With your five senses, you absorb information every conscious minute of your life. That information is stored as memories. Sometimes you can recall that information on command. Other times memories arise unbidden. For instance, a certain smell will trigger the memory of a person you haven't thought of in years. Amazing, yes, but not terribly efficient.

"But you can also train your brain to store information in compartments. That way, the information is there when you need it. Try to picture your brain as a large chest with an infinite number of drawers."

"Or like the world's biggest Kunstkammer," added Henry drowsily, subconsciously recalling a section from the *Guidebook*.

"Very good! Now then, I want you to start with a drawer labeled 'astrology.' Visualize opening this drawer and looking down at rows of compartments, each one empty."

"It's open," said Henry.

"Your job is to *listen*, something that very few people know how to do. You *hear* things, but unless you listen with the intent to understand, you will not learn." Coralis's voice suddenly changed. The spoken words became deep and full, rich with substance. And at the tail end of each word was a barely perceptive musical tone—a mezzo piano bell tone that was meant to be felt more than heard. "So I will talk and you will listen. And I will tell you where to file each item of information, just as I have them stored."

Henry twitched as something horrible occurred to him. "You're not emptying your drawers to fill mine, are you?"

Coralis forced himself not to laugh while reverting to a normal voice. "No, Henry, I cannot forget what I have learned. And besides, it would take many lifetimes to transfer the entire contents of a single drawer. We will start with basic information. Within time, you will learn to create sub-compartments and drawers within drawers."

"Will I live as long as you have?" asked Henry.

An innocent question, thought Coralis. But how to answer it? Now was the time for honesty, not cagey riddles and half answers. And yet a truly honest answer might do more harm than good. Troubling times lay ahead. Not for the first time, he questioned whether he was doing the right thing— dragging this young boy further into the gaping mouth of danger. He could easily make a call to Molly and drop Henry and his sister at the next station.

But instincts were as important as knowledge. Coralis knew that Henry was a key player and very likely the first of his kind—the eighth generation of two strong Wandmaker lineages. And Coralis had almost missed him entirely. He chastised himself for becoming such a recluse and hiding safely within the walls of his castle. He owed Randall a debt of gratitude, for without his interference, whatever awaited them would have spiraled unchecked and unchallenged.

So he answered honestly. "No one can see the future, Henry."

But he avoided the question.

"Astrology is not to be confused with astronomy," Coralis began. "Astronomy is the scientific study of the universe, which includes planets, galaxies, and an entire host of phenomena that occur beyond our atmosphere. There are many areas of expertise within astronomy, such as aerolithology, the study of meteors. And astronautics, the study of space travel.

"But astrology tells us how all those celestial objects combine to affect our daily lives. It is something that is felt more than seen, which is why scientists will never be able to fully grasp it."

"Excuse me, Coralis," Henry interrupted. "Exactly what am I supposed to put in the drawer?"

The barest hint of a smile tugged at Coralis's lips. "Just listen, Henry. I'll tell you when to begin filing."

"Do you really think my brain is big enough to hold it all?"

"Without a doubt." He clutched Henry by the hands, his voice stern yet sympathetic. "Henry, I have put this off for too long already. We are entering into uncharted territory. Events await our arrival that cannot be foreseen. In many ways, I have been a fool with my head buried in the sand. I have ignored my responsibility to protect the Earth. Many, many years ago I was a young apprentice, full of hope that the positive side of human character would dominate for the good of all mankind. But the things I have seen . . ." He paused. "I became jaded and began to lose that hope. I neglected my charge as a Grand Wand Master because I knew that power and greed could never be eliminated. There would always be an alpha ram who would lead an ignorant flock of sheep to do his evil bidding. All the wars, all the genocide, all the senseless slaughter of innocents . . . it will never end."

Henry winced as Coralis's grip tightened. He wriggled free and Coralis leaned back.

"I was wrong to give up. I see that now." Coralis's voice was etched with pain and regret. "I am also beginning to understand the heroic efforts of Randall."

It took a moment for the name Randall to connect. "The falcon?"

"Not always a falcon. Once, my brightest apprentice. A shining star in the dark vastness of space."

It took Henry a moment to process that information. "That falcon used to be a boy?"

Coralis chuckled. "Indeed. And how that boy could get on my nerves. But despite all the challenges and disobedience, he flourished and grew. And when he didn't think I was teaching fast enough, he found ways to experiment on his own.

"Not since the days of wand enlightenment in the time of the first Council of Aratta had anyone constructed a Urania Wand with such extraordinary power."

"A Urania Wand? Like the planet Uranus?" asked Henry.

"Mmmm . . . almost. In Greek mythology, Urania was the muse of astronomy. But in our realm, the Urania Wand is an invaluable tool to help forecast events as they would occur if left unchecked. The best ones are made from meteorites.

"Randall disappeared for several months, as he was prone to do when we argued. I thought nothing of it and assumed it was his form of a temper tantrum. But when he returned, he brought with him a piece of moldavite of unparalleled purity. Are you familiar with this stone, Henry?"

He thought hard but couldn't place the name.

Coralis read the look on Henry's face. "It is a very rare crystal found only along the banks of the Moldau River in a remote area of Bohemia—now the Czech Republic. It arrived on Earth millions of years ago when a large meteorite hurtled through the atmosphere."

"The one that killed the dinosaurs?" Henry asked eagerly.

"No, not that one. But no doubt it too created a powerful explosion. Moldavite is a dark green crystal. The piece Randall found was so pure you could almost see the constellations trapped within. It was also large enough that he was able to form seven individual wands." He held up Henry's hand. "About the size of your pinkie finger but half as thick." He frowned, recalling the memory. "We argued over that as well. I told him it was criminal to intentionally dismantle that singular specimen. But Randall has a gift: intuition that borders on the paranormal. I did not see where his instincts were leading him.

"Then one day he came to me with a dire warning."

And then Coralis went silent. Not just a pause, but an extended break that made Henry uncomfortable. He was clearly struggling with himself. Henry turned to Brianna, who was still sleeping and snored in soft whispers. His own instincts were telling him to wait it out.

"I used to think he was obsessed with the moon," Coralis said at last. He whispered it so softly that Henry wasn't sure if he even meant to say it aloud. "Out of all the celestial bodies in the universe, he was fixated on the one closest to Earth."

Coralis cleared his throat and turned to address Henry once again. "Many people fail to grasp the importance of the moon and how much it influences our behavior.

"Before science truly understood the causes of insanity, people blamed it on the phases of the moon. In the Middle Ages, the full moon was thought to be the cause of all sorts of things, from simple acts of violence to seizures caused by diseases. Over time, so-called experts have attacked the lunar theory in an attempt to disprove it, which they can . . ." A cagey smile creased his face. "To a point."

He leaned toward the window to look at the night sky. "But just because you can't see something doesn't mean it doesn't exist. And to simply dismiss something as powerful as moonbeams as if you were throwing out yesterday's dish-water is ignorant and foolish. Anyone who relies on the Earth's resources to make a living knows how to use the phases of the moon to his or her advantage. Fishermen use it to increase their catch. Farmers use it for harvesting crops. Over the years, they've given its phases names like harvest moon or hunter's moon."

Coralis leaned back, and as he did so, the glow from the waxing gibbous moon that had begun to rise reached the quartz ring on his finger. The moonbeam trapped inside it swirled in a cloud of dark vapor, as if angry at its containment.

Henry breathed in sharply, recalling the painful extraction. *Has it really only been a few days?* Everything was happening so fast.

Coralis extended his hand closer to the window. The moonbeam pushed and prodded against its prison cell. "In a way, Henry, you are fortunate. You have experienced what most people can only theorize. Through your careless experiment—" He waved a hand, quieting Henry as he started to object. "It's okay, Henry. It was careless, but I understand your curiosity, and there was no way for you to know."

Outside, the train rolled past field after field of cornstalks—a surreal landscape that contrasted greatly with the conversation inside.

"You have been given a taste of the power of moonbeams." He glanced upward at the darkening orange of a fading sunset. "On a normal night under normal circumstances, people absorb moonbeams without having the slightest idea they even exist. They bask in the glow of that giant romantic ball of light, never giving it a second thought. But moonbeams affect many things in many ways.

"The more evil a person has in his or her heart, the greater the absorption of bad energy. It's as if they were magnets collecting stray pieces of metal. But in the case of the bad moon, all that metal is sharp, dangerous, and deadly. Those moonbeams have succeeded in igniting wars and riots over the centuries.

"Even as an apprentice, Randall knew this as well as any Wand Master, and he exposed the seven moldavite wands to seven phases of the moon under unique circumstances that included things like immersion in rare water and exposure to extreme heat. Many other elements were involved. The entire process was amazingly complex. Looking back on it, I realize now that Randall was probably one of only a handful of Wandmakers in our entire history who had the knowledge and, more important, the intuition to achieve that level of success.

"Two of the moldavite wands disintegrated. Gone in an instant—poof! Four of them contain extraordinary power that the average Wandbearer would have difficulty controlling. And one of them . . . one of them transformed into the Urania Wand."

"Can I see it?" Henry asked excitedly.

Coralis squirmed uncomfortably. "I don't have it. The wand belongs to Randall, and only he can use it. As I said, we had quite an argument over his treatment of the moldavite specimen. Concealing the Urania Wand from me was Randall's way of punishing me."

Henry was puzzled. "If Randall had a wand that helped him see into the future, why wouldn't he share it with you? You're the Grand Wand Master. If anyone could stop something from happening, it would be you."

Coralis mumbled something that sounded to Henry like "horse feathers."

"What's that?"

"I said I had the hubris of a fool!" Coralis nearly shouted.

Henry jumped back, banging his head on the wall behind him. "Ow!" He rubbed his scalp and narrowed his eyes. A reaction like that would have panicked him when they first met, but he was becoming accustomed to the old man's rapid mood swings. No wonder Randall did things behind his back.

"What is that word, *hubris*?" he finally asked.

"False pride," Coralis mumbled. "I can tell you, I'm not proud of it now. I had become bitter and cynical. And my ego would not allow me to admit that a mere apprentice could accomplish what thousands of talented Wandmakers before him had failed to do."

"You said he came to you with a warning. Was it something he saw with the Urania Wand?"

A grave and ominous undercurrent crept into Coralis's voice. "Exactly that. He saw the bad moon on the rise. He used an odd phrase—called it the mother of all bad moons. He told me he foresaw Dai She, that malignant son of Malachai, causing massive destruction by channeling the power of the bad moon. Had I believed him and given him adequate training in reading the visions sent by the wand, we would not be barreling blindly ahead. And I wouldn't be forced to jeopardize—well." Coralis broke off, as if the thought was too terrible to voice, and he looked guiltily to Brianna, who continued to doze.

Henry didn't know how to react to this. To finally meet the man he revered, only to find he was as flawed as any human could be—and to know that Coralis's flaws had put him and his sister in danger—left him confused and somewhat . . . angry? "Didn't he tell you anything useful?" he snapped. "You know, like how Dai She plans to do it? Or what kind of destruction? Or how we can stop it?"

Coralis scowled. Henry immediately knew he had reacted poorly and braced for the Wand Master's reply, yet Coralis surprised him.

"Fair enough," Coralis said with a growl. "I made a few mistakes and am paying the price for them. But, for your sake, I will not make them again. And with that in mind, let us resume your training, beginning with some filing in that astrology drawer."

Coralis slipped back into the voice with musical tones that mesmerized Henry, who listened with rapt attention. But in the back of his mind, he realized Coralis never answered his questions. And he wondered: Did that mean Coralis didn't know the answers?

Or was he afraid to share them?

Some time later, they retired to the dining car, where a meal of surprisingly good lasagna awaited them. Afterward they ventured to the observation car, where Henry and Brianna were treated to a panoramic view of the countryside. Minutes later, the train rumbled over a long bridge that crossed the mighty Mississippi River. Barges carrying coal downstream mixed with sailboats dotted with their ant-sized occupants. As they sped past Fort Madison, Iowa, the terrain changed from flat fields to rolling hills.

Inside the car, an Amish family of six sat together in silence while a troop of Boy Scouts raucously played cards. In one corner, a woman sat alone, taking pictures and sketching in a pad. Opposite her, a man in his early twenties with his cap on backward listened to his iPod while playing solitaire with a deck of cards.

It was hard for Henry to believe that so many people went about their daily lives never suspecting the evil that was about to erupt. But then, up until very recently, he had been one of them. His carefree life had been interrupted by events beyond his control.

Coralis caught Henry staring and nodded knowingly. "This is how it has always been," he said softly. "This is why we do what we do. Every day, in other countries, soldiers fight to protect this way of life, and for the most part the average person never gives them a second thought.

"You are a Wandbearer now, Henry. A soldier in a different kind of war. No one will know who you are or what you will do to protect them. But it is good for you to remember these many faces. You are forevermore charged with protecting them."

Henry thought he should be scared stiff. But Coralis's words filled him with pride.

TWENTY-TWO

D ai She paced impatiently outside the front door of the small shack. "What's taking you so long?" he shouted.

Another minute went by before Markhor emerged holding a dangerous-looking dagger, upon which several small scorpions were impaled. "You asked if it was safe." He held the dagger close to Dai She. Two of the arthropods squirmed and thrust their venom-filled tails forward.

But Dai She did not flinch. "Ah, *Centruroides suffusus*. Fine specimens! They'll make a nice treat for Viktor once we roast them." He turned to the vulture squatting on the ground next to him. "And you deserve a treat for being such a good boy," he said, patting the bird on his bald head.

Markhor turned away and rolled his eyes. "This is all I found, but there is still a chance more are hidden."

On the outside, the shack was unimpressive, made up of dry-rotted wood planks in various stages of decay that hardly seemed capable of holding together. Two of its four sides contained a single window, filthy beyond cleaning. The entire structure was only about four by four meters, with no rear door—although someone with a dry sense of humor had painted one.

Dai She roughly brushed past Markhor to enter the shack. Inside wasn't much better, but at least the gaps and holes in the wood provided some ventilation. Two rusted, steel-framed cots, one beneath each window, looked more like gurneys in a morgue than beds for sleeping. Wooden crates ranging from completely intact to totally demolished were scattered around the single open room.

"Where is the restroom?" Dai She asked. It had been a long ride over many miles of washboard dirt roads that jolted, bounced, and rattled his innards. His bladder was at the bursting point.

The door was still wide open, and Markhor pointed into the distance. "I believe it might be that somewhat dubious structure out there." And while he wanted to be able to laugh at Dai She's discomfort, his need to use it was just as urgent.

The two men groaned and trudged up the incline, neither looking forward to what awaited them inside.

<hr />

Years of traveling to remote corners of the world had taught Markhor how to prepare for extended stays in inhospitable environs. He unloaded supplies from the car, which included packs of food with extended shelf life—survival food that was meant for the avid explorer.

Dai She didn't appreciate the foresight. "Blech! What kind of drivel is this? Viktor eats better from the roadside."

Markhor chewed a strip of teriyaki-flavored beef jerky thoughtfully before answering. "It might not taste like much, but it contains everything you need to live for a long time."

Dai She snorted. He waved a chubby hand at the room. "Why do you think anyone would have abandoned such a decadent mansion?"

"I'm not sure it's been abandoned. The door was closed when we arrived, and it opened freely, meaning someone's been using it. The crates that are still intact are positioned with the open ends down, which indicates they might be used as seats. The mattresses, while thin and stained, don't show signs of dry rot. And . . ." He looked upward. "There are no cobwebs."

Dai She, who was sitting on a cot, shifted uncomfortably. As he followed Markhor's explanation, he became mad at himself for not observing the obvious. "Then why are we here? What if the owners return? No doubt they will be armed."

Markhor opened the door and peered into the darkness. A gentle desert breeze curled inside and cooled the shack. Gazing upward at the awe-inspiring display of stars, he said, "I'm playing the odds. This terrain has been rougher than I anticipated and has slowed our progress. We need a place to stay for the night, and whoever uses this place doesn't live here. I figure the odds at seventy-thirty in our favor that we will get a good night's sleep and be on our way in the morning, and no one will ever know we've been here."

He walked outside and Dai She called after him. "Where are you going?"

He poked his head in quickly, startling Dai She. "To feed our falcon friend. I think it's best that we keep him alive."

The sound of a car motor didn't wake them. It was the sound of breaking glass. Dai She rolled off his cot, falling with a loud thump. Just as he hit the floor, a rough hand clamped down over his mouth before he could cry out.

"Quiet!" Markhor whispered roughly, his mouth pressed close to Dai She's ear. "We have company." He released his hand slowly as the wild look in Dai She's eyes returned to normal.

"Who is it?"

"Vandals, from the sound of it. They're having a bit of fun with our car. It will be only a matter of minutes before they work up the courage to barge in here." Markhor quickly crossed the room and gathered the few items they had brought in with them.

"Where are you going? There's no way out of here!" Dai She's voice rose to a hoarse whisper. "This is all your fault! You and your odds. You got us into this!"

Markhor spun on his heels and leveled a glare that stopped Dai She in midrant. His eyes glowed red with a fury that shone in the darkness like fiery embers of coal. He quickly got his temper in check. Dai She thought he was in charge and Markhor had to keep it that way, though it was becoming increasingly difficult. "I know. And I will get us out of it. Now drag that mattress over to the doorway and get behind the door."

Dai She mumbled something about heavy lifting but did as he was told, listening carefully to Markhor in the pitch-darkness. "They won't be subtle. When they storm in here we will need to react quickly. We don't know how many there are or what kind of weapons they have, but we have darkness on our side. You will need to close your eyes. I will flash-blind them with my wand, which you will be able to see through your eyelids. The mattress should cause them to stumble.

"As soon as you see the flash, use your wand to slam the door closed so hard it will burst off the hinges. That should take out whoever is waiting on the outside." It wasn't the best plan, but it was all he could come up with until they could see what numbers they were up against.

The car thumping ended and hushed whispers took its place as the partyers gathered their mob courage. Seconds later, as Markhor predicted, the door burst open and two large thugs fell forward, landing heavily—one on the mattress, one on the floor next to him.

Before they could gather their wits, Markhor blazed the power of full sunlight directly into their eyes, making them shriek in pain. As he was instructed, Dai She let loose the full fury of a repelling spell through his wand that sent the door viciously in the opposite direction—with unintended but fierce results. The second intruder had not fallen completely into the room, and the force of the door broke both of his legs below the knee. Everything happened so quickly that it took a moment to register.

And when it did, the chaos began.

Blood-curdling screams erupted from both the victim and the remaining two people outside—both women—who were hit by the splintering fragments of the door. Markhor advanced to the doorway, using a spell that gave the illusion of a large animal. He growled with the ferocity of a caged lion.

"Chupacabra!" one of the women screamed in terror. She painfully yanked a large wedge of wood from her thigh and hobbled quickly toward the off-road buggy, her partner right on her heels.

Markhor let the illusion vanish as the taillights faded into the distance. He turned to the wimpering, wounded man and roughly dragged him to the center of the room, bringing forth another agonizing scream.

Dai She stepped clear of his hiding spot. Moonlight illuminated the frightening duo as the men scrambled desperately to get away. The last night of a waxing moon was clear of clouds and they raised their arms in unison, allowing their auras to absorb the full force of evil moonbeams. They began to glow as brightly as the moon overhead, feeling the power surge within them.

"We don't appreciate uninvited guests." Markhor's voice dripped with venom. He looked back at the battered car, a wicked smile creasing his face. "Perhaps we should teach these hooligans a lesson."

And the screaming began anew.

And the only one who heard it was bound and hanging from the outer back wall in a burlap sack. Several hours later, shivering uncontrollably, Randall heard the unmerciful end.

Markhor had urged Dai She to get back on the road as soon as possible, just in case more people showed up. Shortly after midnight, they resumed their journey. The car rumbled and moaned, but it ran. The battering at the hands of the unfortunate vandals only served to make it look more ominous as it fought the rock-strewn roads that resembled horse-drawn paths.

Inside the car, the air was tense with a darkness that mirrored its exterior. The two occupants glowered in silent reflection of the evening's events. Neither felt any remorse. If anything, they felt slightly giddy with power, having absorbed an abundance of moonbeams.

Dai She concentrated on one of the myriad spider cracks in the splintered windshield. He focused, making it lengthen millimeter by millimeter. He pushed it upward, where it connected with another and another.

"Stop that." Markhor had been watching, his heightened senses aware of every subtle use of energy. He was acutely aware of the increase in Dai She's power—as well as his own. But the level of Dai She's cruelty far surpassed anything

Markhor would have done. Interfering would have been a sign of weakness, something he could not afford. He angrily slammed shut the image in his head and snapped at Dai She. "I still have to be able to see where I'm going."

Dai She bristled. He turned his attention to the rear window, snapped his stubby fingers, and watched it explode into tiny fragments that glittered like diamonds in the road.

Markhor jerked the steering wheel and slammed on the brakes, wiping the smirk off Dai She's face as he banged his head on the passenger window.

"I get it," Markhor said while grinding his teeth. "You're feeling happy with yourself. You had a good night. But unless you plan on walking the next thirty miles, I suggest you flex your muscles in another direction."

He expected Dai She to throw another of his tantrums, but was surprised when he calmly grinned in response. "What is it you think happened back there? Do you think I enjoyed torturing those miserable lowlifes?"

Markhor sensed where this was going and remained silent.

"You think you are a Wand Master. That one day, history will revere the deeds of the infamous *Markhor*." The grin spread to a malevolent sneer. "You are nothing compared to me. My power is without limits! Last night was to give you a taste of what true power can do. And . . . to give you ample warning. Don't mess with me, *Markhor*.

"Do you think I missed the significance of your name? The snake eater? Ha! I am a snake unlike any other. I will strike without warning or mercy at those who oppose me.

I will strangle all who step into my path. And I will crush the life out of *you* if you dare to get in my way."

The two glared at each other. Seconds ticked by and the silence grew until Markhor shifted gears and pulled the car back onto the road.

Markhor was growing weary of his irritating traveling companion. He glanced again at his image in the rearview mirror. His connection with young Henry was strong—built on a foundation of love, no doubt. Perhaps it was time to have a little fun. No father should be denied the opportunity to play games with his son. Even if those games contained a certain element of . . . danger.

A test, then. Something scary with a bit of a bite to it.

Are you ready, young Henry?

The train arrived in Kansas City almost two hours late due to mechanical delays. The conductor announced repairs would take about thirty minutes, which gave them time to stretch their legs and get some fresh air before resuming their trip to Winslow, Arizona. It was just past midnight and Henry should have been tired, but sitting for hours on a train being tutored made him antsy. He jumped from the train and sprinted the length of the platform, then back to Coralis.

"Is that all?" the Wand Master asked.

Henry seized the moment and sprinted again, returning breathless and sweaty. "Okay, that felt good." He smiled.

"As will a hot bath someday." Coralis led them to a row of vending machines, where Henry selected several candy bars and a large plastic bottle of soda, and a granola bar for Brianna. Coralis settled for a mix of nuts and dried fruits. No one seemed to take notice of Brianna, who was perched in the upper pocket of Coralis's trench coat.

The twenty ounces of soda Henry consumed in record time ran right through his kidneys.

"Come back straightaway, Henry. You don't want the train to leave without you," Coralis teased.

Henry turned to him, belched loudly, then ran off before Coralis could yell at him. He followed the restroom signs and jogged to the station waiting area, only to find it blocked off for maintenance. Seeing no other signs, he quickly exited the far side of the building.

The urge to pee now had his feet dancing and his legs flapping. He couldn't hold it too much longer, but there was still no sign of a restroom. He hurried down a dimly lit sidewalk past several restaurants and shops. Finally, he spotted what he was desperately seeking. As he crashed through the door and it closed behind him, a sinister figure went to work . . .

Theodore Burnhardt had once had a promising career ahead of him. As the youngest-ever assistant curator at the Chicago Field Museum, he had been well on his way to fulfilling his dream of taking over the top spot. And if he could somehow get his boss to retire early, the job would be his before he turned thirty.

So he put a little something extra in the boss's soy latte. Nothing fatal. Just a blend of rare herbs that had an adverse reaction on ligaments and joints.

Unfortunately, the boss intercepted a shipment of one of the herbs and put two and two together. Which left Theodore in financial ruin following a crippling lawsuit. He was lucky he didn't go to jail.

Fortunately for him, there was only one source where those rare herbs could be purchased—and it was one that the Scorax kept a close eye on. Within a week, Theodore had been recruited as the organization's newest member, willing and ambitious.

The Scorax influence spread far and wide. And through it, they were able to place people in positions that one day might become useful. Which was how Theodore, despite his sketchy résumé, was handed the job of director of the Science Center at Union Station in Kansas City. The same Union Station where Henry's train was now parked.

Until yesterday, his life had become dull, routine, and boring. But now he had an assignment. He couldn't imagine what was so special about the young Leach boy. Frankly, he didn't care. This was his moment to shine.

Only last week, he had received a shipment of two dozen black squirrels from New York City. They had been fed daily by a little old lady. When she passed away, no one took over and the squirrels became very aggressive. They were trapped and scheduled to be relocated to a forest upstate when Theodore became aware of them and asked if he could have them.

He wasn't sure exactly why he wanted them at the time—perhaps to stuff as part of an exhibit. But now they would come in handy.

Once Henry had finished his business, he attempted to avoid eye contact with the mirror as he washed his hands. But it was like trying not to look at an accident on the side of the road. He turned on the faucet and glanced up for a quick peek. Hit the soap dispenser—took another peek. Rinsed his hands—took another peek.

Nothing. He breathed a sigh of relief, dried his hands, and grabbed the door handle.

He should have taken one last peek.

Henry stepped outside, nearly tripping into a barricade. He thought it was odd that he hadn't noticed it on his way in. The barricade was the type of portable metal fencing used to control crowds at parades and concerts, and it blocked him from going back in what he thought was the direction that he had arrived.

Attached to the end of the fence was a length of yellow CAUTION tape that extended to the far end of the building. Henry hesitantly followed it. The alley was deserted, yet an uneasy feeling of being watched nagged at him. As he reached the end, a light went out, leaving him in hazy darkness.

He decided to backtrack when something in the darkness skittered past like a shadow that moved of its own accord. He nervously rubbed a hand through his hair and turned around, only to run smack into the barricade. He spun in a circle, looking for someone who might be playing a trick on him.

He caught a glimpse of more movement in the darkness. Suddenly, the light that had gone out began to flicker on and off rapidly like a strobe light.

His feet were riveted to the pavement as several black animals the size of large rats appeared. Within seconds, six of them were in place, sitting in a perfectly straight line less than ten feet away. He rubbed his eyes, as the strobe effect made him feel disoriented. Squirrels? He had never heard of a black squirrel, and his imagination began to churn up images of some kind of genetic mutation that liked to eat young boys.

He took two steps backward. They took two steps forward, but no closer. Another step back. He expected to feel the barricade behind him. He didn't want to take his eyes off the creepy squirrels but glanced quickly, only to find the fencing had disappeared.

His temporary good fortune turned bad as more and more squirrels appeared, blocking him in a tight semicircle with his back against the wall. In the distance he could hear voices as groups of people were leaving restaurants. He could shout for help . . . but didn't know how the squirrels would react.

The train whistle blew. It sounded so far away. Coralis was going to be furious. Just as Henry decided to make a move, the squirrel directly in front of him jumped on top of the one next to it. He watched, fascinated and horrified, as the two squirrels became one larger one. *This isn't good,* he thought.

A third, a fourth, and a fifth squirrel jumped into the mix. With each addition, the original squirrel got bigger. Henry kept count until number fifteen, at which point he had the urge to pee again . . . this time from fright.

When it was finally over, Henry had no doubt he was in serious trouble. Magnified by a factor of twenty-something, the beady little eyes of a squirrel became glistening balls of hate. Teeth and nails the size of toothpicks transformed into fangs and claws that would look more at home on a veloci-raptor. The creature towered over him.

The train whistle blew again—a long, urgent blast telling him he was doomed to be left behind. The squirrel twitched its enormous tail and flexed its claws.

"Kuk, kuk, kuk!" The squirrel barked warning sounds that bounced off the walls and hammered back at Henry. It leaned in close enough that he could smell rotting acorns on its breath. It was trying to tell him something, but it was like listening to a dog bark in an alien language.

As Henry began to edge sideways along the wall, it whipped its tail around to block his path. Another quick twitch of the tail knocked him to the ground. In a panic, he scrambled crablike backward, knowing it was pointless. His wrist buckled and he fell to his side, landing hard on the gold nugget from his footlocker. Pain erupted through his body like a jolt of electricity. He attempted to scream but nothing came out.

The effect on the squirrel was nothing short of extraordinary. It was as if the gold and the animal could sense each other. The squirrel thrashed its head wildly and screeched a long, keening wail, sounding like a cat being tortured. Henry knew then that this was some kind of dark power at work.

But how could he fight it? He concentrated on Coralis, willing him to appear and save the day, yet knowing the train had probably left by now, and Coralis with it. Hopelessness engulfed him as the mammoth squirrel recovered, leaning over him, gnashing its teeth.

Somewhere out of sight, people nearby shouted like cheerleaders, "Rock chalk, Jayhawk!" over and over. It wasn't until the fourth or fifth time he heard it that he connected the dots.

Jayhawk. Blue jay. His wand! The one that had gotten him into all this trouble to begin with. He had nearly forgotten it.

He recalled the time he'd witnessed a savage attack in his backyard, when a mother blue jay had been forced to defend her baby from a squirrel. What if . . . ?

There was no time for second-guessing. He whipped the wand into the face of his assailant and yelled, "Attack!"

The squirrel reared back in confusion. It jerked its head from side to side, ears twitching madly. Seconds later, an entire flock of blue jays swooped around the corner of the building, blindsiding the squirrel in a powerful attack. They stabbed at it repeatedly, driving it backward until it tumbled into the far wall. Chunks of concrete cascaded across the sidewalk.

Henry pulled his knees to his chest and huddled on the ground while stones and bricks rained down on him. The deafening war cry of the birds assaulted his eardrums as they fearlessly pummeled their monstrous enemy. Finally, a loud POP! exploded in the alley, followed by an eerie silence.

He worked up the courage to open his eyes. Three normal-sized squirrels looked at him curiously before scurrying off. There were no birds in sight. As he sat up, several people jogged up to him, asking if he was okay.

"Henry!" A familiar voice cut through the confusion. "There you are, son. We must hurry if we want to catch the train." Coralis brushed Henry off and quickly led him back to the train station just as a conductor yelled, "All aboard!"

"I thought for sure the train had left," he said breathlessly, his voice shaking.

"For some reason, a herd of cattle decided to take a nap on the tracks. And at this hour of the night!" Coralis winked at him. "Let's get you cleaned up. I believe you have a story to tell."

As the train resumed its journey, an announcer told the passengers they would try to make up as much time as they could on their way to Topeka.

Back in their room, Coralis heated some water and made a special blend of tea to relax Henry, who shivered despite being wrapped in a warm blanket. Brianna roamed up, down, and around Henry, sniffing curiously. "You smell like nuts."

Her remark brought back the terrifying memory of the giant rodent. "Stop it," he whispered hoarsely, nudging her off him.

For a change, she had no smart comeback. She waddled to Coralis and tucked tightly against his leg.

"How did . . . what was . . ." Henry struggled to comprehend what had happened. He shifted and the blanket slid from his shoulders. Then he stood and angrily whipped it off, tossing it into a corner. "Why was I just attacked by a giant squirrel?" he exploded.

"That would explain the nuts," Brianna said.

"I don't think I'll ever be able to eat another one," said Henry.

"Not even peanut butter with marshmallows and bananas?" She was doing that thing with her voice again, but he didn't mind. It calmed him, and he began to rationalize things.

"It was a warning, wasn't it?"

"That it was, Henry. And you met the challenge admirably." Coralis removed his long coat for the first time since he arrived in the States. "It was also a test," Coralis continued. "Everything that has happened to your father, your sister, your mother . . . you. It is all connected. The clues your mother left are leading us to where we need to be. But in a way, we are marionettes and several forces are pulling the strings.

We have no choice. We must follow this thread to the end and see where it leads." He smiled wanly. "This is some kind of adventure, isn't it?"

Brianna looked up at him. "You're kidding, right? My brother almost gets eaten by a giant squirrel, and that's fun to you?"

"No, he's right, Brianna," Henry said confidently. "If that was a test, I passed it. But I also showed my hand. And so now they know what I can do."

Coralis was impressed. "Indeed, our enemy will be wary."

"So we should turn around and go home. Right?" Brianna said hopefully.

Henry laughed aloud. "No way! I just beat a giant squirrel! A giant squirrel!" Henry picked her up and rubbed her face in his. "Do you have any idea how good that feels? I can't wait to see what's next!"

"That's the spirit, my boy!" Coralis clapped him on the back.

Brianna shook her head slowly. "I hope insanity doesn't run in the family."

T he rays of the morning sun streamed through the window—an invitation to start the new day. Henry consumed a hearty breakfast consisting of a short stack of pancakes, two eggs, hash browns, and bacon. He ate the meal in enormous chunks, and incredibly fast.

"Can I have seconds?" he asked before he even finished swallowing the final bite.

"I thought only cows had four stomachs," Brianna said from the seat next to Coralis. They had the dining car all to themselves, and she took advantage of the few precious moments alone to stretch out in public.

"How did you know that, young lady?" Coralis was only halfway through his serving. As he watched Henry, the same thought had occurred to him.

"He's not the only one who watches animal shows," she said indignantly.

"I can't help it! I don't think I've ever eaten this much in my entire life!" he said with a huge smile. "Maybe I'm finally going through that growth spurt that Mom has been promising me." He stood and examined his pants. "I think I am! Look, don't they look shorter than yesterday?"

"They're different pants, doofus." Brianna laughed.

Henry blushed and quickly sat down, getting a chuckle from Coralis. "Brain energy consumes a lot of calories. You've had a busy few days, but the next few will really put you to the test. So by all means, eat up, young man."

Young man. Henry liked the sound of that. "Um . . . how about maybe just another order of pancakes?"

He looked to Brianna for approval, but she rolled her eyes and climbed onto Coralis's lap. "Fine. Just let us know when all four stomachs are full, *cow*-boy."

Nothing could spoil Henry's mood. He glanced out the window at the dry riverbeds of Colorado rolling past. "We're out west, Brianna. It's a good place for a cowboy to be." While he couldn't say why, that statement summed up something he had been thinking about. The farther west they traveled, the more at home he felt. His instincts were telling him that this was where he belonged. It wasn't just an adventure anymore. In some odd way, he felt as if he were going home.

He looked up at Coralis, who was staring at him. His thoughts silently entered Henry's mind. *"There will be plenty of occasions going forward when you will experience a sense of déjà vu—as if you've been somewhere or seen something before, even though it couldn't have happened. In this case, I believe it is your tribal roots calling to you, Henry. In a very real sense, you* are *going home."*

Henry's jaw slackened. "How did you do that?"

"Do what?" Brianna demanded. "What did I miss?"

"Nothing." Coralis stroked her head gently with his finger. "Henry and I are just beginning to connect."

"Well, stop connecting and finish eating. I feel a nap coming on." She curled on his lap in comfort.

"Think of the universe as an isolated physical system with a predetermined amount of energy." Coralis flexed his fingers, preparing to resume his role as professor. "No more energy can be created or destroyed. It will change form . . . or re-manifest itself . . . but never disappear."

Henry's glazed look and slack jaw told him he had overestimated his audience. He needed to simplify things.

"The easiest way to explain what is happening is to think of Earth's water cycle. Water evaporates, condenses in the atmosphere, forms clouds, and descends back to Earth as rain.

"It's the same with energy. Energy doesn't just disappear. It transfers. And in the case of bad energy, it is absorbed by the moon and transferred into moonbeams that shower the Earth. You hear the nightly news reports, Henry. There is quite possibly more evil in the world today than at any other time in history. And that makes the moon an extremely dangerous and volatile place. It has now reached a saturation point.

"Look at this, Henry." He held out the hand wearing the quartz ring. Black tendrils writhed angrily in their crystal cage. "This is a single moonbeam reduced to its essence. Can you even begin to imagine what will be released when the moon unloads everything it has stored up?" The lines on his face hardened. "My instincts tell me it will affect millions, if not billions, of people. And we simply cannot allow that to happen."

Henry shifted uncomfortably. Having come to the decision to fight against evil, he suddenly had the feeling he was in way over his head. "What am I supposed to do?"

Coralis carefully considered his reply. "Henry, you are not just a boy. These are not tricks, they are abilities. You are now a Wandbearer! And anyone who assumes that responsibility must act with confidence and without hesitation for the good of mankind. It is not something to be taken lightly, and if I didn't think you had it in you, you wouldn't be here with me."

He leaned forward and grasped Henry's hands. "It's in your blood, my boy. You are just awakening your powers, but I can sense that those powers are very special indeed. Fortunately, Randall could sense this as well, or we might have met under more dire circumstances." Coralis stared into the face of a very frightened young man. He smiled. "You, your sister, your mother, myself, we are not alone in this fight."

"Do you mean Randall? How could Mom possibly know about Randall?"

"Yes, Randall is on our side, but there are others. And when the time comes, our combined power will be exponentially greater than the sum of the individuals."

Coralis's words gave him confidence. He began to relax a little, knowing the burden did not fall entirely on his shoulders. But there was still something nagging at his subconscious. "Where has Randall gone?"

Coralis sat back once more. Grave concern lined the creases of his eyes. "I don't know, Henry. But I hope wherever he is, he is exercising extreme caution. If some harm had come to him, I would have felt it. But that doesn't mean he's not in harm's way. The boy could be reckless at times. For his sake—and ours—let's hope he's keeping himself out of trouble."

TWENTY-FIVE

To avoid complications, Dai She and Markhor decided to bind and gag the security guard. The other option was to give him an herbal haze that would immobilize him, but he was old and frail. There was a chance that his bodily functions would permanently shut down if he was kept under the spell for more than a few hours.

The old man was furious, which was good because his adrenaline level would keep him alert. "Do you speak English?" Markhor asked. The old man jerked his head as if he were trying to spit at Markhor through the rag in his mouth.

"I'll take that as a yes," he said lightly. "Just sit tight and relax. You won't be harmed. I'll be back in a few hours to give you some water." Markhor gave him a pat on the head, knowing that if the man hadn't been gagged he would have taken a bite out of his hand.

"Aren't you finished yet?" Dai She yelled from outside the shack. "We have work to do."

"See what I have to put up with?" Markhor asked the old man. Then he took the sack with the falcon and looped it over two hooks so that the opening was stretched apart to allow some airflow. He peeked into the sack and Randall lunged at him. Markhor laughed. "Good little bird." He poured water over its head to help cool it down. "No shenanigans, you two. I'll be back shortly."

Compared to the roads they had traveled to get there, the entrance to the mine was suitable for a high-performance car, paved smooth and lined with electric lights. Since the initial discovery of the Cueva de los Cristales in April 2000, researchers had been hard at work. Their early efforts at preserving the upper caves had resulted in contamination of the crystals, but it made for much easier access into the mine. Dai She was happy, if not grateful for their work.

They walked downhill with relative ease, Markhor carrying the bulk of their supplies. When the electric lighting ended, Dai She switched over to a handheld lantern. Markhor, who had spent considerable time exploring other caves around the world in search of rare elements, wore a hard hat with an attached lamp.

The air thickened with humidity the deeper they descended. Markhor wasn't sure what smelled worse, the sulfuric scent in the air or the sweaty stink of the obese man leading the way.

"I thought you said it was only a thousand feet." Dai She grumbled, stopping to wipe the perspiration from his face and take a long draft of water from his canteen.

"I said the cave we need is a thousand feet below the surface. The tunnel to get there is angled, and as you can see, does not go in a straight line." Markhor wrinkled his nose, pulling even with Dai She. "We still have a ways to go."

"I hope, for your sake, we have enough time to make all the necessary preparations," Dai She threatened.

"And what exactly is there to prepare?" Markhor was irritated. "The crystals you asked me to locate are already in place. They're pure and huge and millions of years old. You'll have everything you need."

Dai She smiled wickedly. "How do you think we will harness the full energy of the moon's beams a thousand feet below the surface?"

Markhor stared blankly as it dawned on him what needed to be done. And knowing all too well that he would be the one doing it. He mentally kicked himself for not putting the pieces together earlier. "Prism alignment," he said dismally.

Dai She nodded enthusiastically. His shrill giggle echoed off the walls. "A crystal anchored at every turn, precisely aligned to reflect and amplify the full power of the moon. When the beams reach the cavern, they will trigger a chain reaction that nothing can stop. The West Coast of the United States will cease to exist. The East Coast will fall into the ocean. Mountain ranges will tumble. Tsunamis will rage across Europe and Asia. Volcanoes will explode throughout the Pacific Ring of Fire. It will be the greatest day in history!"

His voice rose with excitement. "The hydrogen bomb will seem like a firecracker in comparison. And we will be lighting the fuse!" He marched forward, his evil cackle growing louder with each step.

Two months earlier, researchers had noted a fragile fissure in the limestone. They exercised extreme care, keeping the decibel level of their activity to a minimum. A piece of yellow tape on the tunnel wall marked the width of the fissure.

Markhor thought nothing of it as he walked past. And he didn't see it move, ever so slightly.

The entrance to the Cave of Crystals had been sealed by a conservation group. A massive iron door, custom-fit to the opening and bolted to the cave wall, contained dead bolts and padlocks to keep out treasure hunters.

Dai She touched a wand to the center of the door and blew on it as if he were blowing out a candle. The padlocks exploded into tiny pieces and the dead bolts disintegrated. Fortunately, Markhor was standing off to the side, just barely out of range of flying fragments. He was impressed by the power Dai She had at his disposal and the speed with which he could summon it. Dai She didn't just experiment with darkness; he embraced it. Any doubts he had about Dai She's ability to harness the bad moon's energy were quickly disappearing.

The big man grunted with effort as he yanked the door open. Before he could step through, he was met by a blast of heat and quickly slammed the door shut.

"I told you it was hot in there," Markhor said as he turned to conceal the slightest of smiles.

"Then I'll be getting my money's worth out of you, won't I?" Dai She answered maliciously.

Markhor had trained himself to be ready for anything. He reached into his pack and pulled out a heat-resistant blanket similar to one used by men who fight forest fires. He was eager to get started and just as eager to finish. Dai She looked away quickly, but not before Markhor saw a glimmer of admiration. "Ready when you are," he said. "Tell me what you need."

Twenty minutes later, Markhor emerged, drenched in sweat, straining to carry a crystal rod four feet tall and a foot in diameter. A normal man might have lasted only half as long. But a normal man did not have the essence of a Wand Master. He quickly rummaged in his pack and drained the electrolyte fluid from his canteen. He knew water would not be sufficient to prevent dehydration but now worried that he had not brought enough of the life-sustaining fluid.

"I am going to need help."

"Then I suggest you find some," Dai She remarked with little concern. "Perhaps that old man has more uses than just operating a few toggle switches."

Markhor had trouble concealing his growing disdain for the powerful Wand Master. He could not believe this abomination was his—

Quickly he wiped the train of thought from his mind, lest Dai She attempt to tap into it and discover something he was not to know. He had to keep his thoughts and emotions in check. By the end of the day he would be physically drained. Emotions would be the reserve fuel he would need to call upon.

"The old man would die down here. I'll need to get one of the mining carts to move the rest of the crystals."

"Do what you must, but be quick about it!" Dai She yelled. "Time is a luxury you do not have."

When he returned with a freshly oiled cart, he found Dai She leaning against a tunnel wall, grinning from ear to ear—a most unpleasant sight.

A brief glance at Dai She's work quickly explained why he was smiling. The crystal Markhor had pulled from the cave had been polished and honed with the precision of a diamond cutter. The sides were now perfectly planed to provide pinpoint reflection. He reached over to feel the surface, drawn to it like a magnet.

"Don't touch it!" Dai She snapped. "Even the slightest trace of oil from your skin will affect it."

"How did you do it?" Markhor asked admiringly.

"That's none of your concern," he replied. "Maybe, if you're a good boy, I'll show you . . . someday." His high-pitched laughter bounced through the tunnel. And when he heard its echo his sweaty face gleamed happily and he laughed even louder.

Markhor felt a slight tremor beneath his feet, but Dai She was shaking too hard to notice. For the first time he wondered about the stability of the walls and remembered the yellow tape farther back in the tunnel.

"Now hurry along! By my count, we need eight more of them. And don't cheat on size. This one was barely big enough to work with."

Markhor wrapped himself in the blanket, entered the cave, and shut the door, Dai She's incessant cackle bleeding through the seams.

Two hours later, they were almost halfway done. Markhor was glad to see that while the physical effort was taking its toll on him, the use of elemental power was taking a similar toll on Dai She. Still, he needed to rest to recover his strength.

Dai She accompanied him to the surface. The sun sat low in the sky, baking the valley floor. He checked on the security guard and gave him water, which he drank greedily through fits of cursing.

Much to Markhor's relief, he found a cabinet with a supply of energy drinks and electrolyte water. He passed on the former and offered the water to the guard before guzzling another quart himself. He was about to ask the old man if he needed to relieve himself when he saw the dark stain on the front of his pants.

Markhor looked away quickly in shame and embarrassment. "Sorry, old-timer." Then he briefly touched the man's bindings and muttered something softly. The old man probably wouldn't notice at first, but the knot that held him would be just a little bit looser the next time he tugged at it.

Then Markhor took the squirming falcon from the sack, placed it in a corner, and lightly covered it with an old, oily blanket. "Be still," he commanded.

"What took you so long?" Dai She was waiting just outside the door. He peered around the small confines of the cabin suspiciously. Satisfied, he slammed the door shut and pounded his massive frame back toward the tunnel entrance.

TWENTY-SIX

The remainder of the day unraveled at a snail's pace, as days tend to do when one is being schooled. The world opened up to Henry in ways he'd never dreamed possible. The process of creating storage compartments in his brain became easier with practice and proper instruction.

Henry, the willing student. Coralis, the patient teacher.

Layer upon layer was added to each drawer. Pop quizzes taught him how to retrieve the information, the drawers opening easier each time until they rolled on well-greased hinges.

The train continued to speed westward. Henry's ears popped as it proceeded to climb into the mountains of Colorado before changing course southward into New Mexico, where the beauty of the southwestern countryside tugged at Henry's ability to concentrate.

Pictures didn't do it justice. Henry had seldom set foot out of his hometown, and it was as if they'd entered a completely different country. Henry recalled wondering why there were so many colors in a box of crayons, and now he understood. It was all so beautiful and unusual and unique.

At one point the train entered a tunnel that ran directly through a mountain. They were in darkness for over a minute.

Rather than fight the elements, Coralis shifted his lesson plan. They opened a new drawer and labeled it *geology* and discussed the passing landscape in minute detail. Henry absorbed the information like a sponge, his love of rocks and minerals making it easy. When his interest shifted to the amazing rock formations, Coralis turned that corner along with Henry and delved into the formation of land-masses with such detail that Henry thought he must have been there at the beginning of time.

He couldn't stop. He needed more and more. Coralis had lunch delivered to their cabin.

Brianna grumbled—though secretly she was enjoying the lessons almost as much as her brother. When she tired of looking out the window from her perch on Coralis's shoul-der, she curled on the seat next to him, feigning sleep.

The train continued west through New Mexico, finally entering Arizona in the early evening. "This feels . . . right," Henry said with difficulty, unable to pinpoint why.

Coralis wrapped his hands around Henry's. "The blood of the First People runs strong in your veins."

"First People?" Henry had never heard the term before.

"Those you call Native Americans—Navajo, to be pre-cise. This is their home, and you can sense that."

Henry had to admit, he did feel at home in this glorious land of color and majesty. It surpassed anything his imagina-tion could create on its own.

Brianna had silently crept next to Henry. "We belong here, don't we, Henry?"

"Do you feel it, too?"

"I feel something different," she said. "It's a good feeling, but it's kind of scary, too. It's like I don't know who I am."

Henry smiled but refrained from saying *You're a hedgehog.* Instead, he said what he felt. "Do you see how beautiful the sky is? I think you're a part of it, Brianna. And every time I see a sky this color, I'm going to think of you."

She blushed, bringing a light flush of lavender to her face, and curled onto his lap.

Coralis knew when to stop. He had not witnessed a moment like this in a very long time. Not just the bonding of two children, but the bonding of a team. A family.

Coralis had thought he had stopped growing many years ago. But with each turn of the train's wheels, he felt the hard shell in which he had encased himself begin to crack and crumble.

He turned away from the children and pulled out a worn photograph from his coat pocket, the image now distorted from many creases. Love cracks, Gretchen would call them. A loved photo was carried, handled, and abused with affection. This one was a grainy image of a young boy, eleven or twelve years old—he'd forgotten exactly how old. Randall had finally settled into a comfortable routine at the castle. He had just given life to Willoughby and the look on his face was a priceless mix of wonder and pride. A smile couldn't stretch any wider.

Coralis often thought back to his first encounter with the boy . . .

His trip to London had been unexpected. He had heard from a gem collector about a rare find and was set to enter the premises to negotiate a price when a small voice spoke from a nearby alley.

"I wouldn't go in there, sir." A pale, thin boy with unruly pitch-black hair showed himself but stayed to the shadows, where only Coralis could see him. Used to being accosted by the street urchins of London, Coralis was ready to move along when the boy did the most unusual thing. He wiggled both ears simultaneously.

"What's that you're doing, young man?" he asked, suddenly curious.

"Getting your attention, sir. And it worked." The boy flashed a perfect smile of triumph.

"And why shouldn't I go in there?"

The smile disappeared so quickly it might have been mistaken for an illusion. "He's a fraud, sir. Has a couple-a goons. He'll take your pounds and lay you up in the alley like the rest of 'em."

"And did you warn the rest of them?"

"Course not, sir. They wasn't you."

"And I'm special, am I?"

"Oh, yes, sir! All gold around the edges!"

And that stopped Coralis in his tracks. The young boy was speaking about his aura. Only a person with extended age, experience, wisdom, and valor achieved a golden aura. And it took a very special person to be able to see it. "What is your name, son?"

"Randall Elliott Hawthorne at your service, sir."

"Well, Randall, for starters, you can drop the act. You're no more a street urchin than I am an opera singer."

"Whew! Thanks for that. Do you know how hard it is to play that role?"

Coralis smiled. *"Why don't we go for a walk and you can tell me all about yourself."* For the next several hours, Randall talked, hardly taking a breath. He was ten years old—in an orphanage for the past two after his parents died in a freak accident while searching for something in the Himalayas.

"Some la-di-da thing," he said sadly.

"What were their names?" asked Coralis.

"Evelyn and George Hawthorne, 'last of the great explorers.' That was Dad's big joke. Guess the joke was on him."

"Would you like to come live with me in a Romanian castle, Randall?"

He did, of course. But there were two things Coralis never shared with the boy—or with anyone.

First, he'd known Evelyn and George. They were on a mission to Shangri-la when they'd met their untimely deaths in an avalanche.

Second, he adopted Randall.

Coralis stood suddenly, excusing himself as he left the cabin. There was something he needed to do—for himself, for his family. He quickly passed from car to car, seeking the end of the train. Then he laughed at himself when he came face-to-face with the wall that was the rear of the train. In his absentminded state, he momentarily forgot he was not on a train of yesteryear, which would have had a caboose—an open-ended car at the tail end where one could stand to see the tracks behind them.

He reversed his steps and came to the connection between the sleeper cars and the crew's quarters. Wrapping his long coat tightly to his body, he willed himself to become unseen. Though the space between the cars was totally enclosed, he tapped his wand against the side to create an opening that closed as soon as he stepped through. Lithely gripping the side of the train, he climbed a ladder and sat on the edge of the roof. Unperturbed by the force of the wind, he crushed a unique crystal in his palm and began to chant an ancient spell.

And somewhere in another country, in the stifling-hot trunk of a battered car, a family member in the form of a falcon heard him.

The average body heat of a bird is higher than that of a human. But there is a limit to the amount of heat it can tolerate. To regulate its internal temperature, a bird will resort to openmouthed breathing or panting, or it can hold its wings out away from its body in an attempt to cool down. Being tightly bound and gagged and shoved in a sack, Randall could do neither.

He was approaching his limit. Twice he had faded to the edge of unconsciousness. Both times he managed to force himself back to a drowsy state of awareness. He could not afford to miss any vital piece of information.

He had given up cursing at himself for allowing the brief lapse in concentration that placed him in this dire predicament. Instead, he embraced it as fortuitous. He could not have gathered the details of his captors' heinous plans if all he had done was follow them from a lofty altitude.

But the dangerous combination of extreme heat and lack of oxygen was causing him to lose his grip on reality. To cross the plane from reality to hallucination would be disastrous.

Through the Urania Wand, he had foreseen the ruins— the aftermath of some horrendous calamity. The nightmarish future that would come to pass if he did not succeed in stopping it. These were the thoughts that motivated him.

He firmly believed in everything the Wandmakers' Guild stood for. His only desire was to see mankind into a better future and to thwart the evil that tried to do otherwise.

Coralis.

Randall loved the old man dearly, but was constantly frustrated by his lack of attention to the world around him. The final straw had been when he refused to believe in Randall's discovery of the evil that was about to unfold. He knew he had to take drastic action to wake Coralis from his malaise.

It was no accident when he transformed into a falcon. It was no accident when he located Henry and forced a connection between the old man and the boy. He could only hope that Coralis had followed through.

His feathers ruffled at the thought of Coralis digging in his heels and wrapping himself within the safe confines of his castle in ignorant bliss. He became agitated with anger and felt pressure building in his brain.

Coralis!

"Hello, Randall." The old man's voice sounded faintly in his head. He thrashed violently, fearing hallucinations that could compromise his mission. *No!*

"Calm down, boy!" He stopped, suddenly still as a statue. Would a hallucination answer him? Did the old man anger him so much that he now invaded his subconscious?

I am not hallucinating. Randall decided to play along. If this was what it took to keep him awake, then he had nothing to lose.

"Hello, old man," he silently spoke through his thoughts. *"Long time, no see."*

"Still a disrespectful lad, I see."

"I find it hard to respect a dream."

"This is not a dream and we have no time for idle chatter." And with that admonishment, Randall understood. It was indeed the voice of Coralis. He must be using an ancient art to communicate with his thoughts.

"Coralis, where are you? Please tell me you're not eating a bowl of Gretchen's stew at the castle."

"Yes . . . Gretchen's stew. What I wouldn't give for a piping-hot bowl of it. No, unfortunately I am far from that. I am effectively following the trail of bread crumbs you've been dropping. And the fact that this connection is coming through loud and

clear means we are fairly close—geographically, that is. But we have no time to waste, so listen carefully. I am on a train with Henry and his sister."

In concise terms, Coralis told Randall the essence of everything that had transpired in the past few weeks. Randall then reciprocated with his side of the story. When he got to the point of his capture, he could sense tension and worry. When he told of the night in the cabin, he could sense the old man's fear. And when he detailed what he knew of Dai She's evil plan, he felt Coralis recoil in horror.

"What I don't know is how they plan to do it."

"And what of Henry's father?" Coralis asked.

"I'd say he's a very willing accomplice. But there are indications they don't see eye to eye. There's somewhat of a power struggle between them. And I sense something else about him. Something beneath the surface that is extremely powerful. If indeed he is Henry's father, he is much more than he seems to be."

"Randall, I hate to ask this of you, but—"

"No need to ask," Randall interrupted. *"I got myself into this mess and I plan to get myself out of it."*

There was no reply from Coralis for several minutes, until finally: *"I'm sorry, Randall. Sorry I didn't listen to you. Sorry I . . ."*

Randall could sense the connection weakening. *"It's okay."* Proving the old man wrong should have given him some measure of satisfaction. But it didn't. And the apology was just making him uncomfortable. *"Whatever is going to happen, it's going to be soon. I'll do my best to find out. Keep in touch, sir."*

"Unfortunately, this is a one-time arrangement. The distance between us is great, and I have used the last of my crystals to make this link. It's already starting to fade."

A long gap followed. The connection was gone . . . almost.

"Be safe, my son."

The pressure eased in Randall's mind. The connection had been broken. And now he was more focused than ever. There was a plan for mass destruction, and he was the only one in place to find out all the details.

But there were also plans for him. He didn't know what they were, but he knew they couldn't be good.

"Epifanio Corsini was not only an exceptional Wand Master, he was also an intuitive cartographer—a mapmaker, and a very good one. He was able to draw a map of the entire world in such detail and precision that it puts today's maps to shame. And this at a time when most thought the world was flat! But what really made his map special was that it was alive. Everything he used to make this map, from the trees used for the papyrus to the water from which the ink was made, was highly specialized and seasoned with the expertise of a Wand Master.

"And when the map was completed, when the final strokes had been laid to the paper, it took on a life of its own."

Henry and Brianna listened intently as Coralis spoke. The Wand Master had returned to their small room looking pale and grave. They understood why as he added, "I've just learned the map has fallen into evil hands."

"Why even make such a thing if it's so dangerous?" Brianna asked.

"Corsini never imagined it would be used as a weapon," Coralis answered. "Along with the map, he developed an extraordinary healing wand—the one-of-a-kind Coisa Wand. A simple touch of the wand to the affected area of the map could prevent an earthquake, stop an avalanche, put a quick end to a forest fire. It was an extraordinary thing.

"Following Corsini's death, the map and wand ended up in my care. They should have been safe. But in 1185, the castle came under siege by members of the Mongol horde. Do you know the name Genghis Khan?"

Henry perked up. He'd encountered the name in the course of his translation research. "He was a ruthless conqueror. His army conquered all of Asia and kept going west, as far as the Khwarezmid Empire—modern-day Iran."

Brianna made a theatrical snoring noise.

Coralis nodded. "An impressive force of battle-seasoned warriors, to be sure, but they should have been no match for a castle full of Wandmakers. Yet by the end of it, twelve Wand Masters had lost their lives. And the Corsini Mappaemundi had been stolen."

"How?" Henry asked.

"Treachery!" Coralis thundered. "My own apprentice—a brilliant young man named Malachai—was secretly in league with Genghis Khan, and had lured a sizable portion of the man's forces to the castle with the promise of riches.

"Malachai left with the map and the wand, but he never returned to Khan—and neither did the small army that helped him. He killed every last one of those men on a narrow mountain pass, where he used the map to cause a landslide that buried them alive.

"And thus was Corsini's legacy tainted for all time. The map was eventually reclaimed, but we kept it hidden. Apparently, Malachai's wicked spawn, Dai She, has found it. And it now falls to us to stop him."

An uneasy silence settled over the cabin. Finally Brianna spoke. "Are you scared, Henry?" she asked softly.

Henry fidgeted. The answer was obviously YES. But if he were to admit it in Coralis's presence, would he think him a coward? Would Coralis have second thoughts about taking him any farther on their quest? Or possibly even abandon him at the train station?

"I don't know about Henry, but I certainly am," Coralis said. Brianna curled onto his lap. "Are you scared, Brianna?"

"Yes," she answered quickly.

"That makes two out of three. Will you make it unanimous, Henry?"

He was making the choice too easy. Henry couldn't help but feel as if he were walking into a trap. "Yes," he finally admitted.

"Good! I would hate to be traveling with companions who had no common sense." Coralis reached into his robe and took out a packet of M&M's, offering some to Henry and his sister. "It's good to be afraid. Fear will sharpen our senses, but we cannot allow it to cloud our judgment."

"Is that some kind of riddle?" Brianna asked, annoyed.

"No, not a riddle. I only mean that fear can be a good thing in situations like this, but only if we use it to focus on the task at hand. If we allow fear to overwhelm us, it will give the advantage to our enemy because our decisions will become irrational. If we understand our fear, we can control it." He hesitated for a moment. "I have never entered a battle without being afraid. And I almost always won."

"What?!" Brianna squeaked loudly. "Almost always? What's that supposed to mean?"

"Shush!" Henry warned.

"No! No shushing. He's saying we could lose this battle. He's saying we could die!"

"What I'm saying is that if we all keep our wits about us, we have a much better chance of winning. Have you ever played sports, Henry?"

The two moaned as if in pain. "Please don't tell us we need Henry's baseball skills to win." Brianna buried her face in her paws.

"Hmmm . . . perhaps that's a bad example." Coralis thought for a minute. "Have you ever been bullied?"

Brianna groaned again. "Just kill me now."

Henry glared at Coralis. If he was trying to make him feel bad, he was doing a good job of it. "Of course I've been bullied! Look at me. I'm a nerd, Coralis! It's not cool to be a nerd!"

"Nerd?" Coralis said calmly. "Because you apply your brain over brawn? Because you choose to seek education and information over athletics and video games? Nonsense. Do you think the star quarterback can save the world by pitching a no-hitter?" Henry started to correct him but saw the old man smile. "I was never very good at sports trivia. But I am very good at spotting character, potential, and intelligence.

These are the things that make a winner. These are the things that have helped mankind to survive. And these," he said directly to Henry, "are the things that you possess in abundance. Be afraid, Henry. But always be in control."

The train began braking as it approached the Winslow station. They all turned their attention to the window, each immersed in their own private thoughts about what awaited them.

"We will win this battle, children."

Henry thought of a phrase he had heard somewhere. *They won the battle but lost the war.* What was Coralis not telling them?

"Patience, Henry." Coralis spoke silently into his mind. *"It will become clear all too soon."*

The train shuddered to a stop. Through the window, they could see a lone figure seated on a low brick wall. The children stared at her.

"Grandma?"

"Hello, Henry!" She hugged him tightly. "My, how you've grown."

This was the same old woman they had seen in their driveway. The one their mother called Mom.

She hadn't changed since they'd seen her that day. Tan, wrinkled face, warm brown eyes. Salt-and-pepper hair pulled back into a tight bun. The strength of her hug was much greater than Henry expected from her small, slender frame.

"Coralis." She released Henry and shook his hand vigorously. "I never thought I'd actually get to meet you. It is an honor, sir."

Coralis winced from her grip. Henry chuckled. "A pleasure to meet you, madam. But I'm afraid you have me at a disadvantage."

"I am Henry's grandmother, Gailene Granoble. I was sent to pick you up." She looked past him at the few passengers departing from the train. "But where is Brianna?"

A blue nose poked out from Coralis's coat pocket. "Hello, Grandma," Brianna said timidly.

"Oh my." Gailene blinked several times, flustered. But more surprisingly, she rubbed her hand briskly over her own hair, the spitting image of Henry. "Well then. I . . . um . . . perhaps we should go." She grabbed Henry's backpack and strode across a set of train tracks, disappearing behind the well-manicured landscaping on her way to the parking lot.

"So much for grandmotherly love," said Brianna.

Coralis tapped her lightly on the head. "I believe she thought she was surprising us, when clearly the surprise was on her." He laughed.

She giggled. "It was kinda funny."

Henry smiled, too, but for a different reason.

Grandma Gailene led them all to a familiar van, white with GRANOBLE'S GRANARY printed in big green letters.

They all climbed in, Henry taking Brianna in the back with him.

"You kids have never been out here before, though goodness knows I've begged your mother to bring you. Just wait till you see the stars! Billions of them. It's going to make you feel very small."

She started the van and pulled onto the main road. "The train station is beautiful, isn't it?" she said, apparently recovering from the shock of seeing Brianna. "There's even a small bed-and-breakfast attached. The only passengers arrive on the Southwest Chief. But more than one hundred freight trains a day roll through here. Back in the old days, the Chief would carry movie stars out here from Hollywood. They made a lot of Westerns on the reservation. I even got to meet John Wayne!" Her eyes lit up and her face beamed with pride as she looked at Henry in the rearview mirror.

Clearly, he was supposed to be impressed. But he racked his brain and came up empty, finally shrugging his shoulders.

Coralis chuckled. "I'm afraid they are from a different generation."

"I guess you're right," she said sulkily. "But *you* remember the Duke, don't you?"

Coralis twisted uncomfortably in his seat. "The duke . . . ah! The Duke of Devonshire!"

She sighed. "Maybe we should talk about something else."

There wasn't much in the town of Winslow for Henry to see, except for a statue of a man standing on a corner. The window behind him had an image of a woman in a pickup truck. People were taking pictures, and Grandma Gailene explained that the sculpture and picture were a scene from a well-known song.

Once they turned left to head north on State Route 87, there was even less. But in *his* eyes, it was the most beautiful land he'd ever seen. The sun was setting on one horizon while the moon was rising on the other. Large boulders that dwarfed the van cast shadows in abstract shapes that stretched as the sun dipped lower.

Suddenly he felt an overpowering urge to look in the opposite direction. Staring at the moon made a chill run down his spine. He absentmindedly rubbed a hand through his hair.

Brianna picked up on it. "What's wrong, Henry?"

"It's hard to say." He kept his voice down. "It's almost like something is pulling at me. It's like a whisper in my mind telling me to do bad things."

"Well, don't listen to it." Brianna softened her voice, musical tones woven into her words. "You must think of Coralis and how important it is to succeed in our mission, whatever it may be. Think of Mom, Henry. Ignore the voice. Push it away!"

As she spoke, Henry calmed down. He tenderly scratched Brianna's head. "Thanks. I'm okay now." But when he looked up, the two adults were looking back at him.

Coralis held the ring on his finger up for all to see. The black swirl had clouded the entire crystal. It pulsed with evil energy. "We have no time to waste."

A short while later, Grandma Gailene needed what she called a "pit stop for her aging kidneys." She pulled over at a small roadside shack where tourists bought souvenir pottery. The others piled out of the van to stretch their legs.

"How are you holding up, Henry?" Coralis asked.

"I'm okay now." He relaxed noticeably as he realized it was the truth. Whatever had come over him had not resurfaced. He strolled past the cars to watch a group of old men playing cards in front of the shack.

Coralis stayed near the van and gazed at the rising moon. "Young lady, I don't know where you learned to use Voice, but you are as natural with the gift as I have ever seen—and I've seen many. You may not understand this now, but your transformation, however uncomfortable, may turn out to be fortuitous. I think you should stay with Henry at all times from now on.

"As I feared, I was not able to extract all of the evil from the moonbeams that entered your brother. Your talent may be needed again—and soon. So please remain alert for any signs that he might be slipping."

She fluffed up her fur with pride. "Well, if somebody has to do it, it might as well be me."

The road twisted and turned. Grandma explained that they were driving through the Hopi Indian reservation as they passed by the village of Old Oraibi. "How long have you lived out here?" Henry asked.

"All my life," she answered proudly. "Many Navajo children, like your mother, think the grass is greener in the outside world. They leave, but they take their heritage with them. And sometimes they come back."

"Mom was born here?" the children asked together.

"My goodness. Has she told you children nothing?" She shook her head sadly. "Yes, she was born and raised on the Navajo reservation. But she went to study at the university in Flagstaff. That's where she met your father." Her disdain was evident. "I don't know what came over her. I assumed it was hormones." She smiled sadly. "Your father was quite the charmer."

Coralis frowned. "But it wasn't anything as simple as hormones, was it?"

"No." Grandma's back stiffened. "Lois—your mother— has a gift." Henry glanced at his sister. "Even as a child, she was supernaturally perceptive. It was as if she could sense which way the wind would blow. I don't think it was an accident that she met your father. I suspect she knew about his Wandmakers' Guild lineage before he told her about it. But she *was* surprised when he revealed a dark truth he kept tucked away in his heart. He confessed he felt an unnatural craving for power. She was able to persuade him not to give in to his darker nature. But the temptation would always be there. And she swore never to leave his side."

"Wow," Henry said, unsure how to process that information. His parents' lives were clearly far more complicated than he'd ever imagined.

Grandma carefully navigated the dark road. She gripped the steering wheel tightly. "Your parents loved each other very much. And though they moved far away, Lois kept in touch with frequent letters. She wanted a 'normal' life for them—for you." She took a deep calming breath and exhaled slowly. "Then one day the letters stopped coming. I could sense something was not right, so I drove several thousand miles to check on her.

"It was not a pleasant reunion. She would not even allow me into your home. She said I could ruin everything just by being there. When I left, I was so worried about her . . . about you." She stopped and took another deep breath.

"But she let me know that everything was under control. That I should go back to the reservation and wait. Waiting can be difficult—especially when you don't know why." She tapped the brake suddenly as a large animal scampered across the road. "Coyote. A good sign."

Streetlights appeared in the distance. A road sign read TUBA CITY, HOME OF THE WARRIORS. They turned right at an intersection, passing a supermarket and a fast-food restaurant. "Let's stop for a snack," she said in an attempt to brighten the mood. "I love Tater Tots with cheese and chili."

"Ah, health food," Coralis said sarcastically.

"As vices go, Tater Tots isn't so bad." She laughed and broke some of the tension. "Besides, there isn't much between here and Kayenta and it's getting late. Can you eat Tater Tots, young lady?"

Brianna's nose twitched excitedly as she read the menu. "Only if I wash them down with a chocolate shake!"

"Yes," said Coralis hungrily. "A chocolate shake will improve any situation."

TWENTY-EIGHT

Henry and Brianna were asleep in the back of the van when it pulled to a stop in the parking lot of the Blue Coffee Pot Restaurant in Kayenta. "Henry." Grandma Gailene shook him gently. "There is someone who needs to meet you."

Henry rubbed his eyes, and Brianna yawned widely. "If they only need to see Henry, I'll just stay here and sleep." She curled up on the seat.

"You should come, too," Grandma said sympathetically. "The invitation is a rare one."

"Where is Coralis?" asked Henry.

On cue, Coralis emerged from the restaurant with the sour look of a man who had sniffed rotten vegetables. He held a Styrofoam cup at arm's length, quickly glanced to see if anyone was watching, and ceremoniously dumped it in the trash. "I'm not sure what was in that cup, but it couldn't have been what I asked for," he grumbled.

"They must have given him the tourist blend," Grandma Gailene whispered. "The good coffee is reserved for the locals."

Coralis continued his show of displeasure, hacking like a cat bringing up a fur ball, wiping his tongue with a napkin. Henry stifled a laugh, unsure of Coralis's mood but picking up a bit of mischief in the old man's face. "Bahtzen bizzle?" Henry asked.

"Indeed, young man!" Coralis laughed. "But watch your tongue. There are ladies present."

Grandma Gailene led them into the restaurant, where the hostess nodded a playful smile at Coralis, who winked and said, "Touché."

The tables were three-quarters occupied, every patron clearly of Navajo descent and mostly men. They wore flannel shirts, rugged jeans, and wide-brimmed hats. Henry's stares were answered with barely perceptible sideways glances. He recalled what Grandma Gailene said about a rare invitation and suddenly understood. This was a place for locals, not tourists. And whatever kinship Henry felt for this place, he was at best a newcomer and at worst an outsider. He was suddenly self-conscious.

They walked to the rear of the restaurant and entered the kitchen, where cooks ignored them as if they were merely pots and pans sitting on a stove top. Tucked into the back corner was a door. A thick oaken door surrounded by runes and ancient symbols. A door Henry recognized from an underground cemetery in New York City.

Coralis grunted in satisfaction. "Ah, now we're getting somewhere." He studied the symbols. "This is no common entrance. There is sacred ground beyond this point."

Grandma Gailene motioned for him to continue, and he raised a wand and lightly touched symbols in each of the four corners. The door latch popped. Coralis opened the door and stepped through.

Henry swallowed hard as he crossed the threshold—hesitant and unsure of himself. Coralis's words of wisdom came back to him: No one is ever ready for the odd and unusual turns of life. It made him feel a little better.

The first flight of stairs ended in a basement the likes of which he expected to see in a restaurant. Cans of food lined shelves along one wall, while boxes of cleaning supplies were stacked along another. But he could sense there was more to this space than met the eye.

Coralis advanced to the center of the room and withdrew another wand—weathered and off-white, slender, with several knobby protrusions. Henry gasped as he realized it was a bone. Coralis whispered over it and the bone glowed with a subtle green hue. "Green," he said curiously. "This should be interesting."

Before Henry could ask what he meant, Coralis laid the bone wand down and flicked it into a spin. It slowly gained momentum, but once it got going, it quickly morphed into a circular blur. Directly beneath it, the floor began to change, smooth concrete turning to dust. The diameter widened by a foot.

Coralis had returned to Henry's side. With a light touch to his shoulder he held the boy fast as the glow rippled beneath their feet. A tingling sensation traveled up Henry's leg, and when it reached his heart, a feeling of euphoria engulfed him. His earlier trepidation was replaced with a giddy sense of joy.

When the ripple met the walls, Henry laughed aloud. Inch by inch, the walls and everything on them wavered like a mirage before disappearing. But it didn't stop. The ceiling disappeared as well.

The glow, once again circular, closed in upon itself until it was the size of a quarter, then a dime, then the tiniest pinprick of light that popped out of existence. The bone stopped spinning and sagged like an exhausted runner.

They were left standing at the entrance to an awesome cavern, the size of which should not have been possible so close to the surface. Henry did not recall seeing a mountain behind the restaurant, yet the enormous cavern could only exist within one.

"That would explain the green." Coralis's voice echoed. "The wand I used was a Revealer. It can be used only once." And before the echo stopped, the wand crumbled to dust. "Did you sense anything before I used it, Henry?"

He nodded. "I felt there was more here than I could see . . . but I never expected something like this." His voice cracked as if parched.

"How is this possible?" asked Grandma Gailene.

Coralis examined her with curiosity. "They haven't confided in you, have they? They sent you as the messenger, but didn't tell you why."

"I am not as gifted as my daughter," she replied softly. "And those who have skills like the men and women of your Wandmakers' Guild—those with the power to call upon the very Earth—are extremely rare. Even among full-blooded Diné."

"What does that mean?" asked Brianna from Henry's hand. "What is Diné?" She pronounced it *Din-eh*, as her grandmother had.

"It is the name of our people before we were known as Navajo. The Navajo Nation was once the Dinétah."

"Come." A deep voice rumbled through the cavern. In that one word, Henry could feel something that had been dormant and ancient come to life within his chest. With his free hand, he gripped the wand in his pocket and felt a warmth that comforted him.

"Come," the voice said again, but this time another word was fed directly into Henry's mind. *"Welcome."*

It wasn't until they had walked half the distance across the cavern that Henry noticed it was he, not Coralis, leading the way. He glanced worriedly at the Wand Master, who motioned him to keep going. As they got closer, he could make out the shape of a pile of rags at the base of the far wall. And closer still, the rags became a man—one so ancient he appeared to be made from the earth around him.

"Sit," said the voice in his head. It was kind but insistent. Henry sat across from the Navajo man. *"Diné,"* the voice corrected him. Coralis and Grandma Gailene

flanked either side of him. A small pile of fist-sized rocks lay between them and the Diné chief—*for what else could he be,* thought Henry. He placed Brianna on the ground and saw the briefest flicker of surprise in the old man's eyes. And that's when Henry recognized him. The face from his mother's mural.

"We meet again," he said to Coralis slowly, deliberately, as if unaccustomed to speaking more than a single syllable at a time.

"It has been a very long time." Coralis bowed his head in respect. Something unspoken passed between the two men. The image of two heavyweight boxers sizing each other up before a big fight occurred to Henry.

"Ah, forgive me," the Diné chief said to Grandma Gailene and the children. "I am Joseph." He leaned forward and rearranged several of the rocks in a peculiar pattern, then pondered them for several minutes before speaking to Coralis. "He has the blood."

Coralis nodded. "And the talent." He added, *"And the innocence."*

Joseph acknowledged the silent message. "You are his grandmother?"

"Yes," Grandma Gailene said hoarsely.

"The generations are important, especially now. There is much at stake. I have foreseen this day. Evil will rise tonight, but the form it takes has not been revealed. Perhaps the great Coralis has knowledge of it?"

"Not all," Coralis said uncomfortably. "But with some luck, we will know what we are facing."

Joseph coughed. Henry realized he was laughing. "Luck? You entrust the fate of the world to luck?"

Coralis's back stiffened. Henry shifted closer to Grandma Gailene, expecting him to explode with anger. "Knowledge and wisdom are important, but in battle, luck can swiftly shift momentum."

"Then we will need our share," said Joseph. He held out his hands with his palms facing outward as if he were warming them over an imaginary fire. Henry felt something tug at a knot in his stomach, a gentle but firm pulling sensation. As Joseph's hands moved, so did the knot, from one side to the other, then up into his chest.

A strong scent of incense, musty and bitter, drifted into Henry's nose and filled his mind with hazy images, like figures moving in smoke. Gradually, the shadowy forms took concrete shape, and Henry was witnessing a battle scene. A man who could only be Joseph in his youth led a company of warriors against a pale-skinned invader. The man wielded a wand that controlled wind and fire. The essence of evil oozed from his pores.

Henry flinched as the man looked directly at him and pointed the wand. Fire erupted and Henry screamed, breaking the trance. "What just happened?" His voice echoed loudly. No one answered. Coralis, Joseph, and Grandma Gailene sat with their legs crossed, palms facing upward on their knees, eyes closed. Brianna lay next to him, asleep—and in human form!

Before the shock could register, incense again pervaded his senses, and he was back at the scene of the battle. But this time Henry stood alongside the foreign man, who smiled at him. "So, you've chosen to join me after all," said the man in a familiar voice. Henry looked into the man's face: the face of his father.

He screamed and woke again. This time everyone was awake and staring at him—and Brianna, to his sadness, was still very much a hedgehog.

"You have failed him, Coralis." Joseph's voice was barely a whisper.

"I did all I could," Coralis answered with the tired edge of a defeated man. "But the moonbeams had already merged with his aura, and to pull any more out of him might have killed him."

"He may yet choose to be our enemy," said Joseph.

Coralis shook his head gravely. "His heart is true."

"Perhaps," whispered Joseph. "Perhaps."

"When the time comes, he will not fail us," Coralis insisted.

"And the girl?" Joseph asked, motioning toward Brianna. "The change in her goes beyond her physical appearance."

"When the time comes, she too will be our ally. I give you my word."

Joseph arched an eyebrow. "I hope the word of Coralis is

enough." He stood and pressed his back against the cavern wall. The rock melted away, revealing an opening as dark as pitch. "Come," he said. He stepped into the opening and the darkness swallowed him whole.

"Because a blind man cannot see, his other senses become more acute—more sensitive. He can smell or hear things before others can. The man with sight takes things for granted. The blind man truly appreciates that which he cannot see." Joseph led the way in darkness, his voice trapped within the walls of a narrow tunnel that left only enough room to travel in single file. "Follow my voice. Extend your senses. Do not be frightened by the dark."

Brianna giggled and Joseph stopped. He turned to see a dull glow emanating from Henry, and sighed.

"Sorry." Henry shrugged.

"Fine." Joseph sighed again. "Just keep up."

Behind him, Henry heard what might have been a muffled laugh coming from Coralis. *"It's good to keep him on his toes,"* he said directly into Henry's mind.

Henry wasn't too sure about that. He liked the old man and wanted to show respect. He cursed the residual moonbeam that would not let go, and swore to himself to fight against it.

They walked a great distance. If there were any twists or turns in the tunnel, they were so gradual that they were imperceptible. Occasionally, Joseph muttered words in a language unfamiliar to Henry.

Time seemed to slow down—their steady pace might have taken them miles before they came to the end. A solid wall blocked their path and Joseph knelt. He began to hum, then chant to a rhythm that sang to the earth. Coralis and Grandma Gailene stood to either side of Henry, each taking a hand and gently squeezing. Joseph's voice rose in volume, the chant assuming a sense of urgency.

Then it abruptly stopped.

He picked up a twig—an item out of place on the otherwise bare ground. He stood and touched the twig to four points on the stone wall, the outline of a door that silently opened outward.

Despite all that Henry had seen over the past weeks, he gasped.

Joseph beckoned him to enter. "Come and meet our allies, my son."

The labor was exhausting but Markhor found his rhythm. As did Dai She. By the time he had extracted the next crystal from the chamber, Dai She had transformed the previous one into a perfect glasslike pillar. With great relief, he hauled the final crystal to the mouth of the cave. What appeared to be one last obstacle was quickly overcome when Dai She used a wand to melt a hole through the pavement so the crystal could be mounted into the earth beneath it.

Markhor wiped the sweat from his forehead, so physically spent that he momentarily lost his concentration, revealing his true self. He looked upon Dai She with a mixture of pride and regret. A split second before Dai She looked up, he regained his composure, but Dai She had noticed something.

"What was that?" he snapped.

"What was what?" Markhor asked innocently.

"Your face," he said suspiciously. "For just a second—"

"We are both exhausted," Markhor interrupted. "I suggest we get some rest. No point in going through all this work only to make a careless mistake from lack of sleep."

Dai She continued to stare untrustingly at him.

"If you're seeing things that aren't there, perhaps you are already too tired."

Dai She flushed red with anger. "There will be no mistakes! It is you who are weak." He bristled with energy. Markhor thought he would lash out at him . . . and he'd seen what he was capable of. But he settled down and the energy dissipated. He walked into the shade of the tunnel. "Get me something soft to use as a pillow. You take first watch. No more than an hour."

A shadow shifted and they both looked to the horizon, where the top edge of the full moon had just crested.

"What are you waiting for? Do it now!"

Markhor used what energy he had left to mask his disdain—and to imprint a sleep spell into Dai She's mind.

Dai She yawned, long and widemouthed. Markhor smiled. He nudged Dai She's leg to make sure he was out, then let the facade of Henry's father completely dissipate as he raised his arms to soak in the rays of the bad moon.

The new cavern was nothing like the one Coralis had revealed earlier. This one was much smaller—or perhaps it only seemed that way because of the number of people in it. Henry counted off a group of ten and estimated there must have been close to a hundred people gathered. "Allies," Joseph had called them. Men and women with power over the Earth.

Flaring torches lined the roughly circular walls at regular intervals, bathing the cavern in an eerie red glow.

Joseph signaled for everyone to sit. All but one obeyed the command. A young girl about Henry's age stepped forward, weaving her way through the assembly. She carried a single wand, delicately carved and finely polished. In the cavern's dim glow, the wand looked like an extension of her hand, matching her slim fingers. She pointed it at him.

Suddenly Henry grimaced in pain! He fell to his knees as agony exploded in his head. Then as suddenly as it appeared, it was gone. And in its place was a vision of a world untamed by man. It occurred to him that if there was a picture of the world "in the beginning," this was it.

The vision rushed at him, revealing plains of long grass that bent before him as he soared past. He crested a small rise and gasped in awe. A herd of bison stretched from horizon to horizon. He floated above them, close enough to reach out and touch them.

As he crested the next rise, a herd of wild stallions appeared, as vast as that of the bison. He zoomed past one horse after another, until he came to a regal beast the color of night. His coat was flawless, as if painted with purest black, then dipped in lacquer.

As Henry approached, the horse reared up on his hind legs and kicked out in fury. Searing heat interrupted the vision. It faltered and Henry panicked. He felt himself falling and was afraid of crushing one of the horses. Or worse, getting trampled by the herd. But just before he touched the ground, something lightly brushed his shoulder and the cavern came back into focus.

The young girl stood back and smiled. Henry swallowed, hard. Despite all he had just seen, the only thought in his head was how pretty she was. He felt the heat returning, but this time it was from blushing.

Joseph made a few soft noises that erupted into laughter. And suddenly everyone was laughing. Henry's initial reaction was anger, but one look into the face of the girl and it dissipated as quickly as it appeared. "What just happened?" he asked her.

The laughter died and the assembly rose up.

"You have just seen the past and the future," the girl said.

Henry had no experience with describing such things, but from the way authors described things like this, he'd say her voice was the color of the rainbow and the scent of wild flowers. "Who are you?" he managed to ask.

"I am your dream girl . . . figuratively speaking, of course."

"Of course," he answered, though her answer made no sense to him.

"My name is Serena."

Henry could not think of a more appropriate name. With no effort at all, he saw her aura. It was . . . peaceful. The most beautiful arrangement of light and color he could imagine. He wanted to ask if she was a goddess, but realized how absurd that would sound.

"Never be afraid to ask a question, Henry." It was Joseph's voice this time.

Henry looked from Joseph to Coralis. "I wish you two would stop doing that."

Serena giggled, and the lightness of it made him happy. She reached for his hand. "Come with me. We can get better acquainted on the journey, but there is no time to waste."

She led them through the throng of people, who parted for them. Grandma Gailene had joined their ranks. "I will see you when you return, Henry."

Still in somewhat of a fog, he walked with Serena, vaguely aware of Joseph and Coralis following behind. And from the fold of his jacket, the voice of Brianna sang softly, "Henry has a girlfriend."

At the far end of the cavern they entered another tunnel, also lined with torches, and much shorter than the previous one. They traveled in silence. Serena never let go of his hand. Henry didn't object. But on the list of things he never saw coming, this was close to the top. The longer she held his hand, the more confident he felt—as if their combined energy could defeat anything.

There was no door made of stone at the end. The tunnel opened into a sheltered space carved out of pure rock. A short distance away, amazing structures of rock sat like sentinels, rising hundreds of feet above the valley floor. "Let's sit for a minute," she said. A shallow pool of water several feet wide was in the center of the arch. "We are in the map room," she teased.

It took only a second for Henry to catch the reference to one of his favorite movies. He looked up at the top of the arch, dozens of feet overhead; a perfectly round hole was carved out, through which he could see the fading light of day. "Indiana Jones was here?"

She laughed. "No, but it looks like the scene from *Raiders of the Lost Ark*, doesn't it? Many movies were filmed here in Monument Valley, though mostly Westerns. My grandfather met John Wayne and many other actors."

It was the second time Henry had heard that name, and he made a mental note to look him up.

"Those movies introduced our land to the world. And naturally, the tourists followed." She didn't sound very happy about that last part as she paused for a second. "Things change, and not always for the better. But sometimes, we have some small control over the future. Which brings us to what we must do tonight. What *you* must do, Henry."

She stopped, and he felt the weight of intense gravity pushing down upon him. "What must I do?" he asked warily.

Her lips tightened. A warning of danger flashed briefly in her eyes.

"You must save the world."

As the moon began to rise in a cloudless sky, moonshadows from the large stone monuments reached toward them like the grasping hands of giants. The vibrant red, yellow, and orange landscape was now muted in dusky hues, but it was magnificent nonetheless. Henry watched as the incredible mural his mother had painted came to life before his eyes.

Serena whistled sharply. Then she stood beside Joseph and Coralis and looked off into the distance. At first all Henry could see was a small cloud of dust on the horizon. The cloud quickly took on a shape as three horses galloped toward them. In the lead was the magnificent black stallion from his vision. As it drew near, he became frightened. It was so much larger in real life!

"Midnight," he said softly, the name emerging from his subconscious.

"Yes, Henry," said Serena. "His name is Midnight. You have chosen him, and he has accepted."

The horse walked calmly up to Henry and lowered his muzzle, his flanks glistening with sweat from the exertion of galloping. He nickered and huffed in Henry's face.

He reached up to touch the horse while Brianna attempted to burrow through his clothes and under his skin. "Easy," he said, more to her than the horse, but both listened.

"Have you ever ridden a horse?" Serena asked.

Of course he hadn't! He was even further out of his element riding a horse than he was playing baseball. But the look in Midnight's eyes told him otherwise. Those coal-black eyes were intimidating, with the fierce energy of an untamed beast. But there was kindness and understanding in them too, and a startling intelligence. The horse stomped a powerful front hoof three times within inches of Henry's feet, then circled away and reared high on his hind legs, braying loudly for all the valley and the world to hear.

"He is telling you that he is yours to command," Serena explained. "And you must trust that he is up to the challenge."

Henry looked to Coralis and Joseph. What were they expecting from him? How could he help them when he had such little control over his own abilities?

Suddenly Henry felt something. Another presence. The small pool of water began to shimmer, rippling as if from a nonexistent wind. All eyes were drawn to it. Henry tentatively approached the pool and saw his own face reflected in the water. Afraid to get any closer, he touched the surface with his foot.

It was as if someone had cannonballed into the center of the pool. A single wave radiated outward and left in its wake a still, glasslike plane.

Looking through the glassy surface was the face of his father, whose eyes bored into Henry's. Henry was paralyzed, his feet staked to the ground.

His father shifted his attention to the rest of the group, eyes landing squarely on Coralis. His mouth moved as if he were speaking, but there was no sound. Instead, a bubble formed beneath the surface, growing to the size of a grapefruit before floating up, detaching from the pool, and hovering two feet above the reflection, which was now smiling demonically. A hand, formed completely of water, reached up from the depths of the pool and popped the bubble.

A voice sounded from the bubble: "We meet again, Coralis."

The voice did not belong to his father. The image in the pool wavered, and another face appeared—one that had not been seen for hundreds of years.

The cannonball effect hit the water again, and the image was gone. Henry's feet were suddenly free to move again. He stumbled backward and fell roughly on his behind, only then realizing he had been trying to pull away all along.

"Who . . . ?" he began.

Coralis blanched. His skin was pale, and his eyes wider than Henry had ever seen.

"Malachai."

PART THREE

Malachai always did enjoy a good fight. It seemed only fair to let Coralis know at this point just who he was actually up against. The look of shock on the old man's face had been almost reward enough for the months of scheming.

But Malachai had more scheming to attend to while Dai She slept.

He returned to the guard shack and found it empty. Nothing but the rope and tape that had been used to bind the old man and falcon remained in hastily tossed heaps on the floor. The small carrying case that held the miniature wands was also gone. If his suspicions were correct, the falcon had found a way to get the old man to strap the case onto its back. A clever design for a clever bird.

Clever and odd.

There was something about that bird that didn't add up, but he was certain now that the bird was working with Coralis. That old fool had been in hibernation so long he'd thought he might have actually given up. But one look at the wand Henry exposed while they were together in his father's study told him otherwise.

Malachai recalled the fortuitous fate that led him to meet Henry's father. Little did Malachai know at the time that it would provide a connection directly to Coralis. The matter of young Henry was disturbing . . . yet exciting. It was obvious he possessed power—raw, untrained, unfocused, and to Malachai's delight, slightly tinged with darkness.

He stepped back into the last dusky minutes of daylight. The disabled truck was still parked where Malachai had left it, the electrical system fried from a burst of wand energy. There was no way the old man could reach civilization in time to bring back reinforcements. Dai She's plan would proceed . . . as would Malachai's.

He smiled and scanned the skies. No sign of the falcon.

But the smile abruptly faded. He quickly paced around the exterior of the shack, hopeful that he was wrong, cursing himself for the oversight. The grounds were totally void of any signs of life. No falcon . . . no old man . . .

No Viktor.

Randall was in trouble. He landed next to a black sage shrub and sought protection underneath it while he worked out the cramp in his wing. The old guard had been terrified—which had made it easy to influence him into fastening the wand case to Randall's back. But it was on just a little too tight. Normally that wouldn't be a problem, but he'd been bound so long, and bounced around in such awkward positions, that his wings were not functioning properly. He was dehydrated as well, which caused more cramping.

He could maintain short bursts of speed, but was having difficulty gaining altitude. And without height, he couldn't get into the thermal currents that would help him glide.

He was stretching his wings and rotating them backward when he noticed a lone smudge far overhead. He knew immediately that Viktor had followed him.

Half of the moon was now visible above the horizon, an ominous warning that time was not his ally. He slowly folded his wings and pulled farther into the shrub, knowing that Viktor's keen eyes would detect the slightest movement. He weighed his options. Outrunning a healthy vulture wasn't one of them.

The tiny belt that cinched over his breast feathers pulled against him and gave him an idea. Probably a bad one, but it was the only one he could think of. And he had to get the full details of Dai She's plan to Coralis—or die trying.

He turned his head and stretched to retrieve a wand from his back. He then hopped into the open and flapped his wings, hoping to look like a bird in distress . . . which was not far from the actual truth.

Within seconds, Viktor had taken the bait. He soared down with the speed of a dive bomber, misjudging his landing and tumbling to an ungraceful stop several feet from Randall. The two birds eyed each other warily. Viktor approached, his beady eyes watching distrustfully.

This was not a carcass, but soon would be. And nothing tasted better than a fresh kill. Just the thought of warm innards sliding down his gullet made him oozy with delight.

The falcon was holding a small stick that it waved from side to side. A feeble weapon. Viktor squawked, the equivalent of a vulture laugh, and hopped closer. The falcon continued to wave the stick in a slow circular motion.

Viktor watched . . . and watched. He couldn't take his eyes off the stick. He was still hungry, but it no longer mattered. The stick mattered. The stick that now moved even slower. Back and forth. Back and forth.

Viktor's head ticked from side to side, following the rhythm of the stick. When the stick stopped moving, so did Viktor. He was frozen in place. His brain was empty.

Then a thought entered his mind—a suggestion that sounded like the best idea he'd ever had. With one final hop, he covered the remaining distance to the falcon and landed squarely on its back. He firmly gripped the wand harness and flapped his mighty wings, taking off with as little grace as he'd displayed when he had landed.

Randall moaned softly as sharp talons raked his skin, but he kept his concentration as the vulture struggled to lift off. When they were finally high enough, Randall directed his new set of wings northward.

To where he knew Coralis was waiting.

After Malachai's grinning visage had faded, the desert erupted in a blur of activity. Coralis and Joseph easily mounted their own stallions. Serena grabbed Midnight's flowing mane and lithely hopped onto his bare back. She reached a hand down to Henry. "We must hurry."

The reality of what he was about to do suddenly registered. "Without a saddle?"

She smiled reassuringly. "Trust me."

Midnight's head swiveled toward him. They were all waiting, and Henry felt nothing but panic. "Get on the horse, Henry." Brianna's head popped up. "Look on the bright side. Even if we die, you'll be riding on a horse with the girl of your dreams."

"Bahtzen bizzle!" Coralis exploded in anger. "Get moving, boy!"

He needed no more encouragement. He clasped Serena's hand and hoisted himself onto Midnight's back. At once, they urged the horses forward, quickly picking up speed from a trot to a gallop. Henry wrapped his arms around Serena and held on for dear life, somewhat comforted to see her blushing almost as much as he was.

At first he flopped and bounced around, threatening to make them both tumble from their mount, but with some encouraging instruction from Serena he found the horse's rhythm. "Don't fight the movement. Become one with the horse. Imagine it is you that is running." When he did, he felt the ground fly past beneath them, just as he had seen in his vision.

The three horses sprinted side by side, the urgency of the riders spurring them on to greater speeds. Monuments of stone rushed past, each more majestic than the last. He hoped he would have a chance to see them again. And that's when it hit him.

He hoped he lived long enough.

THIRTY-ONE

Serena pointed out rock formations as they rode past, turning back to shout their names to Henry. There was Sleeping Dragon, Big Fat Man, Indian Chief, Three Sisters—names the Diné had given to describe the massive rocks. Other than Sleeping Dragon, Henry couldn't quite match the names to the shapes. To the ancient Navajo, it must have been like staring at cloud formations, where abstract visions of dog heads would float past.

Serena shouted something in the Navajo language, and the sound of her voice echoed back at them. "Talking Rock," she said with a smile, pointing to a red rock mesa that rose hundreds of feet in the air. They rode close enough to the base that Henry could see petroglyphs—ancient scenes engraved on the rock.

The horses slowed to a trot as they emerged from behind a tall outcropping. They stopped in front of the formation she called the Skinny Elephant, and she hopped off the horse with the agility of a gymnast.

Henry just knew he was going to fall trying to dismount. He could see nasty bruises, welts, and scrapes in his immediate future. Fortunately, Coralis came to his rescue and offered to help him down.

"Ow, ow, ow!" Henry hobbled as he rubbed his backside.

"You did very well for your first ride," Joseph assured him. Henry mumbled a thank-you, then noticed an earthen mound that nearly blended in with the base of the Skinny Elephant. The mound was some kind of structure, for it had an open doorway—and a woman stood within it. From where he stood, she could have been a carving made from driftwood, until she raised a hand in greeting to Joseph.

Joseph returned the gesture, but then he led Henry in the opposite direction. "Does that woman actually live out here?" he asked Serena.

"Yes, she does. Do you see that structure?" Serena asked. "That is her hogan. It is the traditional living quarters of the Navajo people—made from mud but very sturdy. Someday I will show you the inside of one. But not now. There is no time."

They hurried toward a seam in the elephant's leg, where Joseph was already waiting. He once again performed his magic, revealing a concealed entrance to yet another tunnel. This one, however, appeared to be man-made, as it was lined with timber support beams. Joseph must have noticed Henry's puzzled look. "This is an abandoned mine shaft," he explained. "Not so many years ago, our people mined precious minerals on this land. This shaft was quickly closed when tribal elders heard about it, however. You will soon see why."

They proceeded into the darkness and turned a corner, which cut off the remaining light from outside. Coralis and Joseph reached for their wands, but not before Henry gave off a little moonglow of his own. He heard Serena gasp. "It's a long story. I'll tell you all about it when we visit that hogan," he said, trying to deflect his embarrassment by impressing her.

A short distance later they once again hit a dead end of solid rock. "This is why we closed the mine, Henry." Joseph began to hum, a sound that seemed to amplify within the rock. Stone walls flickered like a holographic projection switching off. The area beyond the wall was cloaked in pitch-darkness until Coralis and Joseph tapped their wands against the rock to either side of the doorway.

The cave responded by coming to life. A bluish-green iridescent glow spread quickly around the room—for that's what it was, a room, more square than round. The ceiling extended about twice Coralis's height, rising slightly in the center like a dome. Bookshelves lined two of the walls, holding ancient bound volumes. Petroglyphs lined the other walls, elaborate scenes of life and death in incredible detail. It was awe-inspiring. But there was a warmth to the space as well. The kind that made you feel like a guest in a stranger's cozy home.

Henry was immediately drawn to a wall of books. The shelves had been carved into the very rock itself. He ran his fingers lightly over the dusty, cracked-leather spines, and as he touched them, titles appeared, each in a language he had never seen. At the end of the shelf were several dust-free tomes. Their titles were printed on the spines, but wavered like an optical illusion. He smiled briefly, recognizing the books from his father's study.

In the center of the room was a table of the biggest slab of wood Henry had ever seen—probably twenty feet across, and cut from a single tree. He didn't have to count the rings to know that the tree must have been thousands of years old. He couldn't fathom how something so big could have even gotten into this room.

He ticked off a list of at least a dozen questions, not sure which to ask first. Until he saw something else. Someone sitting at the far end of the table.

"Mom?"

It didn't take a genius to know that Randall was in a race he couldn't win. There were limits to Viktor's speed, especially while carrying Randall. He would never get to Coralis in time. He desperately attempted a mind-link with the Wand Master, but he couldn't do it. They were going to have to land so he could use the Earth's power to boost his own abilities.

The Chihuahuan Desert far below stretched out endlessly. He knew the area was rich in mineral deposits. In the distance, he saw what he needed—a valley between two rolling hills. Using Viktor like a hang glider, he directed the vulture toward the valley, searching for something he knew had to be there. On the second pass he spotted it. He detached himself about thirty feet up and landed safely without the weight of Viktor possibly crushing him. But as he did so, his mind connection to the vulture was broken. Now thoroughly confused, Viktor flapped vigorously and continued on in search of a meal—never once questioning how he'd gotten there or what he was doing.

Randall was on his own. It was a worst-case scenario. If he was not able to connect with Coralis, the entire journey had been a waste. He twisted his head and selected a wand from his pack with his beak. The valley floor was rich with copper and silver deposits. Randall wasn't familiar with the effect the minerals would have on his mental energies, but since they were excellent conductors of electricity, he hoped they would do likewise for thought waves.

Gently but firmly pressing the wand to the rock, he chanted an ancient spell. The wand flared with light as it fused to the rock. He sat, still as stone, in meditation, summoning every ounce of concentration he could muster. Precious minutes passed. He pushed himself harder. His head began to pound from the strain. He had just reached the limits of his mental endurance when, suddenly, he connected.

But it wasn't with Coralis.

As much as Henry wanted to vault over the table and smother his mother with hugs and kisses, a slow-burning spark of anger held him in check.

"Henry?" Her head tilted quizzically.

"You left us" was all he could say without choking on words. Water welled in his eyes. He angrily wiped the tears away before they could fall. All the suppressed emotions of being abandoned and forgotten suddenly surfaced, and he lashed out at her. "How could you leave us? Do you have any idea what we've been through?"

He wanted to yell and shout and scream at her. To make her feel bad. To make her feel guilty. To make her beg for forgiveness.

Slowly she stood. "I had to, Henry. For so many reasons—I had to leave right at that moment." She circled around the table to approach him. "There were things I had to do that couldn't wait a second longer. But more important, there were things you had to do, too. You had to be ready for this moment, son. And there was nothing I could have done to better prepare you for it than to leave you on your own."

"That's not true!" he shouted. "You could have told me . . . something! Anything!"

She stopped a few feet away. "I am truly sorry. I thought the more you knew, the more danger you would be in. Your father had become erratic . . . frightening. And he was fixated on you and on the Books of Elements that his family had been charged to protect. I took the books and brought them here, the only place I knew he couldn't get them. By the time I felt it was safe enough to return to you, you'd already begun your own voyage. And now look at you." She straightened with pride. "You've grown in so many ways in such a short time. Do you think you would be the strong, confident young man who stands before me had I held your hand the entire way? Never! And not a day has passed that I haven't worried myself sick thinking about you and Brianna . . ." Panic creased her face. "Henry! Where is your sister?"

"Relax, Mom." Brianna poked her head up from Henry's jacket. "Still think leaving me alone with Henry was a good idea?"

Their mother tried several times to speak.

"Check it out, Henry. She looks like a fish out of water."

His anger cracked and a smile tugged as if seeking permission to come out.

"Ahem." Coralis stepped forward and extended his hand. "We haven't met yet. I am Coralis."

"THE Coralis?" She shook his hand—reverently at first, then hard and harder. "I never thought . . . OMG!" She squealed like a delighted child.

"Did Mom just say OMG?" Brianna asked Henry. "Well, LOL."

The dam holding Henry back broke with a vengeance. He laughed long and loud and raced into his mother's arms. "I missed you so much." The words gushed out as they squeezed each other in a death grip until Brianna interrupted, "You're killing me here!"

"Brianna, is that really you?"

"Either that, or he's turned into a world-class ventriloquist."

Their mother laughed again in a carefree way that reminded Henry of simpler, happier times gathered around their kitchen table.

"I'm sorry to interrupt," Coralis said softly. "But we don't have much time. I think it's best if—"

"Coralis?" The voice came from Brianna, but it wasn't her. It was a young man's voice, with a distinctly British accent. Henry was about to congratulate his sister on her new talent when the Wand Master cut in.

"Randall?"

"Of course it's me. Who else would it be?" Brianna— *Randall*—swiveled to survey the room. His gaze lingered on Serena for a few moments longer than necessary, and Henry was surprised to feel a quick pang of jealousy.

"Where are you?" Randall and Coralis asked simultaneously.

Coralis answered first. "We are in a sacred cave in Monument Valley. Are you nearby?"

Brianna/Randall considered this for a moment. "No. I am in a valley somewhere in Mexico in the Chihuahuan Desert.

I was attempting a mind-link with you but ended up with . . . this." He looked up at Coralis. "Curiouser and curiouser."

"Indeed." Coralis frowned, rubbing the beard stubble on his chin. He turned toward Joseph, and Henry saw they were communicating wordlessly—two ancient minds trying to piece together a puzzle.

The longer the silence lingered, the more worried Henry became.

Finally Randall spoke. "The wand I am using has been out of my possession."

Coralis's frown deepened. He nodded as if Randall's admission was the key to solving the mystery. And when he spoke, his voice was grave and solemn. "Your wands have been contaminated." Then he added, "By Malachai."

The hedgehog's head snapped forward. "But that's impossible! He's long dead."

"As impossible as it may be, it is the truth. He has shown himself to me. He is in possession of the aura of Henry's father."

"No!" Lois cried. Henry gripped his mother's hand.

"That would explain a lot, actually," Randall said. He turned Brianna's eyes to Henry. "For what it's worth, I believe your father is fighting him as hard as he can. Otherwise, I'd probably be dead." Then he asked Coralis, "Is it possession or replacement?"

"It would appear to be possession. There are severe limitations to both, but there are more risks with replacement. However, for possession to work, a constant mind-link with the one being possessed must remain intact at all times. Only someone with the level of Malachai's talent could sustain it for any length of time."

"So the father is still alive. That's a good thing, right?" Randall asked.

Coralis nodded, successfully masking the thought, *It depends on how you define alive.* He placed Brianna on the table and sat facing her in an ornately carved chair. "Tell us everything."

"In a nutshell?" Randall took a deep breath. "Dai She is holed up in a cave deep in the earth with the world's largest crystals, aided by the elder Leach—who, I guess, is actually Malachai—and when the full moon peaks in about an hour and a half, he will focus all that bad energy into the crystals, and by using the Corsini Mappaemundi, will rip apart the surface of the planet."

Coralis sat heavily in a chair as the full gravity of the situation registered. "That's about as bad as it gets."

Randall nodded. "I also don't know how much longer I can keep this connection."

"Why?" Coralis leaned forward, concerned. "What has happened to you?"

"Let's just say I haven't been treated with kid gloves." He smiled. "But I'll be fine."

"Randall . . ." Coralis paused. "When this is over, come back. I've been a fool and you were right to task me. But there is much to be done, and I will need your assistance."

"Will do." He turned away, hiding any emotion he might be feeling, but suddenly stopped, as if remembering something important. "Coralis, if my wands have been contaminated, how am I able to connect with . . . whatever this is?"

Lois reached into her bag and snapped open a compact mirror, holding it up for Randall to see. "That is my daughter, Brianna."

"Huh." He examined his image from several angles. "Cute but not very useful. I prefer being a falcon."

"To answer your question," said Coralis, "the energy that caused the girl's transformation included moonbeams from the bad moon. Malachai has been building his strength from exposure to that same energy—hence the connection. I had not considered what effect this energy was having on her until now, but it bears keeping an eye on."

"You don't think she'll turn on us, do you?" Randall asked.

"Hey!" Henry yelled. And in that moment something triggered inside him. Brianna wasn't an annoying little brat any longer. She was an important ally. No! She was as much a part of him as his own aura. And he knew, there and then, he would protect her at any cost. "She's as much on our side as anyone else in this room, so back off!"

Randall smiled coolly. "The kid's got some backbone." Then he suddenly grimaced in pain. "Gotta go now. Good luck, everyone."

The hedgehog wobbled, struggling to remain upright before falling forward on her nose. "What . . . who . . ." Brianna's words slurred.

Lois picked her up and cradled her like a newborn child. "It's okay, baby. You just helped us in a huge way."

Brianna rubbed her face furiously with her paws. "Good . . . I guess. But why do I feel all yucky?"

Henry laughed. "Because Randall was using you to talk to Coralis!"

"Oh, gross! Mega-cooties!" And she rubbed her face viciously against her mother.

"Thanks to Randall, we know what Dai She is planning to do," Coralis said gravely. "But I fear that knowledge may have come too late. The instruments he has at his disposal have power far beyond anything we can counteract. I know of these crystals. It was big news when they were discovered. The media referred to the cave as Superman's Ice Palace—though I'm at a loss to explain the meaning."

"It's a reference to the Fortress of Solitude," Henry explained. "It's Superman's secret home somewhere in the Arctic, and it's made of enormous ice crystals."

Coralis stared blankly at him, and Serena stifled a giggle.

Brianna rolled her eyes. "Geek."

He blushed. "Just trying to help."

"He can leap tall buildings in a single bound," said Joseph. "Did you know that in the original comic, Superman could not fly? Only later did he exhibit powers like flight and X-ray vision." He smiled widely at the perplexed faces of the group. "What? Did you think an old chief could not enjoy a good comic book?" And into Henry's mind he said, *"Later I will show you my collection."*

Henry was immediately pumped. He felt like he, too, had superpowers. "Let's beat this guy! C'mon, Coralis, look at us! We're the underdogs, but we're a force to be reckoned with. All we need is a plan."

"Henry." Coralis sighed. "All cultural references aside, we are talking about the ultimate lethal combination." He ticked off on his fingers. "The greatest natural powers of the Earth, energy from the most evil moon in centuries, the resurrection of the vilest Wand Master in history, and the Corsini Mappaemundi—one of the most powerful instruments ever, created by a Wand Master of the original Council of Aratta." His voice had risen in volume with each point.

"Ah," said Joseph. "But we also have a secret weapon." And he smiled like a cat that had just swallowed a canary.

THIRTY-THREE

"I told you earlier that the tunnel leading to this room was an old mine shaft, which we had closed," said Joseph. "The mining activity encroached on the sacred room, and we couldn't allow that. But another reason we stopped it was that the miners were approaching the richest and most pure layer of uranium known to man."

"Not to burst your bubble or anything, but isn't uranium radioactive?" Henry asked warily.

"Uranium is radioactive, but at a very low level until it is processed and refined into something much more dangerous. The real danger, as many of our people found out too late, comes when you disturb the rock that contains the uranium. As the ore is mined, a toxic gas called radon is released. Many Navajo died because they were not told. Men in power wanted the ore to create their weapons of war and withheld this information." He relayed the story as if reciting from a textbook, but there was a bitter edge to his voice.

"The Diné people have known great misfortune, but in closing this mine and preserving its uranium, they have provided us with a tool that just might help us defeat our enemy."

"And save the planet," added Lois.

"Indeed." Coralis rubbed his chin again.

Henry could see the wheels churning in the Wand Master's brain. Yet the thought of working with something radioactive scared him. People died horribly from exposure to radioactive fallout from atomic bombs. He had seen pictures and watched documentaries. Saving the planet while dying in the process wasn't high on his wish list. He looked up to see Coralis and Joseph staring at him. "Are you reading my mind again? I wish you would stop that."

They turned away, chastised, as Henry tried to come up with a reasonable rationale to continue this seemingly hopeless quest.

If only radioactivity would work on him the way it worked in comic books. Spider-Man and Hulk both got their powers from it. And while the thought of spinning a web and clinging effortlessly to skyscrapers had its advantages, the idea of changing into an oversize green monstrosity held much less appeal.

Hulk smash! He almost smiled. Peter Parker and Bruce Banner couldn't help what happened to them any more than he could, but they did their best with what they had. If he turned into a boy who glowed in the dark—and he was already halfway there—or grew hardened scales for skin, then maybe he'd become a superhero himself.

"You already have greatness within you." Joseph implanted the thought.

"And with great power comes great responsibility," he responded, quoting Spider-Man.

Henry gasped audibly. It was the first time he'd said something back through telepathy, and Joseph and Coralis gave him a congratulatory pat on the back.

"What's . . . going . . . on?" Brianna drummed a paw impatiently on her mother's forearm.

Henry pointed his wrists at her like Spidey would do. "Thwip thwip!" He could tell she didn't see the effect of those beautiful sticky strands, cocooning her in an unbreakable web. "Let's do this."

Joseph led them deeper into the mine shaft. "Thirty-seven minutes," Lois stated like a countdown to liftoff.

"I don't understand," said Brianna. "Isn't the moon already full?"

"It just looks that way," Lois answered. "From way down here on Earth, the moon appears full for several nights in a row. But a true full moon lasts less than a minute."

"And that's our window," Coralis said gravely. "A matter of seconds."

"It's just a little farther," Joseph said. Henry could sense the tension in the man's body language. But he also sensed something else—the raw power of the Earth.

A yellow mineral peppered the walls. He searched through the geology drawer he had created in his mind. "Carnotite," he said.

"Very good," Coralis replied.

Then the walls began to show traces of something silver-gray. Like veins on a human arm, they ran in streaks before

branching off. The farther they walked, the greater the concentration of gray, until the entire tunnel was nothing but a
solid silvery sheen.

He reflexively reached for the wand in his pocket. If his
instincts were right, he would need it soon. As he started to
take it out, something began to vibrate in his other pocket.
Panic and dread hit him like a bulldozer, and he stopped
dead in his tracks.

Coralis pulled up short behind him. "What's wrong,
Henry?"

"It's the gold nugget," he said fearfully. "Something's
happening to it!" When he brought it into plain view, it
flashed a brilliant green. A tongue of flame erupted from it
and struck at Coralis. No, not at Coralis—but at the quartz
ring on his finger.

Coralis shouted and whipped his hand away a micro-
second before the flame could reach it. The ring responded,
the angry tendrils of energy twisting and surging to be
released. Coralis screamed as it began to burn his finger.

"Joseph! The uranium!" He gripped his wrist with his
free hand, willing the power in the ring into submission.
The smell of burning flesh permeated the tunnel. "Joseph!"
he yelled again.

With speed belying his age, the Navajo chief withdrew a
wand and blasted chunks of rock from the tunnel wall. He
grabbed one of the larger rocks and pounded at a smaller
one, reducing them both to gravel. "Place your hands over

the rocks!" he said with such urgency that it frightened Henry.

Coralis's face was drained of color and etched with pain as he struggled to the tunnel floor.

"Henry, on the count of three, toss the gold piece into the uranium!" Joseph shouted.

Henry stared at the gold nugget, suddenly mesmerized by the wisps of energy that continued to flare, searching longingly for Coralis's ring.

"One!"

He felt warmth penetrate his hand and creep up his arm. The flares subsided and the globe pulsed with a singular inner light as if the evil energy within it no longer needed the ring.

As if it had found a home in Henry.

"Two!"

He stared deeply into the energy and felt himself giving in. Here was the power he'd imagined. The power to teach Billy Bodanski and everyone like him a lesson. The power to save his parents—and to make them respect him.

All he had to do was accept it, to drop his defenses and absorb it. He was looking into the face of evil—and he was *liking* it!

Joseph was focused on the uranium and apparently oblivious to Henry's distraction. It was only when he shouted "Three!" that he looked up to see Henry losing control. "Brianna!" he shouted. "Bite him . . . hard!"

She didn't hesitate. She raced up his chest to the closest exposed skin and sank her teeth into his neck.

"Ahhh!" He screamed and yanked her away with his free hand. "What's wrong with you?" he yelled.

"He said 'Three!'" she snarled angrily.

One glance at the two old men on the ground snapped him back to his senses. He could never give in to evil. Everything that was wrong in the world had the corruption of power as its source. He was determined to use his power to protect and defend. Fury arose in his chest and pushed outward like an electrical charge in a thunderstorm. "Nooo!" he yelled in pure rage. But instead of throwing the gold into the uranium, he closed his hand around the gold and squeezed it, tighter and tighter. His knuckles turned white from the strain, and the glow from the energy radiated through his skin, revealing his bones like an X-ray.

With an audible CRACK! the energy leapt from the nugget in a blinding streak of lightning. At the same time, Coralis yelled in pain as the quartz ring exploded, releasing the moon's evil beam and tossing the Wand Master aside like a rag doll. The energies from nugget and ring coalesced into a single ball of malevolent gaseous energy. It swirled in the dark tunnel, expanding, threatening to infect them all.

Acting on pure impulse and instinct, Henry thrust his wand into the center of the energy. The gas reacted. It changed from hot white to pitch black to raging red as Henry focused his willpower—and finally drew the ball of gas into his wand.

"Now . . . three!" he shouted, pointing the wand at the uranium and shooting the energy from his wand like a ray gun.

Joseph slammed his own wand into the ground at the exact moment the energy streamed from Henry's wand into the uranium rubble. Activated by Joseph's wand, the uranium erupted with a field of wavering energy of its own, encircling all of the bad energy and clamping down on it like an iron fist.

Henry fell to the ground in exhaustion as the uranium finished the job, squeezing the bad energy out of existence and leaving the tunnel in deafening silence.

Lois was the first to react, rushing to her son's side. "Are you okay? Oh my God, you're bleeding!" She pulled a tissue from her pocket and pressed gently on his neck.

"My sister the vampire," he croaked weakly. All attention focused on Brianna, who lay in a limp heap at Henry's feet. "Brianna?" He reached for her but pulled back sharply as her outline flickered. For just a nanosecond, the form of a small girl appeared. Then, just as quickly, it winked back into a hedgehog.

"What happened?" Brianna sat up groggily.

Serena picked her up gently. "You saved us."

"Yeah, right." But when she saw their faces, she knew it was true. "Well . . . I couldn't let Henry have all the fun."

"Modesty is a fine trait in a young lady." Serena gave her a quick kiss.

"Are you bleeding?" asked Brianna.

"Don't you remember? You bit me." Henry smiled.

Brianna blanched. "Cool." Then she passed out.

"It would appear we have our answer." Coralis addressed the group as they gathered in a circle on the floor.

"What came out of the uranium?" Lois asked.

"Gamma rays," said Joseph. "I attended government hearings while trying to get them to close the mines. Many of our people became sick—some died—from exposure to radon gas and gamma rays. I suspected uranium might provide some help in defeating our enemy . . ."

"Suspected?" said Henry.

Joseph smiled coyly. "Call it an educated hunch. But you showed us something else. How did you know to release the energy from the gold?"

Henry shifted uncomfortably. The gold nugget in his hand was just a nugget now—Coralis has declared it completely devoid of the moon's energy. "I didn't *know* anything. I don't even know why I did that. It was like something took over my body. I was so angry, and I was afraid . . ." He hesitated. "I was afraid we were all going to die."

"Ha!" Coralis beamed. "I knew you had it in you, my boy. From the moment you made the sun flare in the car." He stood, energetically brushing the soil from his coat. "Enough talk. Lois?"

"Thirteen minutes."

"Lucky thirteen," said Brianna.

"Lucky indeed. We have bigger fish to fry," Coralis exclaimed.

"Like the size of a whale," Brianna quipped.

"Technically, a whale is a mammal," said Henry. "Perhaps a whale shark?"

"You might be a decent Wandmaker, but you're still my brother the nerd."

"I'll take that as a compliment." Henry smiled, but another thought nagged at him. "If just a small amount of gamma radiation could kill us, what's going to happen when . . ."

The group was lost in silent thought as another minute ticked by.

Coralis extended a hand, helping Henry to his feet, a black circle of burnt flesh where the ring once resided. "We will take our bumps and bruises, but we will not be defeated," he said with intensity. "This is not the first time a small legion of Wandbearers has confronted overwhelming odds. We will do this," he said directly to Henry. "And then we will return to my castle. And you will help me rebuild a powerful council so we will never again be caught flat-footed."

Henry smiled. But just for a moment.

"Ten minutes."

Dai She rubbed his hands together in giggling glee. He had come a long way from the tortured little boy with the blotched white skin and blistering disposition. All the suffering and shame of his childhood had been locked away—encased in a hardened shell and buried deep inside him. It was a shell filled with really bad mojo. Over the years, he had allowed that shell to open only by the tiniest of cracks. It provided a source of adrenaline in times of need. Not the kind that an athlete would use to win a race, but the kind an evil overlord bent on revenge would tap into.

And now, with only two minutes to go until the vilest moon in centuries would achieve its perigee, he picked that shell fully open. No longer confined, the darkness oozed, puslike, soaking into every fiber of his being. It spread outward, filling him with bitterness, rage . . . and an undeniable appetite for vengeance.

There was no reason to contain it any longer. He was about to bring this planet to its knees.

And when he was done, he would get rid of that sniveling worm of a self-appointed Wand Master, Markhor. Dai She had no more use for him than a cactus had for water. He would never have what it took to become a true Wand Master and Dai She's trusted general. Markhor had spent too many years creating relationships with people—creating weaknesses within himself.

But Markhor had served his purpose and, despite his occasional hostility, served it well. And for that, Dai She would reward him with a quick, merciful death.

Speak of the devil, he thought as Markhor strode toward him, glancing at his watch. "One minute."

Dai She nodded. He checked the positioning of the Corsini Mappaemundi, hovering his stubbly fingers over the surface, unwilling to touch it lest he disturb something before the time was right.

"Thirty seconds."

Markhor's voice betrayed his tension. There was no turning back. He had allowed Dai She to use him. Ever since he had occupied this body, Malachai had known that he would have only one chance to draw Coralis out into the open. To see what defenses the Wand Master had left, what kind of network remained of his old empire. Malachai had plans— *big* plans—and he didn't want that old fool to get in the way.

Of course, he couldn't allow Dai She to get in his way either.

He glanced once more at his only son. He would have no remorse when this was over. Dai She could have been good, but never great. There were mental and emotional flaws that could not be overcome or corrected. In the language of war, he was expendable.

"Open the door!" Dai She squealed with delight.

Markhor shifted his eyes in a look that could kill, and obeyed one last command.

Tainted or not, Randall withdrew the Urania Wand. It seemed like eons had passed since he'd last used it; the day that changed his life forever. Whether it was luck, skill, or a remarkable combination of both, the wand had given him the power to foresee the future. What he saw had brought him to this place at this moment.

He hadn't foreseen all the random events and detours that had led to hitching a ride on a vulture, but that had only added spicy seasoning to the adventure.

Using the wand wasn't an exact science, after all. It could foresee a future, but not tell what might happen to alter it.

With the moon's greatest shower of evil power just moments away, he needed to use it one more time. *Interesting,* he thought, *I almost said one* last *time.*

The time for speculation had passed. With no further hesitation, he grasped it firmly in his beak and willed it to show him what he needed to know.

Unfortunately, his earlier thought was correct.

Henry, Lois, Serena, and Joseph positioned themselves as corners of a square. Coralis stood in the middle. At his instruction, they withdrew their wands. "This is not the time for gadgetry. We must focus every ounce of our essence through our wands and into the uranium. Joseph, I'm assuming you've prepared your students?"

"They await my mind-link. You will have the full power of my people behind you," Joseph answered proudly.

"I will gather our collective energy and focus it into a single stream," Coralis said. "The only way to win is to create a chain reaction that will ignite every gram of uranium and use it to form a shield that will take the bad energy head-on."

"What if it's not enough?" Henry nervously rubbed the top of his head.

"Then we will need a bit of luck." Coralis honestly didn't know if there were any more lucky cards in his charmed deck, but they were out of options. He closed his eyes and reached out with his mind to connect with the other four warriors. *Once more unto the breach,* he thought. *One more time.*

Interesting, he thought, *I almost said one* last *time.* Then he realized that thought had come to him from another place. *Good luck, my son,* he projected to a solitary figure in a lone valley.

When he opened his eyes, a universe of stars swirled deep within his pupils. He could already feel the power of many Wandbearers building within him. He hoped he would be able to handle it. "On the count of three."

The wand-bearing warriors were emitting a constant energy flow—all but Henry. His power fluctuated wildly. It came at Coralis in raging torrents, threatening to engulf him one moment, then winding down to a trickle the next.

Coralis struggled to harness and modulate the energy. He told them to touch their wands to the tunnel walls.

"Focus!" he commanded, bringing them to a heightened state they didn't know was possible.

"Now!"

Markhor opened the door. Immediately the crystals began to glow.

Dai She shouted, "And evil shall reign!" With one hand he took his personal wand and touched the crystal pillar next to him. With the other hand, he touched the Corsini Wand to the map. He sent a stream of energy outward, an invisible streak of lightning that connected pillar to pillar up the tunnel until it reached the one at the entrance.

The moon had reached its perigee at the precise moment that it could no longer contain the centuries of evil it had accumulated. To the untrained eyes of billions of people around the world . . . nothing happened.

But within the diabolical mind of Dai She, a flood of evil coursed outward and latched on to every single thread of moonlight. For just a second, the moon darkened as if a cloud passed before it. A single second was all it took for the moon to return to its original luster.

A meteoric pulse of energy rocketed toward the Earth at the speed of light and collided headlong into Dai She's snare. The first crystal pillar nearly exploded, but it held fast and allowed the energy to pass, streaking down the tunnel and into Dai She.

The Wand Master strained and bucked as he began to glow, his eyes the color of crimson fire, his body red, purple, and black.

Markhor edged away from the opening. For the first time, fear etched his brow. He crept along the wall, steering clear of the crystals. He knew he had to escape from the tunnel before Dai She released the energy but could not tear his eyes away. To witness destruction on this scale was simultaneously horrifying and thrilling.

And he wanted to witness it as himself. He allowed the glamour of his facade to dissipate, revealing himself as Malachai.

Dai She saw the shimmer at the outer edge of his peripheral vision. Through red-stained eyes, he imagined it was his father and not the sniveling Markhor who was about to witness his greatest achievement. When he felt his body was about to burst, he concentrated on the map and unleashed the power into the giant crystals all around him.

The map began to buckle . . . and the Earth along with it.

Having the senses of a falcon, Randall felt the tremor in his mind a few precious seconds before the Earth trembled beneath him. There was no turning back. The Urania Wand had foretold his future.

But as a falcon, he would be unable to use his full power. Unlike Malachai, he was not using a glamour—reverting to his original form would not be easy. Doing what he feared most, he gathered his wands beneath him and lay flat on the ground against them. He recited in his mind the phrases that would reverse the transformation. The Earth shuddered from one source of power, and he from another. A wing became an arm; a claw became a foot. He was using valuable energy and hoped it wouldn't cost him in the end.

Finally, a naked young man emerged, glistening with sweat and gulping air into his expanded lungs. The transformation had left him stunned and shaken. A sound in the distance got his attention: rocks tumbling from cliffs and rolling down mountainsides, small ones at first but followed in quick succession by an avalanche of boulders the size of houses.

With the effort of a gladiator thrust into a den of lions, he grabbed every wand from his harness, held them tightly in his fist, and rammed them into the ground.

Coralis absorbed energy much like Dai She had done, but his eyes glowed with the white-hot intensity of the sun. In his mind's eye, legion upon legion of warriors were gathering at the crest of a hill, readying for a gallant charge. And when he, too, could no longer contain it, he jammed his wand into the packed earth.

The impact nearly threw him, but he held steady, gripping the wand as searing heat drove through him and into the uranium.

The reaction was not instantaneous. The walls began to glow, but slowly. He needed more power, and there was only one source.

"Henry!" he shouted above a deafening roar. "Let yourself go!"

Henry gasped. Surely Joseph, Serena, or his mother was capable of greater power than he. What was he to let go of? He was doing all he could to help.

And yet a part of him was holding back. His imagination was haunted by the fear of turning Monument Valley into a mushroom cloud of destruction. Everything he had ever read about uranium, all the documentaries he had seen about atom bombs . . . If he were to accidentally do something to trigger a holocaust . . .

"Listen to Coralis." Henry glanced down. Brianna had crawled into his pocket. "You must trust him, Henry."

Sweat dripped down the side of his face. Droplets rolled from the tip of his nose, moistening the dirt at his feet. Brianna spoke again, but this time her voice hummed with persuasion. "If you don't act now, evil will win. Millions will die. People are counting on you. Those who love you know what's best. You must not be afraid, Henry. Concentrate on your wand. It will not let you down."

He knew she was right, of course. Besides, if he failed . . . he'd be dead. Not a comforting thought, but superheroes didn't save the world without taking chances.

He focused. Hard. He pushed every other thought from his mind but one. He let himself go.

Coralis reeled from a jolt of power the likes of which he had never felt. With a massive effort he channeled that energy into his wand. The uranium in the walls around them began to glow brighter until suddenly the chain reaction fired.

The uranium wanted to explode. Coralis couldn't let it. He cried out in agony as he fought to contain the explosion and reshape its energy into a shield. The earth shook beneath their feet. Chunks of rock fell all around them, but the walls held fast as the streaks of uranium fused together. When he reached the limit of his endurance, at the moment he would cross from living to dead, he released the power.

The effect was magnificent. Bright green light illuminated the tunnel as the power surged out in all directions, connecting molecule to molecule. The light flooded through the mine shaft in an instant to race outward into the valley and beyond the uranium-rich Navajo Nation.

Infrared images from space would later reveal a subterranean network of veins that glowed like molten rock and would be mistaken for volcanic activity—stumping scientists for decades.

It continued to spread beyond the borders of states and into Mexico, where it collided with the energy of the evil moon that Dai She had released.

And the two forces collided at the precise point where a young boy named Randall would feel the full impact.

Malachai had seen enough. He turned his back on his son and ran. The fissure he had seen earlier had widened to more than a foot. He had no doubt the tunnel would collapse, entombing Dai She . . . and the map! He skidded to an abrupt halt, nearly stumbling into the path of the crystal pillars. To lose the map would be devastating. To go back for it would almost certainly mean death. Malachai cursed his son—his biggest failure—then continued to run.

As he reached the mouth of the cave, he heard the final cry of a terrified man.

"Father!"

The valley was no longer a valley. Mountain peaks split and crashed downward hundreds of feet, adding to the tremors.

Tectonic plates that had been silent for millions of years pushed upward with incredible speed, forcing their way skyward. Randall was afraid but he held his ground.

Giant cliffs rose all around him. The quaking earth pushed him to the ground. He strained with every ounce of strength he could muster. The Urania Wand had revealed his fate, and he was ready for it.

Not to be contained, pulses of evil energy pushed outward, trying to break through the bond that threatened to crush it. It thrashed and pummeled the uranium shield. Randall sensed a crack beginning to form. If he didn't act quickly, the shield would splinter and all would be lost.

The battle was at a standstill. He needed something that would give him one last burst of power. Good must triumph over evil.

Good versus evil! He nearly laughed aloud as he realized what was missing. The final ingredient.

With one final gasp, he rose from the ground, ran to the nearest cliff, and rammed the Urania Wand into the rising wall. Waves of green light poured from the face of the cliff at the same time that waves of evil energy suddenly recognized Randall as the source of its obstruction and turned their full fury upon the small boy. He screamed as it ripped at his soul, consuming him in a river of malignant hatred, turning him into a pillar of crimson light.

And at that moment, he blindsided the hatred that consumed the evil with every ounce of love in his heart. It peeled off in layers—his love of the Earth he had sworn to protect, the parents he had lost. His love of Gretchen. And finally the love of the man he thought of as his second father—that crotchety old man who gave his life purpose and believed in him.

The wall cracked ever so slightly, but it was all the edge Randall needed. Every second of his short life passed quickly through his mind, followed by every act of evil possessed by the moonbeams. He willed the uranium shield toward him and it responded like an iron fist. The shield could not separate the boy from the evil that consumed him. It bore down upon the evil and crushed it within its grasp.

And then the valley was no more. A mushroom cloud exploded. Swirling clouds of green and red rose high into the stratosphere beyond the pull of Earth's gravity, scattering the precious remains of one heroic young man into the infinite cosmos of space.

THIRTY-SIX

In the humble room of a hogan, an old Navajo woman served an herbal broth in wooden bowls to five warriors on the brink of exhaustion. There should have been joy— they had won the battle. Instead, they were filled with remorse. Coralis had told them of Randall's fate.

"He was a hero," Lois said softly.

"Bahtzen bizzle." Coralis's curse had no bite to it. He could not even summon enough emotion to shout. He did not tell them that he had reconnected with Randall and had stayed with him to the very end. He could never tell them how he had let the love flow from his own heart, adding it to that of that brave young lad. His son.

He wanted to tell them that Randall's sacrifice had been for the greater good. He wanted to tell them that it had been for the best. But he could not find the words. He wasn't entirely sure he would believe them if he could.

One thing he did believe: He would never forgive himself for his role in these events. It would never have come to this if he hadn't been so stupid, lazy, and shortsighted. He had failed Randall.

"But you still have me." Henry sent the thought to Coralis. The old man smiled. *"Indeed I do,"* he sent back. He stood, brushed the dirt from his coat, and walked out of the hogan. Joseph and Serena followed him.

"Mom?" Henry hung his head, afraid that if he were to look up, the tears he had been holding back would overflow. "What's going to happen to Dad?"

Lois rushed to his side and embraced him in a loving hug. "Oh, Henry." She sighed. "I don't know. But he's still out there. There's still hope." Her body shook with quiet tears, and Henry could not hold his own back any longer. He allowed himself to cry. All the stress, tension, sadness, and joy of the past week were released in waves of tears.

He wept for Randall—that poor falcon he had trapped in his garage so long ago. He wept over what he had done to his sister. He wept for whatever Malachai had done to his father.

When the tears were gone, he felt no better. Brianna curled onto his lap. He picked her up and kissed her on the nose. "I'm so sorry."

The old Navajo woman looked upon the scene in silence. She said something in her native language and motioned for Henry to hand over his sister. Murmuring so softly that only Brianna could hear, the old woman cradled her in her hands and left the hogan.

"It would appear," said Lois, "our journey is not yet over."

THIRTY-SEVEN

"**A**ch! Not again! Shoo, Sophia! Shoo!" Gretchen ran after the bear, flapping her apron like a matador's cape. Like a child caught with a hand in the cookie jar, the four hundred pounds of fur scooted out of the garden and, with great effort, through a hole in the perimeter wall of the castle compound.

Overlooking the drama from high above on a battlement, Coralis bellowed, "You can't win, you know. That mangy beast eats better than we do."

"I see." She squinted into the morning sun. "Well then, perhaps you would like to make your own stew tonight."

He dismissed her hollow threat with a wave before continuing his walk.

"He seems slightly less grumpy these days," Henry said to Gretchen as he ran his hand through fresh rosemary to release its aromatic scent. Coralis had insisted that before Henry could begin his apprenticeship in earnest, he needed to immerse himself in the wonders of the natural world—as transcribed by the Wand Masters.

Upon returning to the castle three months earlier, Coralis laid down the ground rules for beginning Henry's training—all with Gretchen. For the first month, he never caught even the slightest glimpse of the Wand Master. Despite his queries, Gretchen protected the old man like a fox protecting her den of pups. "Someday you will understand," she said mournfully.

But he did understand. The loss of Randall had taken its toll on Coralis—a two-fisted blow to his self-confidence and his ego. By the second month, the Wand Master appeared just often enough to chastise Henry for falling behind in his studies. Though how Coralis could know how his studies were going baffled him. At times he suspected there were hidden cameras. More than once, Gretchen caught Henry making faces and sticking out his tongue at paintings or at corners of the ceiling.

His time in the garden with Gretchen was his favorite. Her knowledge of plants and herbs was more thorough than any textbook, and had Henry believing she must possess the reincarnated soul of a medieval healer.

The reading assignments, involving books from Coralis's private collection, were more difficult. While Henry was experienced in using the ulexite translator, he struggled over the meaning of ancient phrases. But he plowed onward, understanding the importance of every shred of knowledge.

Yet more than once, his mind wandered to thoughts of Serena. Henry suspected Coralis had his reasons for leaving her behind, but he couldn't help feeling that they would benefit from studying side by side. He wondered what she was doing right now . . .

"That is not a weed, young man," Gretchen chastised. "Sometimes I don't know where your head goes."

"Sorry," Henry mumbled as he replanted the seedling he'd just torn from the ground.

"Apprentice!" Coralis yelled down. "Report to the dining room at once!"

Thankful for the interruption, Henry rushed to his feet.

He arrived to a meeting already in progress. The first surprise was seeing Lois. "Mom! When did you get here?" He hurried into her arms for a hug and squeezed, nearly lifting her off her feet.

"Oh my! Coralis, have you been sending him to the gym every day?"

"Not hardly. The boy has the energy of a sloth. The only workout he gets is eating, and of that he never tires."

He motioned for them to be seated. "Recently, I received word from Joseph that there had been a development."

Henry groaned.

"It is not what you might think," Coralis said. "It was good news, which your mother has decided to deliver in person."

Henry thought back. Around the start of his third month at the castle, there were subtle changes in Coralis's demeanor. The Wand Master began showing up for breakfast. He offered lively conversation and occasionally even harrumphed in between bahtzen bizzles. Henry had assumed a time of mourning had passed and accepted it without question, happy to think the Wand Master might soon take over as his full-time mentor. But perhaps there was more to it.

His eyes roamed the large room and settled on something in the far corner that hadn't been there this morning. It was an object covered in what appeared to be a bedsheet. A statue, perhaps? Had his mother taken up sculpting? Why would she bring it with her instead of shipping it? The sheet moved ever so slightly. He frowned and looked questioningly at his mother, whose face lit with a teasing smile.

"Bahtzen bizzle! I cannot stand dramatics!" Coralis strode to the corner and whipped off the shroud to reveal two young girls.

"Serena!" Henry rushed forward before skidding to an awkward stop.

"Oh for goodness' sake, Henry." Serena closed the gap and wrapped him in a bear hug, which he eagerly returned. His smile stretched from ear to ear.

"Are you here to stay?" he asked hopefully.

"Yes!" she shouted, and hopped in place. "I nagged at Joseph so much he finally gave in."

"That's awesome!" Henry gushed. "I can't wait till you see—"

"Ahem." The second girl rolled her eyes. She stood with arms crossed over her chest while impatiently tapping her foot. She looked to be about his age. Long auburn hair framed a face that was both familiar and not. She fixed her gaze on Henry, and a mischievous smile tugged its way into the open. With a slight turn of her head and flip of her hair, a streak of blue came into view.

"Brianna?" he whispered in shock. His mother laughed and clapped her hands like a grand play had come to an end. "But . . look at you . . . you're . . . older!"

"Seriously, Henry?" Had her voice changed, or was it just that he hadn't heard it coming from something other than a hedgehog for so long? "That's the best you can do? What about beautiful? Effervescent? Dazzling?"

"Vain?" Coralis suggested.

"But how?" As much of the impossible as Henry had seen, this topped all of it.

"The Navajo woman did it," Lois said joyfully. "She finally managed to restore Brianna. Isn't it marvelous?"

Henry was still stumped. "She certainly is . . . older."

Brianna rolled her eyes. "Okay. You're hung up on the age thing. Think about it. I was a hedgehog for several months. How many years does a hedgehog age in one human year?" Henry shrugged his shoulders. "Ha-ha! I've stumped my brother the nerd! The answer is twelve. So for every month I spent as a hedgehog, I aged one human year."

"Which means you two are almost the same age!" said Lois. "Isn't it wonderful? I always wanted twins!"

"No," Henry said sternly. "It is not wonderful! I've ruined her childhood. This is terrible!" The thing was, Henry had actually grown to like being an older brother. Over the course of their adventure together, he felt that, for once in his life, he had done something she could look up to him for and be proud of. This wasn't the way it was supposed to end.

"You may not like it, young man," said Coralis, "but there is a threat awaiting all of us. An evil that will make Dai She look like a child with a beach ball. Malachai has resurfaced, and we will need your sister's help to stop him. The fact that she is older can only serve to benefit our cause."

"Yes, sir," he said humbly.

Gretchen burst into the room wheeling a cart laden with fresh-baked bread, delicious cheeses, and succulent fruit. "Ach!" She stopped suddenly at the sight of two more guests. "More mouths to feed. Well, no bother. At least they are old enough to help with the chores."

"Chores?" Brianna groaned.

"Yeah." Henry smiled mischievously. "How about that."

ACKNOWLEDGMENTS

Not long after I began writing, about seventeen years ago, I started to fall in love with what would soon become a full-time hobby. Working in a warehouse, surrounded by children's books, I read voraciously, my brain devouring aisle after aisle of other people's stories. And I thought . . . I can do this! But little did I know what I was getting myself into. I was truly a rookie. I had no style and no voice. I wasn't sure how to fix it—or if it could be fixed.

Liz Szabla, a long-time friend, recommended I do two things: read Anne Lamott's *Bird by Bird* and join the SCBWI. Smart woman, that Liz. Entering the world of authors and illustrators who approach their craft with dedicated professionalism has been a life changer. Hearing tales of rejection from people whose works I deeply admire, listening to their revision horror stories, and most of all knowing I wasn't alone in my struggle to make it work gave me hope.

I have met countless people over the past seventeen years who have left an imprint on my authorial soul—too many to name. I am fortunate to count among my friends and mentors many librarians, reading instructors, and media specialists. Their passion has been contagious. Every writer needs a critique group. Mine was nothing short of exceptional. Brad and Darlyn Kuhn, Marcea Ulster, Jackie Dolomore, Alison

Jackson, Laura Murray, Anna Khaki, Angie Greenwood, and Leslie Santamaria. So many thanks for your amazing insight. Lezlie Laws and Mary Ann de Stefano, we should write around town more often. Everyone at SCBWI, but especially my Florida peeps, led by the inimitable Linda Bernfeld—good times, great meetings!

Many thanks to Alan Boyko, leader of the pack, who saw something in that early writing and took a chance on me. Thanks to my incredibly dedicated coworkers all over the country who are in this business for all the right reasons. You are a daily source of inspiration. Great heaps of gratitude to the biggest fixers of all—my agent, Marcia Wernick, and my editor, Nick Eliopulos. Nick, I will never understand how you turn my pile of scraps into an edible feast. And to my wife, Barbara. Writing takes time. Carving out spare time means taking away share time. Your endless patience and steadfast encouragement have been the keys to our success.

ABOUT THE AUTHOR

Born in nineteen something, Ed Masessa is the second oldest of ten children. He was raised in the small town of Middlesex, New Jersey, where he lived until moving to the sweltering swamp known as Florida. He has undergraduate and graduate degrees from Rutgers University—neither of which pertains to his current job.

Ed has been a child all his life, subscribing to the Chili Davis philosophy that "growing old is mandatory, growing up is optional." Formerly employed as a grease monkey, office cleaner, fast-food manager, forklift operator, truck driver, warehouse supervisor, sales rep, and automotive purchasing manager, he has spent the past nineteen years at Scholastic Book Fairs, where he has devoted his life to finding books that will turn every child into a lifelong reader.

After reading many, many, *many* books, Ed began to write himself. His second book, *The Wandmaker's Guidebook*, had a nine-week run on the *New York Times* bestseller list, including two weeks at #1. He has also written several works of nonfiction. *Scarecrow Magic*, his first picture book, received a starred review from *Publishers Weekly*. *Wandmaker* is his debut novel.